PRAISE FOR GARRY DISHER AND *BITTER WASH ROAD*

'*Bitter Wash Road* is superb.'
Australian, 'Hot reads for summer'

'Easily one of the best Australian crime novels of the year.'
Canberra Times

'Garry Disher hits the ground running with *Bitter Wash Road*...
never letting up on pace.' *Guardian Australia*

'Peter Temple and Garry Disher will be identified
as the crime writers who redefined Australian crime fiction
in terms of its form, content and style.' *Age*

'Disher shows he's a top-class writer.' *The Times*

'One of Australia's most admired novelists...Disher turns out
to be a superb chronicler of macho cop culture.' *Sunday Times* UK

'Moves at a cracking pace.' *Launceston Examiner*

'Disher's terse, spare prose never falters.' *Dominion Post*

'Disher at his brilliant, hard-edged best.' *Weekend Herald*

'The writing is sharp, with both wit and depth, and the story
engages the reader from beginning to end.' *Otago Daily Times*

'A master class in how to write a tense,
atmospheric crime thriller.' *The Crime Factory*

'Garry Disher has been giving us highly intelligent literary
thrillers for decades and he gets better and better.' *Australian*

'A first class mystery, with writing of the highest calibre,
neatly crafted and strongly evocative.' *Sunday Mail*

'The Australian Garry Disher deserves to be
better-known in the UK, and *Bitter Wash Road* shows why.'
'Joan Smith picks her top thrillers', *Sunday Times* UK

'This is the complete crime novel. It's alive with fully formed
characters, vivid Australian scenery and a plot full of subtle twists
and satisfying turns.' *Australian Women's Weekly*

ALSO BY GARRY DISHER FROM TEXT PUBLISHING

Bitter Wash Road

The Peninsula Crimes series:
The Dragon Man
Kittyhawk Down
Snapshot
Chain of Evidence
Blood Moon
Whispering Death
Signal Loss

The Wyatt novels:
The Wyatt Butterfly: Port Vila Blues / Fallout
Wyatt
The Heat

GARRY DISHER has published almost fifty titles—fiction, children's books, anthologies, textbooks, the Wyatt thrillers and the Peninsula Crimes series. He has won numerous awards, including the German Crime Prize (three times) and two Ned Kelly Best Crime Novel awards.

garrydisher.com

GARRY DISHER
UNDER THE COLD BRIGHT LIGHTS

TEXT PUBLISHING MELBOURNE AUSTRALIA

textpublishing.com.au

The Text Publishing Company
Swann House
22 William Street
Melbourne Victoria 3000
Australia

First published in 2017 by The Text Publishing Company

Cover design by Text
Cover images by Yuko Hirao/Stocksy, iStock and Shutterstock
Page design by Imogen Stubbs
Typeset in Adobe Garamond Pro 12/16.5 by J & M Typesetting

Printed in Australia by Griffin Press, an Accredited ISO AS/NZS 14001:2004 Environmental Management System printer.

National Library of Australia Cataloguing-in-Publication entry (pbk)
Creator: Disher, Garry,-author.
Title: Under the Cold Bright Lights / by Garry Disher.
ISBN: 9781925498882 (paperback)
9781925626087 (ebook)
Criminal investigation-Fiction.
Suspense fiction.
Dewey Number: A823.3

for Tony and Helen

1

ON A MILD OCTOBER morning near Pearcedale, south-east of Melbourne, a snake slid over the edge of a veranda on a shortcut to somewhere. Nathan Wright, blearily contemplating his parched lawn from the front door after breakfast, caught the movement in the corner of his eye: a big fuck-off copperhead rippling over his veranda. Heading where? Towards his wife and daughter? Jaime was pegging jumpsuits to the clothesline on the side lawn, Serena Rae on a pink blanket at her feet.

Finding his voice after a few seconds—weeks—Nathan pointed and squeaked, 'Snake!'

Jaime straightened from the clothes basket and followed his pointing finger. Dropping a tiny pink singlet, spitting a peg from her mouth, she scooped Serena Rae from the blanket and stumbled backwards with a little squeal of terror. The snake slid on, over the patchy grass and dirt, towards a weathered concrete slab the size of a couple of tabletops. No one knew the original purpose of the old slab. The base of a garden shed, now demolished? Chook shed? It was cracked and holed here and there but seemed solid enough and

Jaime had set a garden seat on it, crosswise in one corner, where she liked to read in the sun, shell peas, nurse Serena Rae.

The oblivious snake stuck its nose into a hole that seemed to Nathan impossibly small and began, with a series of long, muscular pulses, to squeeze its way under the concrete. Soon a quarter of the body length had disappeared. Jaime and Nathan watched, appalled. Serena Rae popped her wet thumb and pointed. 'Yes, darling, snake,' said Jaime shakily.

Nathan roused himself from paralysis. A snake living right beside the house? No fucking way. He ran to the lean-to behind the garage where he stored the firewood and garden tools.

'Nathan!' Jaime clamped Serena Rae to her chest. 'Where are you…'

'Axe!'

She gaped, then understood: he was going to chop the snake in two. She watched him vanish, then reappear with the axe, charging the visible half of the snake at a clumsy gallop.

'Don't!' Panic in her voice.

He pulled up, confused. 'What?'

'It could be pregnant.'

Something she'd read, dozens of baby snakes escaping from a severed body, disappearing in all directions to thrive and breed and bite baby humans.

'Plus,' she said, trying for calm—Nathan looked even more rattled than she felt—'snakes are protected.'

'What? Fuck that.'

'And what if the head section comes back out to bite you?'

This seemed unlikely to Nathan, but he hadn't fancied getting close to the snake to begin with, and now it was too late. The snake had disappeared into its burrow.

Still. The fact remained: they had a snake.

Nathan lumbered back to the lean-to and picked up a couple of old red bricks. Approaching the concrete slab as if it was a bed of hot coals, he skittered across the surface, plonked the bricks over the snake hole and retreated. Brushed the brick dust off his hands and joined his wife, who had withdrawn to the veranda.

She seemed unconvinced by his command of the situation. 'What if there's another hole we can't see? What if it knocks the bricks off? What if it digs another exit hole?'

'Jesus, Jaime.'

Nathan resembled any young husband of the district: a little beefy, lawnmower haircut, baggy shorts and surf-brand T-shirt, a couple of meek tatts, sunglasses perched on his baseball cap; given to belligerence when he didn't grasp things. Which happened often enough that Jaime had developed a habit of impatience.

'We need to call the snake catcher,' she said sharply, masking the jitters she still felt.

'Oh for...' Nathan remembered Serena Rae in time to bite off his words; she gazed at him as if she shared her mother's view of him.

'The number's by the kitchen phone,' Jaime went on.

Nathan knew that. He'd stuck the snake catcher's name and number there himself after reading a story in the local paper. Baz the snake catcher advising residents it was going to be a 'good' season for snakes, particularly copperheads, tigers and red-bellied blacks.

'*Na*than...' said Jaime, her tone carrying the rest of the sentence.

'Okay, okay.' He stomped back along the veranda to the front door. Christ, he'd left it open. Who knew how many snakes had slithered into the house? Quick glance back over his shoulder: Jaime was still eyeing the slab, jiggling Serena Rae on her hip. Serena Rae was eyeing *him*. He gave her a sickly wave, entered the kitchen and dialled the number. Waited. Gazed over his yard to the side fence and the neighbour's pine trees and the acres of undulating grassland all around him. All of it crawling with snakes.

*

3

EVENTUALLY BAZ ARRIVED, wearing a blue Snake Catcher Victoria polo shirt, jeans and heavy boots. A cap shaded his face, his big mitts clasped a long crook. Staring from Nathan to Jaime, he said, 'Lead the way,' as if time were valuable.

Nathan indicated the slab and Baz shook his head. 'Jesus, you're not making it easy on me, are ya?'

'That's where it went.'

Behind them Jaime said, 'Can you catch it?'

'Give me a jackhammer and a Bobcat, maybe,' said Baz.

Nathan stood with him, eyeing the slab, and wished he'd just ignored the stupid woman and chopped the fucking snake in half. 'Shoulda killed the bloody thing.'

Baz turned to him, slowly, calmly, and said, 'Bud, I didn't hear that. And for sure I don't want to hear you say it again. It's illegal to kill snakes. You're looking at a six-thousand-buck fine.'

'I'm just saying...'

'Well, don't.' Baz pointed to the discarded axe. 'Even if you chopped it up, the head section is capable of biting you for a long time afterwards.'

'That's what I *told* him,' Jaime said.

Nathan's meaty hands clenched and unclenched. 'So, what, we just leave it where it is?'

'Mate, if it can't get out, it dies,' Baz said. 'By blocking off the hole, you've in effect killed it. Six thousand bucks.'

'You'd report me? Jesus fucking Christ, what the hell are we supposed to do? We've got a little kid. You're saying we remove the bricks so a venomous snake can roam free and me and my wife and kid barricade ourselves indoors for the rest of our lives?'

Baz, unimpressed with Nathan, was nonetheless a fair man. He had kids. He'd even suffered a snake bite, ten years earlier, throwing his family into a panic. He chewed his bottom lip. 'Okay, this is what we do. You need that slab for anything? Intend to build a shed on it, for example?'

4

'You can cart it away for all I care.'

'I'm not carting it away, *you* are. Or disposing of the pieces once we've broken it up, anyway. I've got a mate, a concreter, specialises in house slabs, verandas, foundations. He'll dig it up, no worries. We'll start at the hole, widen it a bit at a time, enough for me to get an idea what's under your slab, like a big cavity or a network of burrows. Soon as I see a snake, snakes, I'll go to work with me hook.'

Snakes, plural. Brilliant. 'What'll you do with it? Them?'

'Release into the wild.'

'Right,' said Nathan. 'And what if your average copperhead has a, I don't know, a homing instinct?'

'Mate, there are snakes all around us all summer. Most of the time, you never encounter them. I get rid of this snake, who's to say you won't see another one in your garden tomorrow?'

Nathan glanced at Jaime. He sighed. 'Okay, let's do it.'

'Might not be today,' Baz said, with a troubled look that hinted he didn't like to think of a snake in distress.

BUT BAZ'S CONCRETER mate agreed to come around mid-morning, so Baz made himself at home—coffee, Anzac biscuits and a chinwag on Nathan's veranda—while he waited. Had Jaime in admiring giggles with his snake stories, the prick.

Finally a small truck trundled in, grey as cement, Mick the concreter himself a grey, powdery wreck of a man in shorts, a blue singlet and heavy boots, his years of heavy labour manifest in a stooped back and bow legs. He shook Nathan's hand with a crooked, lazy grin full of sly knowledge. Nathan blushed, quite sure Baz had said something to make the concreter think he was a dickhead.

'Hear you got a problem,' Mick said, releasing Nathan's hand.

'You could say that.'

'I did say that.' Mick eyed the slab and rubbed his hands together. 'I've been laying concrete all my life. Not often I get a chance to rip it up.'

'Be ready to back off if a head pops out,' Baz said.

'Yeah, well, you be ready with your hook thingy,' the concreter said.

'Be careful,' called Jaime from behind the screen door.

Mick gave the other men a sleepy look and walked back to his truck to fetch a jackhammer. 'I won't start in the middle,' he said, approaching the slab, 'in case there's a thumping great hole underneath and I fall into a nest of copperheads. I'll start at one edge, dig out, say, a square half-metre at a time, check underneath, move on to the next section. What do you reckon?'

'Go your hardest,' Baz said.

Nathan wondered, prise out each section barehanded? Sooner him than me.

Not barehanded: Mick used a crowbar. And after four half-metre-square sections had been removed, it was clear that a large proportion of the concrete had been poured straight onto bare dirt. Except that as the newly bared edges crept closer to the snake hole, a degree of soil subsidence was becoming apparent under the middle of the slab.

'There he is!' Nathan said.

Baz nodded. 'He's trying to burrow deeper away from us.'

'I'll cut out another section,' Mick said.

'Yeah, all right. But be ready to backpedal,' Baz said. 'Our boy won't be a happy chappie.'

Mick cut out a small segment of concrete this time, taking in the original hole. It crumbled as he tried to crowbar it out. 'Whoever the fuck poured this didn't know shit about concreting,' he said, irritated. 'Too much sand, and badly mixed at that.' He reared back. 'Fucking shit!'

The friable concrete had crumbled onto the snake, which tried to strike but was hampered by the masonry on its coils. Baz darted in and pinned the head with his crook. Then he crouched and used his other hand to flick away lumps of concrete until the snake was free. He picked it up, keeping the whipping front section clear with his crook, and poured it into a hessian sack.

'Piece of cake,' he said, grinning at the others.

Who were more interested, it seemed, in a depression under the middle section of the slab.

'What, we got a whole family of the buggers?'

He looked. What they had was a rotting cotton shirt over a rib cage, and a wrist bone encircled by a knock-off Rolex Oyster.

2

ACTING SERGEANT Alan Auhl was late for work, saying goodbye to his wife. Time alone with her was rare. And it wasn't as if the clients of the Cold Case Unit were clamouring for his attention.

'If I'd known I'd be performing cunnilingus,' he said, 'I'd have shaved more closely.'

Liz snorted, cuffed him around the ears and yanked on his greying ginger hair. 'Pay attention.'

He paid attention, and later they spooned and dozed until Liz said, 'I need to finish packing.'

Falling into kissing, followed by falling into bed, seemed to happen to them once or twice a year. They'd glance at each other and something—habit, mutual regard, mutual regret, chemistry, the memory of love—exerted a pull. This time Auhl had merely wandered into his wife's room to see if she needed help with her bags. And, after sex, the spooning, the talking, the irresistible slide into sleep.

Later, when he returned from her bathroom, which was along the corridor from her bedroom and study, Auhl found her on top of the covers, staring unblinkingly at the ceiling. He'd lost her again.

'I didn't so much fall *out* of love with you,' she'd said, tears in her eyes, back when it was clear his general air of distraction and disconnection was never going to change, 'as into a different kind of love.'

Mindful of that now, he bent and kissed her and uttered some banter about the beautiful woman in his bed.

Liz blinked, a flinty intelligence returning to her eyes. 'Last time I looked it was *my* bed. And don't get carried away.'

No. Never that. That wouldn't do at all.

AUHL LEFT HIS WIFE TO finish her packing and went downstairs. Chateau Auhl—three cavernous storeys on a quiet street in Carlton—amplified his footsteps on the stairs and in the hallways. Typically for mid-morning on a Thursday, no one else was at home. Auhl's daughter, and his tenants and waifs and strays, were away until late afternoon.

His bedroom was next to the front door; he shared the ground-floor corridor bathroom with some of the others. He showered, dressed, made two sandwiches and wrapped one for Liz.

And soon she was clattering down the staircase. As she reached the bottom he stepped into the hallway, one hand offering the sandwich, the other reaching to take her heaviest suitcase. She nodded as though both were her due, a lithe, fluid, dangerously attractive woman dressed in a skirt, T-shirt, denim jacket and running shoes. But gone from him now. Distant, untouchable, focused: her mind already on her other life. Even so she was pleasant, almost warm as he carried the bag to her car.

No, she wasn't sure when she'd be staying again.

Drive safely.

Auhl ate his sandwich at the kitchen's chipped and grooved wooden table, Radio National current affairs barely registering.

Her car heads across town, over the Westgate Bridge, down to Geelong.
Auhl mapped it all the way.

AT NOON HE RINSED HIS lunch dishes and walked to the tram
stop on Swanston Street. A generalised anxiety rode with him down
through the city centre and across the river to the police complex.
Liz. The job. The Elphick sisters calling him this morning, as they
did every 14 October, because it was the anniversary of their father's
death and they were still waiting for answers he couldn't give.

John Elphick, born 1942, found dead of head injuries on
his farm in the hills north of Trafalgar, in Gippsland, east of
Melbourne, 2011. Widower, lived alone. His daughter Erica lived in
Coldstream—a nurse, married to a doctor, three kids—and Rosie
was a primary school teacher living with her long-term high school
teacher boyfriend in Bendigo. All had alibis. None had financial
woes. No gambling or drug debts, no iffy friends, no secrets that
investigating police could find. Besides, Elphick had bequeathed
the farm to the Red Cross with his daughters' blessing.

His friends and neighbours also had alibis. None had a reason
for wanting him dead. And without being the life of the district,
John Elphick was well liked and reasonably active: lawn bowls,
church, an occasional beer in the local pub, an occasional Probus
meeting. No lady friend. No young farmhands hanging about or in
residence. 'Lovely old bloke' was the general view.

And that was the extent of Auhl's recall. It wasn't his case,
originally; he'd been seconded to the team late in the investigation,
in the dying days of his marriage and his years in the Homicide
Squad. So you could say he'd been pretty distracted at the time.
And he'd retired soon after that. Fifty years old, burnt out and sad.

But something about him must have appealed to Erica and
Rosie because every 14 October, they'd get together and call him.
Just touching base. Any new developments? And every 14 October
until now he'd been able to say he was no longer with the police. It

hadn't deterred the sisters. Yes, but you have friends in the police, they'd say, you keep in touch. Not really, he'd say.

This morning he'd had to run a different line when the call came. He'd rejoined the police—invited to come back, in fact, ending five years of time-killing. Desultory travel, reading, adult education classes, hopeless and/or disastrous romantic entanglements, a bit of volunteering for various charities.

And somehow the sisters had heard he was back. 'I was just saying to Erica,' Rosie said as Auhl chewed his muesli, 'you're so well placed now.'

'*Extremely* well placed,' Erica said.

In the Cold Case and Missing Persons Unit, to be precise: brought in to free up younger detectives for other duties, mainly. Also valued for his ten years in uniform, ten in various specialist squads, ten in Homicide.

Auhl the retread, expected to run an experienced eye over unsolved murders, accidental deaths and missing persons cases thought to be suspicious. Identify those that might now be solved with the benefit of new technology. Identify those that had been mishandled or underinvestigated; those in which new information had come to light. Liaise where necessary with other squads, including Homicide and Major Crimes. Push for the retesting of old DNA samples. Have another shot at any alibi witnesses who might have fallen out with the suspects. Track changes wrought by time—a crime scene that was now a car park, for example. A key figure since deceased, disappeared overseas, suffering dementia or now married to the chief suspect.

Piece of cake.

Liz had urged him to take the job. 'You're made for it, darling heart.' She still called him that from time to time. Out of habit, probably. She reminded him what he'd been like back in his Homicide days, a case dragging on. 'Obsessive—in a good way.' Meaning he'd agonise that he'd missed something. That a liar had sucked

11

him in. That among the dozens of names he'd collected during an investigation, one was the killer's.

'We have every confidence,' Rosie Elphick had said that morning as Auhl drained his breakfast coffee.

'I can't promise anything.'

'We know that.'

'The coroner ruled it an accident, I seem to recall.'

He didn't, though. What he recalled was that Elphick, J. hadn't been ruled a murder.

There was a silence on the line, a subtle communication of disappointment. 'Wrong,' chided Erica gently. 'The coroner was quite equivocal.'

And Rosie said fiercely: 'Read his findings again, please, Alan.'

AUHL HEADED STRAIGHT for the file room when he reached the police complex.

Hated that room. Thought they'd find his body in there one day, sandwiched somewhere in the massive compactus. Or stretched out on the floor tiles, one hand reaching, desperate fingernail scratches on the door. Back when he worked Homicide he'd rarely needed cold-case files. His cases were hot, or at least tepid. You solved them with shoe leather, phone work, computer searches and questioning. Now he seemed to spend half his time pulling files—and ancient paper files at that. Since the 1950s, two hundred and eighty unsolved murders on the books of Victoria Police. A thousand missing persons cases—of which a third were probably murders.

Looking this morning for *Elphick, J., 2011*, he rolled four grim beige slabs of shelving to the left, creating a narrow aisle. He stepped in, grabbed the file box and stepped smartly out, half-expecting the shelves to abhor the vacuum. Would he even hear a warning rumble?

He took *Elphick, J.* to the small tenth-floor room that was home to Cold Case and Missing Persons. The boss was on the phone in her glass cubicle at the far end of the open-plan room, door closed. One of the detective constables was in court. The other, Claire Pascal, was slumped at her screen with her back to him. Auhl was content to leave it that way. The first time he'd gone out on a job with Claire—a witness re-interview—she'd got in the car and threatened to blind him with capsicum spray if he laid a hand on her.

Dumping the Elphick file box on his desk, he pulled out the contents item by item, scenting the air with a stale mustiness. A bulging file in a rotting rubber band, an envelope of crime-scene photos, crime-scene video. He eased off the rubber band. It broke.

The overview crime-scene photos showed John Elphick on his back in thick spring grass at the rear of his Holden ute, parked beside a wire fence. Closer to, the dead man was heavyset with thick white hair, wearing faded jeans, a flannelette shirt and elastic-sided boots. There were gashes to his head and blood seepage on his forehead, cheeks, neck, shirt collar, down inside the shirt. Auhl thought about that: Elphick was upright when he received the injuries?

Auhl read every report and statement, then turned to the autopsy findings. Elphick had died of massive head trauma. Blood and skin tissue had been found on the roo bar of the ute, which tended to argue against murder. But the pathologist had also noted the pattern of blood flow from head to upper body, and the presence of blood in the cabin of the farm vehicle: he couldn't rule out assault.

And for years now the victim's daughters had politely, gently tried to convince Auhl that he'd dropped the ball back then. 'Inclined to agree,' muttered Auhl now.

'Talking to yourself,' Claire Pascal said, still with her back to him. 'Sad old bastard.'

Auhl ignored her. Name-calling by the youngsters wasn't going to hurt him. He would do what he'd been hired to do.

Next, he slotted the crime-scene DVD into his laptop. Photos were useful for close detail, but a video drew you into the scene. You walked through it with the videographer. When you worked a cold case, a video was the best alternative to having been present.

Auhl saw a hill slope softened by dense spring grasses, a dam at the bottom, half-full, and four nearby gum trees. Distant hills rising to a mountain range in the north and a broad valley to the south—a vista of squares, stripes, dots and dashes that were roads, paddocks, hedges and rooftops. And now here was the wire fence, the ute and the body. At one point the videographer had stood on the tray of the vehicle, the elevation giving Auhl a clearer impression of the body in relation to the fence and the tailgate. Hope the guy cleared it with the techs before climbing aboard, he thought. Pressed pause.

Another benefit of the elevation: he could see *two* sets of tyre tracks in the grass. Elphick's Holden had arrived at the scene after coming through the gate beside the dam at the bottom of the paddock. The second set of tracks ran parallel to Elphick's, but on the other side of the fence. Whoever made them had at some point U-turned and gone back down the slope.

Auhl made a note: *Check who owns or owned the land next door.*

He pressed play again. The video now lingered over the body, top to bottom, soles of the boots, trousers, hands, bloodied head and torso. Then it took him to the cabin of the Holden. Vinyl, the drivers seat sagging, black electrical tape on a couple of splits. Dusty dashboard, also split in a couple of spots. Worn floor mats. Frayed, grubby seatbelts. Air bubbles under the registration sticker, bottom left of the scratched windscreen. A roofing nail, a paperclip and a few coins in the open ashtray. Owners manual, a 2010 phone bill, matches, a pale blue towelling hat and a pair of pliers in the glovebox. In the console between the seats: more coins, Cancer Council sunglasses, a tiny spiral-bound notebook, a chewed carpenters pencil.

Auhl re-read the reports. The investigating detectives had not mentioned the notebook. The crime-scene manager had. Elphick had used it to jot down rainfall figures, shopping lists, reminders: *buy firewood, service mower, re-hang the front gate.*

Auhl went back to the video: the notebook was closed, the cover creased, faded, coming away from the spiral binding. He pressed pause and enlarged the image. Elphick had scribbled something on the cover of the notebook. Random letters. A number? The pencil strokes were indistinct on the shiny surface.

He was dimly aware of Claire Pascal's desk phone, Claire muttering and finally swinging around in her chair. 'Oi, Retread.'

'What?'

'The boss wants us to take a little trip to the country.'

'Concerning?'

'Come on,' she said testily. 'I'll tell you in the car.'

Auhl stood, shrugged into his jacket, checked for phone and wallet.

Pascal wasn't finished with him. 'Don't forget your Zimmer frame.'

3

AUHL SIGNED OUT an unmarked sedan and headed onto the Monash, directed by the encouraging voice of the maps app on Claire Pascal's phone. That voice—he thought she sounded like a Sarah—was his only warm company. Pascal sat centimetres from him, radiating hostility, staring ahead. She didn't want to work a case with him? Stiff shit. Josh Bugg, the other youngster, was in court. So unless the boss wanted to get involved, Pascal had no choice. Auhl felt inclined to wind her up further, keep it down to sixty on the freeway like the old geezer he was. But one of them had to be an adult.

The highway unfurled and then they were on EastLink and, grudgingly, Pascal was telling him where they were going and why.

'Some bloke digging up a concrete slab near Pearcedale, found a body under it. Skeleton.'

'Meaning old and cold,' Auhl said.

She shot him a look. 'Meaning the hotshots from Homicide have handpassed it to us.'

Auhl pricked up his ears, sensing an undercurrent. Personal?

He didn't know much about Claire Pascal's home life. Married, that's all he knew. To a cop? Anyway, it wasn't as if he wanted to trade domestic chat with someone who'd warned him off on pain of a faceful of capsicum.

He glanced at her. Young. Fit. Capable. Still staring ahead, her hair scraped back severely, accentuating the sharpness of face and manner. At the same time, she smelled pleasantly of freshly laundered clothes and a tangy kind of shampoo. He didn't mind her. She did call him Retread, but fair enough, Auhl thought. These days he felt like a retread. Cheaply slapped together. Just about guaranteed to wear down quickly.

The freeway spooled away beneath the car and eventually, by pushing, prodding and offering, he got Pascal to open up. They discussed the boss, the Elphick case, a case she was working on. Time ceased to drag.

Then, after a long pause, she said, 'How come you resigned and joined up again?' and Auhl heard a tone.

He had a pretty shrewd idea of the resentments that lay behind the name-calling and obstructiveness he got from the younger Cold Case and Homicide detectives. He was holding back their careers. He was expecting—and receiving—preferential treatment. He hadn't kept up with technical and investigative advances. Slow, middle-aged, he'd be a liability in life-threatening situations.

Not much of that was true but, in the six months he'd been on the team, Auhl had stepped on toes and asked hard questions. He'd also laid bare instances of laziness, ineptitude and inexperience in some of the original investigations.

Claire Pascal was probably feeling sidelined right now.

He said carefully, 'I was approached. Police forces everywhere are rehiring retired cops to work cold cases. It frees up resources.'

She dismissed that. 'The company line. What I want to know is how come you retired in the first place?'

'Truthfully? Ten years in Homicide, the crime scenes got to

17

me. Awful, some of them. Most of them. You're supposed to grow a shell. I couldn't.'

She didn't call him a princess, tell him to man up—the kinds of rebukes he'd had levelled at him during his long career. She addressed the windscreen: 'It got to you.'

'Yep.'

'I guess looking at old crime-scene photos isn't the same.'

'Nope.'

She lapsed back into moody silence. Then, near Frankston, as Auhl took the exit onto Peninsula Link, she said suddenly, 'I was out of the force for three years.'

'Oh?'

'I was on a raid. Ice lab in a house near Melton. I got shoved through a plate-glass window by one of my own team. One of the competitive types; hates to come last.' She lifted her right hand from her lap, pulled back her sleeve and floated her arm in the space between Auhl and the dashboard. He risked a quick glance: forearm scarring, the skin ridged with threads and cords of mangled tissue.

'Tendon damage. I've got full use back now, or pretty close. But the surgery and rehab took forever and I kind of...lost it. My nerve.'

'Shitty thing to happen.'

'The police medical officer more or less told me to resign on health grounds, which I did, but after a year I couldn't hack it anymore. Rejoined, applied to go back on my old team—they wouldn't have me—got sent to a suburban CIU, way out on the other side of the city, with a bastard sergeant who didn't want a woman on his team.' She paused. 'I learned that the hard way.'

'Uh huh?'

Claire went on as if he hadn't spoken. 'Late shifts. A *lot* of late shifts. Meaning I was alone in the station at the dead of night. Filthy phone calls. Strange noises. Tyres slashed, on one memorable occasion.'

Another pause.

'And if I worked days he'd touch me up, come-ons and little put-downs the whole time. At least you don't do that.'

'Well, I don't want a faceful of capsicum spray,' Auhl said.

She looked at him blankly, then barked a laugh and blushed. 'Yeah, well, you know, ancient history; no hard feelings.'

'Deal,' Auhl said. 'So you applied for a transfer to Cold Cases?'

'And the rest is history.'

Not too much history yet, Auhl thought. She'd only joined a month before him. As they rode in silence, most of the tension gone, Auhl let himself daydream. His house, his daughter, his wife. The students and the broken men and women who sometimes stayed awhile. And niggling thoughts: old Mr Elphick lying on the ground between his farm ute and his boundary fence. The tyre tracks. The notebook between the seats.

The notebook and the jumble of numbers and letters that Elphick had pencilled on the cover…

'*Numberplate.*'

'Pardon?'

'Sorry. Note to self.'

'Old people talk to themselves,' Claire Pascal said. 'I've noticed it before.'

Auhl laughed and let Sarah take them to an address east of Pearcedale.

THEY FOUND THEMSELVES in a land not quite flat, the horizon barely decorated in any direction. Two extremes of human habitation: older gum trees, broad paddocks and cypress hedges marked the original farm homesteads. Dusty razed lots sprouted the colonnades of Mediterranean mansions, cheap kit homes and low-slung tan brick places with broad verandas. Some shrubs and saplings here and there, a miserable replacement for the gum trees bulldozed to ease the creep of the young families. Boats on trailers, bloated

SUVs, satellite dishes. Signs advertised grass slashing, yoga, dog grooming and horse agistment. Now and then a grazing goat, a horse, an alpaca. A guy tearing around in an ATV with a dog on the back.

Finally Sarah told Auhl to turn left and he bounced them along a dirt road to an open gate in a white railing fence. At the end of a gravel driveway, several vehicles beside a new-looking house of outdated design, triple-fronted brick veneer with a tiled roof. Auhl made a mental note of the vehicles as he turned in: a small tradesman's truck, a station wagon, a marked police car, a white unmarked like the one they were driving, a crime-scene van, two SUVs in a carport. Several figures came into view, gathered around a blue poly tent, the kind they always put up to preserve the body and conceal it from the media.

Auhl slowed the car, bumped over the grass, pulled in behind the crime-scene van and they got out, taking a moment to scan the property.

Not really isolated, Auhl noted. People bought five- and ten-hectare blocks out here, meaning they had a sense of isolation but often were no more than a horse paddock away from their neighbours. And this place had untilled land on all sides, with a hint of red tin roof above wattle trees three hundred metres further along the road. The only other nearby structures were an aluminium gardening shed with a lean-to for firewood and a shiny corrugated shed containing hay bales, a horse float, a trailer, a ride-on mower.

Hay bales. Auhl scouted around again and saw two miniature ponies in a fenced enclosure behind the house.

THE HOMICIDE SQUAD was represented by a pair of detective constables, Malesa and Duggan. Auhl knew them by sight, Pascal better than that.

'How's it going, Claire?' Malesa said.

He was a slight, strutting character with a strong stink of

aftershave. Duggan, a gangly gum-chewer, slouched behind with hands in pockets.

Malesa went on: 'Old Retread here showing you how it's done?'

'Something like that,' Claire said. She looked uncomfortable.

'Left his Zimmer frame in the car?' Duggan said.

Auhl was tired of the Zimmer frame jokes. Maybe Claire was too. She said, 'Yeah, thanks guys, hilarious. So what have we got, et cetera, et cetera?'

With Malesa outlining the circumstances leading to the discovery of a skeleton under a concrete slab, they wandered over to the crime-scene tent. A slight breeze flowed over the open fields. The tent walls billowed in, out.

'First impressions?' said Auhl.

Malesa snorted. 'A first-impressions guy. First impressions, the body's been there for a lot of years.'

They paused at the entry. Auhl watched a photographer at work, a videographer, two crime-scene technicians, the latter thigh-deep in a hole in the ground. All wore disposable forensic-examination suits and bootees. The skeleton had been lifted out and placed on a tarp, where another tech crouched over it, brushing dirt from the bones. Auhl could see a belt buckle and a scrap of leather. Scraps of rotted fabric on the upper torso, around the waist and on one leg. Running shoes, synthetic, mostly intact.

Freya Berg, the crime-scene pathologist, knelt on the other side of the remains, watching the brush reveal the bones. She looked up. 'Alan? You on the job again?'

'For my sins.'

That was enough idle talk. Berg peered back down and said, 'Male, shortish, probably young, going by his teeth. By young I mean late teens, early twenties. Possibly shot. There's a chip out of his bottom left-hand rib, a corresponding chip'—she craned her head—'lower spine. So, maybe shot in the chest, the bullet going right through.'

Auhl turned to the hole, the excavated dirt and bits of concrete piled beside it. 'Metal detector find anything?'

The technicians ignored him. Duggan paused mid-chew to say, 'Nope.'

'Shot elsewhere,' Pascal said. She glanced around at the house.

Malesa gave her a twisted grin. 'Hate to disappoint you, Claire, but that gorgeous residence has been there less than two years. Same with the sheds.'

Pascal pointed at the excavation. 'What about the slab? Used to be, what? Floor of a shed?'

'Who knows?' Malesa shrugged.

'Thing is'—Duggan chewed his gum, stopping long enough to rub his palms together, slyly satisfied—'old Slab Man here is very dead. As in, very, very dead. Not our headache.'

'Yours,' confirmed Malesa.

Slab Man, thought Auhl. Everyone's going to call him Slab Man. 'Your boss spoke to our boss?'

Malesa grinned. 'Got it in one.'

Duggan chewed happily. 'So if you two lovers don't mind, we've got a recently dead carcass up in Lalor. Lebanese on Lebanese so no great loss, but we do have to hit the road.'

'Kind of you,' Pascal said.

'We aim to please.'

Auhl nodded at the house, where a man, a woman and a small child watched from a set of veranda chairs. 'They live here?'

'They do,' Malesa said.

'And yes, we've fucking talked to them,' Duggan said. He took out his notebook, tore off a sheet, handed it to Claire. 'They own the joint. Moved in just over a year ago. The house was already here, brand new, never occupied.'

Auhl peered over Pascal's shoulder. *Nathan Wright, 28, Jaime Wright, 29, Serena Rae Wright, 19 months*. Two other names: *Baz McInnes, snake catcher, Mick Tohl, concreter*. He glanced across at

22

the truck, two heads aboard, feet propped on the dash, both cabin doors open. They'd be keen to get this done with.

'Okay, thanks,' Pascal said.

'Don't tire the old bastard out, Claire,' Malesa said. Then they were gone.

'Fuckwits,' she muttered.

Auhl couldn't have put it better himself. 'How do you want to do this?'

'Talk to'—she referred to the paper scrap—'McInnes and Tohl first, so they can be on their way?'

'Exactly my thoughts,' Auhl said.

THE SNAKE CATCHER and the concreter had nothing new to add, but Auhl was curious about the snake.

Baz indicated the tray of the concreting truck. 'Mate, the poor bastard's been in that wheat bag all morning. I need to release it.'

Claire shot a nervous glance at the bag. Took a step back. 'Quick question. Very quick. Do you know who used to own the place?'

'No idea. Never been out this way before.' Baz turned to his mate, who was rolling a pinched-looking cigarette, tickled pink at the drama. 'Mick?'

The concreter finished rolling, wet the tip, patted his pockets for a lighter. 'Wouldn't have a clue. Ask the neighbours.'

Half of police work was asking the neighbours. Claire and Auhl let the men drive away and wandered across the yard to the house, Auhl thinking that properties changed hands regularly in districts like this, a world of smallholdings rather than big acreages that remained in a family's hands for generations. Young families moved in, prospered or didn't; moved on again, chasing a different job, a larger—or smaller—house. Kids finished school and fled to the city for jobs or study, never came back.

Claire was on the same wavelength. 'Might be looking at a few changes of ownership.'

'We might.'

'And it could be days before we know how long the body's been there...'

'So given we're here, let's see what a doorknock turns up before we head back to town.'

She shot him a look. He'd completed her thought.

They reached the veranda, where the little family waited in gloomy acceptance of their new state: under suspicion, the yard a churned-up mess, snakes lurking, death present. Nervous smiles as Auhl introduced himself and Claire.

'We understand you moved in about a year ago?'

'Thirteen months,' Nathan Wright said. He was late twenties, a large, soft man with freckled, hairless forearms. His wife was also stocky, a scowler, brown-haired with blonde streaks, dangly earrings. The child on her lap eyed the earrings and Auhl tensed, expecting to see a little hand yank hard on one of the pretty baubles.

'What was here when you moved in?'

'What you can see,' Jaime said, as if it was obvious. 'House, that big shed, fences.'

'We put in the little garden shed,' her husband said.

'You didn't dismantle any old buildings?'

'Like what?'

Auhl said patiently, 'Was there a chook shed built over the concrete slab, for example?'

They shook their heads.

'You didn't wonder what it was doing there?'

'Not really,' the wife said.

She was like her husband, given to the short view, to immediate concerns. Perhaps she was like most people in that regard, Auhl thought. No inquiring minds anymore.

'Who did you buy the house from?' Claire asked.

'You mean, the agent?' Nathan said. 'Bloke called Tony.'

'You didn't meet the previous owner?'

'Oh, right, I get you. Some agricultural company owned all this'—he gestured at the wider neighbourhood—'and they built our house as like a manager's residence. Then they had second thoughts and subdivided. The agent'll be able to tell you more, I guess.'

ARMED WITH THE AGENT's details, Auhl and Pascal wandered back to the crime-scene tent. The air inside was dense, disturbed soil and faint decomposition.

'Sweating like a pig in this gear,' Freya Berg said, stripping off her gloves and stepping out of her disposable suit. 'Someone else will do the autopsy, probably tomorrow or the next day. Meanwhile, like I said, young male, with what looks like penetrative injuries.'

'Shot, then?' Auhl said.

She waggled her hand, non-committal.

'Anything in his pockets? ID? Wallet? Keys?'

'If you're wondering how long he's been buried, not before 2008,' Berg said. 'Found a 2008 five-cent coin.'

'Where was it?'

'On the ground under the body, possibly originally in the back pocket of his jeans.'

Pascal glanced at the remains. 'Any chance of extracting DNA?'

'Enough for a profile? Yes.'

'How are his teeth?' Auhl asked.

'Intact and in good shape. No fillings, so I doubt you can ID him through dental records.'

'He looked after himself.'

'He was young, Alan,' Freya Berg said.

4

THE FIRST RESPONDERS, a pair of uniformed constables, were still at the house. Lounging in the patrol car, looking bored. Our police force in action, scowled Auhl. Their senior officer hadn't thought to follow up and they'd shown zero initiative, just stayed put.

So Auhl cleared it with a phone call to the local station and put them to work. One to drive Claire Pascal in the patrol car, the other to drive Auhl in the unmarked.

'That way we cover more ground,' he said. 'If we're lucky we might find someone with a long memory.'

Pascal shrugged. 'Soon be peak hour, Alan.'

'Just until we get a name,' Auhl said. 'Or names. Going back ten or twelve years.'

'We could just check property records. There's no hurry on this one.'

'I get that,' Auhl said tensely. 'We can spend all of tomorrow looking at databases. But that won't give us local intel. Maybe there was another house here once, and if so, what happened to it? Maybe someone lived here in a caravan. A shed. Maybe someone noticed people coming and going.'

'You're the boss.'

He wasn't. But he did have the authority of some experience. 'Let's meet back here in an hour.'

HIS DRIVER WAS named Leeton. Young, shy, round-cheeked; mouth permanently ajar. It would take more time than Auhl had to put the kid at ease. They mostly did the house-to-house in silence.

A woman with a toddler on her hip answered the first knock. She lived in a kit home, faux gingerbread with a steeply pitched roof, plonked on a raw new lawn. Fruit tree saplings here and there. She remembered the Wrights' house being built.

'Two, maybe three years after we moved here?'

'What was there before it was built?'

'What do you mean?'

'Anything at all, like an old house, sheds…'

'It was just open paddocks, I think.'

'Do you know who owned it?'

'No, sorry.'

'Did you ever meet anyone coming or going when you first moved here? See any activity?'

'Only the builders.'

A similar story at the next property, an old weatherboard farm-house. After that a dusty converted Melbourne tram, nobody home, then a 1970s brick house where a teenage girl just home from school said, 'Mum and Dad might know, but they don't get back till late.'

Auhl left his number with her and returned to the car. Leeton started the engine, then sat, looking embarrassed.

'What?' said Auhl.

'Sir, my shift ends in half an hour.'

Auhl checked the time: three-thirty. Half a kilometre ahead was a garden supply yard; it suggested the presence of a town and other small businesses beyond it. He pointed. 'A quick word at the garden centre, then back to your partner, okay?'

'Sir.'

They turned in past heaps of firewood, gravel, mulch and soil. Sheds, a weighbridge, a small, high-sided truck. Leeton parked at a log cabin marked OFFICE and Auhl got out.

An old man emerged. Wearing overalls, moving stiffly. Stooped, giving Auhl a view of a lumpy scalp under a thin scrape of greying hair. Watery eyes dismissed Leeton at the wheel of the car, focused on Auhl. 'You here about the body under the slab?'

'News travels fast.'

The man smiled. 'How can I help you?'

'I'm interested in anything you can tell me about the property. Who owned it. Did anyone ever live on it. Vehicles coming and going. Anything at all. Going back ten, fifteen years.'

The old man whistled. 'That long? The rest is easy. Bernadette Sullivan owned the place for donkey's years. Then some foreign agribusiness bought it and built the house that's on there now, then they had second thoughts and subdivided. That's when Nathan and his missus bought it.' He paused, cocked his head. 'You met her, the missus?'

Auhl smiled. 'I did.' Then: 'Tell me about Bernadette Sullivan.'

'Like I said, lived there for donkey's years, her and her husband and daughter. Then the husband passed on and the daughter got married and for a while there, before she sold, Bernie went to live with her daughter and rented the old place out.'

Auhl was confused. 'Rented the land for farming?'

'No, rented the house.'

'An earlier house? Before the present one?'

The old man shot him a look. 'That's what I've been saying. An old fibro place, there one day, gone the next.'

'Pulled down?'

'Far as I know.'

'Do you have an address for Mrs Sullivan, by any chance?'

'Won't do you much good, she's dead.'

Auhl said patiently, 'What about the daughter?'

'Angela. Married and divorced,' the old man said. He jerked his head. 'Lives South Frankston way.'

'Address? Phone number?'

'Come in the office.'

Warped floorboards, ancient calendars and, behind the main counter, a pot-belly stove and a writing desk crammed with a laptop, a phone, a printer and a spill of invoices. A large cat was balanced on the thin upper rail of the firescreen. It blinked at Auhl.

'Here you go,' the old man said, checking a battered ledger, scribbling onto the back of a torn envelope.

'Do you remember any of the tenants?'

'Not really. I think the place was empty for a couple of years towards the end. Before that a couple lived there, but the bloke shot through on the woman, not that I blame him, she was ugly as a hatful of arseholes and nasty with it. Anyway, after a while she left too. And before that a family lived there. Freezing place in winter, I was always delivering wood.'

But Auhl was thinking of the man who'd shot through on his girlfriend. 'What do you recall about the couple?'

'Like what?'

'Names. Personalities. Incidents. Anything about them that bothered you.'

The old man shrugged. 'They were all right. Argued a bit, apparently.'

That's all Auhl was getting. 'You say the house was empty for a time before it was pulled down. How many years before that did they live there?'

'Five? Ten?'

'You wouldn't know where either of them lives now?'

'Not a clue. Angela might know.'

'They were the last tenants?'

The old man looked exasperated. 'They could have been, I wouldn't know. All I know is, I didn't deliver any more wood to the place after the woman left, okay?'

MID-AFTERNOON BY THE time Auhl and Pascal headed back to Melbourne, comparing notes. Claire driving; the outer freeways fast, becoming sluggish by the time they reached the inner city. She had few facts to add to Auhl's, except a name for the woman supposedly left in the lurch by her boyfriend: Donna Crowther.

'She did babysitting around the district, house cleaning, gardening. The woman I spoke to got quite friendly with her.'

'They still in contact?'

'No.'

'Anything about the boyfriend?'

Claire's eyes flicked to the rear-view mirror, the wing mirrors. She changed lanes. A horn blasted. The car twitched. Her hands tightened on the wheel. 'Sorry.'

A nervy driver, Auhl realised, riding the brakes, timid when a bit of push was needed. He rethought his earlier assumption that she avoided driving with a man in the passenger seat and decided she wasn't worried about male criticism or wandering hands. She simply didn't like driving.

'The boyfriend?' he prompted.

'His name was Sean, and apparently he and Donna were always fighting.'

'In which case there could be records,' Auhl said. 'Police, ambulance… We need his surname.'

'You think it's him under the slab?'

'We need to rule him out,' Auhl said. 'Or in.'

'Find Donna Crowther,' Claire said.

5

THE CAR LOGGED in, they headed upstairs to the Cold Case Unit where the boss waved them into her office. There was a vase of coral-tinted roses on the crowded desk. A dozen cards.

Auhl said, 'Birthday wishes in order, boss?'

Helen Colfax gave him a don't-bullshit-me half-smile. The senior sergeant was big-boned and sceptical-looking. Wearing black pants today and one of her range of strangely patterned shirts. Brown hair, apparently uncombed; bright red lipstick. An inquiring tilt to her chin.

Hers was a face that could stare down a cavalry division. Auhl had occasionally seen her express genuine warmth, especially with victims and helpful witnesses. Otherwise she was pretty much unimpressed by the world. She appreciated Auhl's long record, but was quick to remind him that a) he'd been out of the game for more than five years and b) this was her show.

'Sit,' she said now.

Claire Pascal took one of the visitors chairs, Auhl remained standing, his shoulder against the jamb. His life was full of futile strategies for countering sedentariness. Not to mention backache, after almost three hours in the car.

Seeing that he intended to remain standing there, Colfax said, 'Who's on first. Claire?'

Pascal delivered a clear, economical report, at the end of which Colfax said, 'You think Slab Man is Donna Crowther's boyfriend?'

There it was: 'Slab Man' had made it back to base already.

'Could be,' Auhl said. 'Could be the third corner of a triangle. Or it's someone totally unrelated to either of them.'

'And he was shot?'

'Doctor Berg thinks so. Shot somewhere else, then buried.'

'Run a detector over the whole yard, you never know.'

'Under way,' Auhl said.

'And the original house was pulled down? Pity; it might have been the crime scene. The whole shebang: blood, DNA, prints, shell casings, the bullet itself.' She paused. 'Stating the obvious.'

'Someone has to.'

Colfax gave him a look: was he being a smartarse?

Claire Pascal cut in: 'The daughter of the woman who owned the house is probably still around, boss.'

'Talk to her. Soon. She might have seen something. Blood, signs of cleaning, painting or plastering…'

'Will do.'

'Speculating for a moment,' Colfax said, 'why would you hide a body under a slab rather than dump it somewhere?'

Asking for speculation was one of her tactics. Dutifully, Auhl said, 'To stage a disappearance.'

And Claire said, 'Conceal a link to the killer.'

'Conceal forensic evidence, manner of death, for example.'

'Throw us off the scent.'

'Inspirational,' Helen Colfax said, 'seeing two powerful minds at work. Throw us off what scent?'

'Killer and victim were involved in something illegal,' Claire

32

said. 'They attracted unwanted attention and one of them panicked.'

'Or got greedy,' Auhl said.

'Okay, see what the local plods have to say—if anyone remembers back that far. Why a slab? Why not just a hole in the ground?'

'A slab'll sit there for years,' Auhl said. 'Who wants to dig up a slab?'

'But *laying* a slab takes time and effort. And knowledge and… you know, cement, et cetera.'

'This is a quiet back road, boss,' Claire said. 'No traffic, an old house set back from the road. Plenty of privacy, and potentially plenty of time.'

'Anyone who's done a bit of do-it-yourself patching up of a wall or a veranda knows how to mix concrete,' Auhl added.

'Okay.' Colfax shrugged. 'Ask around about this Crowther woman. How strong was she? Was she the *Backyard Blitz* type.'

'Did she have help,' Auhl said.

'So on and so forth,' Helen Colfax said, concluding the briefing.

Auhl returned to his desk and went online. If the configuration of numbers and letters scrawled on John Elphick's notebook *was* a numberplate, then it was probably Tasmanian. He clicked the contact link on the Tasmanian roads department site and emailed a query.

Then it was 5.30 p.m. and he'd promised to collect Pia Fanning from after-school care. He took a tram back across town to the university and walked through the side streets to the gates of her primary school, where he waited with a handful of others—mothers, the odd father and grandparent. He didn't talk and no one talked to him. They barely knew him; he'd rarely had the opportunity to walk Pia to school or pick her up. Besides, she'd only been at this school for three or four months.

Suddenly she was there, hugging him around the waist. Ten years old, a tall, pale, mostly silent child, seemingly ninety per cent elbows and knees. 'A. A.' she called him now, which he considered a good sign. When she'd first moved into Chateau Auhl with her mother, she'd been timid as a mouse.

'Learn much today?'

'Not a thing.'

'Excellent.'

He walked, she skipped, in the general direction of his house on Drummond Street. 'Ice-cream?'

They got ice-creams.

And then Auhl was putting on his conspiratorial voice and murmuring, 'Incoming,' meaning pedestrians, and he and Pia stood stock-still, taking up two-thirds of the footpath, while a straggle of three approached, heads down, thumbs working at their phones.

'Mayhem and chaos,' murmured Auhl. 'Total head-on collisions.'

Pia narrowed her eyes. 'Uh-uh. They have, like, feelers. They can sense us.'

One collided. Two looked up and veered away at the last moment. All were deeply affronted.

'One out of three's not too bad,' Auhl said.

'You've done worse.'

Then, as they neared the house, her playfulness evaporated and she seemed to shrink. Glued herself to Auhl's side, her steps growing smaller, slower. To cheer her up, Auhl said, 'Pupil-free day tomorrow. No school.'

'I'm going to Dad's tonight,' Pia replied, barely audible.

Auhl had been told a fair bit about the father but hadn't yet met him. 'He's picking you up?'

'Yes.'

'What time?'

'He said six.'

'Okay.'

'I'll have to pack. I won't have time to watch crap TV with you.'

An anxious child made more anxious. 'Do we watch crap TV?' asked Auhl lightly.

'That's what you call it.'

Auhl reflected that Pia had been badly in need of crap TV when she moved in. Anxious, solemn, barely knew what fun was.

They reached the house. Chateau Auhl was a three-storey tenement built during the boom that followed the 1850s gold rushes and was at the end of a row of four. The other three—home to a lawyer, a celebrity professor and a pair of surgeons respectively—were well kept. Auhl's was scruffy without quite being a disgrace—apart from the footpath wall. Thigh height, crumbling brick, it leaned inwards and enclosed a narrow front garden of weeds, random litter and dying rosebushes. He'd drawn up a roster but no one paid it any attention so he was the one to clean the little patch of its accumulated cigarette butts, empty wallets, supermarket bags and the occasional tiny sock or children's shoe.

Eyeing the front yard critically, he opened the gate. A McDonald's bag this afternoon. He picked it up gingerly and offered it to Pia. 'Yum.'

'Eeew.'

'I grew up in a hole in the road,' he told her.

After many weeks of sharing a house with him, she was familiar with the old routine but she didn't respond this time. Heart not in it.

Auhl unlocked the front door, a massive slab of wood painted black and decorated with a tarnished brass knocker, tossed his keys into the bowl on the hall table and told Pia to make herself a snack. Then he dumped his wallet in his room, a vast, silent, high-ceilinged chamber with a king-sized bed taking up the centre and a massive wardrobe brooding against one wall. He'd inherited bed, wardrobe and house when his parents died.

Then he opened the curtains and window, admitting air just south of toxic, stepped back into the hall and headed down to the kitchen. A med student occupied the first room after his; he rarely saw her. Then a small room with a spare bed piled with junk, followed by the shared bathroom, the sitting room, the kitchen, the laundry.

Beyond all that was a little suite of rooms: two tiny bedrooms and a mini-bathroom. Known to the household as Doss Down, it faced the tiny concreted backyard and alleyway fence and was cast in a permanent shadow by the terrace row behind Auhl's. He'd lived in it during his teenage years—it was the furthest distance from his parents' bedroom and offered a covert way in and out via the alley—but now it housed waifs and strays.

The tradition began early in Auhl's married life, when Liz's sister-in-law left her husband and needed a place to stay. Then, when she'd sorted herself out, one of Auhl's nephews moved down from Sydney to go to RMIT and stayed for a semester before he found himself a student hovel. And it went on from there. Schoolmates of his daughter, fleeing trouble at home. Old friends between jobs. An aunt from the bush, recuperating after surgery.

And lately, women and kids escaping abusive partners—like Neve and Pia Fanning.

Auhl poked his head into the shared kitchen. Pia was there, smothering bread in Nutella and pouring juice into a glass. He stepped back into the hallway and listened. Above him were two floors and a complex arrangement of stairs, landings and rooms. His student daughter Bec lived at the top, sharing a bathroom with a visiting Sri Lankan biochemist and her husband, who rented a bedroom and a study on the same corridor. Liz lived on the middle floor when she was in town. She had a bedroom, a study, a tiny sitting room and a bathroom.

All those rooms, all those residents, but the house was silent just now. No voices, devices, floorboard creaks. Auhl called out anyway, hands making a megaphone around his mouth: 'Honey, I'm home.'

Presently a muffled clatter and Bec peered down from the upper landing. She held Cynthia the cat to her chest, freeing one hand long enough to waggle her fingers at her father.

'You're home early.'

'No I'm not,' she said.

Well, what would Auhl know? His hours were a mess, and so were hers: lectures, boyfriends, part-time work in a Lygon Street gift shop. 'You in for dinner?' he called.

She shouted yes and disappeared again.

'To be loved and needed,' cried Auhl.

'Cherish it.'

Auhl realised he was hungry. He poured a beer, placed a slice of cheese on a slab of bread and sat at the wrought iron table in the backyard. Some schoolkids walked by on the other side of the alley fence. The jasmine was dying off. Distant cars and voices on the mild spring air, jet streams above. Still hungry, he returned to the kitchen just as the front-door knocker started to reverberate like gunshots along the hall.

Pia's father?

Auhl answered the knock. Found a bulky man on the front step, a towering, soft-looking figure, rolls of flesh above the collar of an expensive grey suit.

'Can I help you?'

All semblance of softness vanished the moment the man opened his mouth. 'Tell Pia I'm here.' Didn't introduce himself. Barely registered Auhl, simply turned around to survey the street. Tapped his polished toecap, shot his sleeve to check his watch. Busy man.

'And you are?' Auhl asked, just to be a prick.

'Me?' Lloyd Fanning swung his great, truculent head around. 'I'm her father, dipshit. I've got her for three days, or didn't the slag tell you?'

He thinks I'm sleeping with Neve, Auhl thought. He opened his mouth to speak but Fanning ploughed on: 'I haven't got all day. Traffic's going to be murder.'

Fanning had stayed on in the marital home and he was dead right. Peak hour down to Geelong, the traffic would be murder. Auhl walked back through the house, knocked on the Doss Down door.

'Pia? Your dad's here.'

And off she went, meek and silent. An unhappy little girl with a well-dressed brute.

6

BY 7.00 P.M. AUHL had cooked tagliatelle in one pot, bolognese sauce in another. He prepared two bowls of the mix, called up to Bec and took his dinner through to the sitting room, where he ate on his lap, watching the ABC news with Cynthia curled hard against his thigh. Bec clomped down eventually, kissed the top of his head and stood behind his armchair, drawn to the movement on the screen.

'Where's Pia?'

'Gone to her father's.'

'Neve?'

'Still at work.'

'Did Mum get away okay?'

Auhl said, 'Yes.'

Bec patted his shoulder, an action she'd repeated many times since her parents split, conveying infinite sorrow, hers included. But the pat also said I'm okay, you're okay, everything's okay. Auhl joined her in the kitchen to chat and watch as she reheated her pasta in the microwave, filled a glass with water, threw torn-up lettuce into a bowl and dripped olive oil and balsamic vinegar over it. 'See, Dad? Greens? Roughage?'

'Impressive.'

She was reddish blonde, with a keen, narrow face. Slight but not fragile, capable of fierce judgments or raucous humour but mostly equable and focused. Black leggings and a loose white T-shirt, nothing on her feet, silver here and there: fingers, ears, one nostril.

Then she was trudging upstairs again. Such was the pattern of Auhl's life. Absent-minded love, reasonable stability, a few secrets.

The best possible outcome of his mistakes and inattention.

NOT IN THE MOOD for crap TV, Auhl curled up in an armchair and read an exquisitely written novel in which nothing happened. He was about to hurl it across the room when the front door opened and closed with a soft click. Neve Fanning appeared from the hallway.

'Oh, Alan,' she said, sounding, as usual, tentative, discomposed and surprised to see him.

'Neve,' said Auhl. 'Hungry? There's leftover pasta.'

A thin, tense, worn-out woman of thirty-four, Neve Fanning ducked her head shyly. 'No, thank you.' She paused. 'Any word from Pia?'

'No. Should there be?'

Neve hovered, expressing apology and neediness, then disappeared into Doss Down. Auhl was betting she wouldn't come out again. Didn't want to be a burden, she'd said, the day she moved in.

Her footprint was pretty small. Used a laundromat on Lygon Street, never took long showers, never left lights on. She worked at the university, cleaning; irregular shifts, the only job she could find after moving to the city. She insisted on paying rent, Auhl insisted it wasn't necessary, and that meant there was now about fifteen hundred dollars in the Neve and Pia Fanning Emergency Kitty.

*

IT HAD TAKEN HER weeks to trust him.

He knew some of the story from Liz. Back when it was all going to hell in the Auhl marriage, Liz, a Ministry of Housing bureaucrat, sought a transfer to Geelong, where she helped set up HomeSafe, a community housing agency for victims of family violence in the south-west region of the state. On the day Neve and Pia came in seeking emergency accommodation, all of the HomeSafe properties were occupied. Why don't you move up to Melbourne? Liz suggested. Away from your pig of a husband. More job opportunities.

Chateau Auhl, with its little apartment out the back.

After a few weeks in residence, Neve Fanning began haltingly to confide in Auhl. 'No one really knows what goes on behind closed doors,' she said one evening.

She wanted him to coax it from her. Auhl obliged, deploying a professional dexterity in the techniques of coaxing and grilling.

Neve Fanning, Pia Fanning, Lloyd Fanning. Lloyd was an accountant, Neve a 'homemaker'. Pia was at primary school, and the little family appeared to lead a charmed life in a spacious house in Manifold Heights, one of the better suburbs of Geelong. 'Everyone thought I was so lucky,' Neve said. 'Married to a great guy—successful, well educated, life of the party, knew all the right people.' She shrugged. 'A nice house here, another in Bali.'

But.

Lloyd Fanning had a temper. Liked to punch and kick Neve, throw her against walls and over tables and chairs, hold a knife to her throat—once when Pia was watching. Not to mention the belittling and controlling.

'One year when I was at a Christmas lunch with the other school mums he came and got me. Dragged me out, saying I couldn't trust those bitches, it was just him and me.'

He didn't allow her to keep a job or make new friends or see her family. She had no money of her own and he'd scroll through her emails, her mobile-phone call log and texts, needing to know who

41

she'd been in contact with. When he wasn't with her he'd call, text, up to fifty times a day.

Eventually Neve found the courage to apply for a one-year intervention order. She left Lloyd and took Pia to live with her elderly parents in Corio. Under the provisions of the IO, Lloyd Fanning's time with his daughter was tightly supervised.

But when the order lapsed, Neve didn't apply for another. Ducking her head as she told Auhl this, as if expecting him to disapprove, she said, 'Lloyd was really trying to make an effort, and it *is* important for Pia to have a relationship with him.'

'You went back to him?'

She shook her head. 'I thought about it, and God knows he put the hard word on me, but in the end I didn't.'

And so Lloyd took his revenge—by way of his daughter. He broke promises, cancelled plans at the last minute, arrived late, returned Pia long past her bedtime. Once when he took Pia to Bali for a holiday, he hired a nanny and left her to it—ignored her for ten days.

'And the way he spoke to me and my poor parents if it was his turn to have her. Threatening. Arrogant. Or he'd sit out in his car and toot the horn. Poor Pia, she'd get in such a state.' Neve shook her head. 'She started wetting the bed.'

Neve, her parents, her daughter—all terrified, so Neve had applied to HomeSafe for emergency accommodation, and to Legal Aid for help in obtaining a no-contact order through the Family Court. The HomeSafe application led her to Auhl's house. The Legal Aid visit was more disappointing.

'The lawyer told me no-contact mums are seen as malicious and I'd need much stronger grounds than just Lloyd being rude or destructive.'

'Neve, he hit you.'

She ducked her head again. 'Anyway, I've asked for restricted time.'

Until that was granted, Lloyd continued to see Pia when it suited him. He'd also hired a very expensive lawyer.

THAT WAS THREE MONTHS ago and in the early days the Doss Down suite of rooms was the Fannings' cave. They hid there for hours. Auhl understood: all those weird strangers in the other rooms; Auhl himself.

But it went deeper than that and Auhl came to realise how unprepared Neve was for an autonomous life. She didn't know how to socialise, was baffled and intimidated by the competence of others, and in awe of Auhl, Bec, Liz, the academics who floated in and out of the house. Auhl's domestic situation she found deeply confounding. If she happened to encounter Liz and Auhl together in the same room, an expression of bewilderment, almost pain, crossed her face: what kind of man puts up with a wife who walks out on him and thinks she can blithely continue under the same roof, coming and going when it suits her?

What she really yearned to comprehend, Auhl realised, was how other people negotiated and managed their friendships and relationships. The life she'd known with Lloyd Fanning was one of hidden shoals and vicious resentments.

No wonder mother and daughter had seemed meek, silent, blunted when they first moved in. Everyone at Chateau Auhl had been patient, however. Not that it was easy. Even now, when Auhl managed to reduce Pia to a fit of the giggles, Neve would dart out and say, *'Pia, shush!'* in a clenched voice, as if Auhl was a man whose temper might turn.

Thinking these things always made him sigh.

Monday was Neve's Family Court hearing, and he'd said he'd attend, moral support. He sighed again, went to bed, set the alarm for 6.00 a.m.

43

7

AUHL'S REGULAR morning walk took him around the Exhibition Gardens and often up and down the backstreets of Carlton. He hadn't a lot of weight to lose, and wasn't losing it anyway, but the exercise toned his mind.

When he arrived at work that Friday, Claire Pascal raised her head absently, nodded hello, returned to her phone call. Joshua Bugg was also there. Auhl hadn't seen him for a few days, was generally glad never to see him. There was something bug-like about Bugg: soft, round, downy. Right now the young detective was leaning back in his chair eyeing Auhl, his pulpy abdomen ballooning against his shirt buttons, flesh gaping like a row of wounds.

'If it isn't Old Man Time.'

'Hello, Josh,' Auhl said.

Bugg heaved away from his desk and over to Auhl's, yanking out Auhl's chair. 'Here, Gramps, let me help you get seated, you look worn out.'

He grinned conspiratorially at Claire, who gave Auhl a faintly sympathetic grimace and said tiredly, 'Give it a rest, Josh?'

Bugg looked put out. 'No skin off my nose.' He returned to his desk.

Auhl was checking his emails—nothing from Tasmania—when Helen Colfax appeared and told him not to get comfortable, they had a post-mortem to attend.

SHE DROVE, CROSSING THE city to the Forensic Science Institute. A fast driver, focused, but even so she spotted the old file on Auhl's lap and wanted to know what and why.

Auhl shifted uncomfortably. 'It's the Elphick post-mortem report. I thought Doctor Karalis could give me a second opinion.' Seeing her scowl he added, 'Two birds with one stone.'

The boss's gaze returned to the road. 'Elphick isn't urgent, Alan. The verdict was open, if I recall.'

'Five minutes, that's all. Fresh eyes.'

Colfax grunted and flicked the car through the traffic.

UNDER THE COLD BRIGHT ceiling lights and in the chilled air of the autopsy room, they pulled on ill-fitting smocks and overshoes and waited. A tap dripped. Finally, the pathologist entered with his assistant. Better-fitting gear, and slightly more flattering: pale green pants, a smock and rubber boots, face masks dangling beneath their chins. The assistant hovered in the background; the pathologist came forward briskly, saying, 'Helen, hello. You're attending for the police?'

Karalis was a tall man, gaunt, a wheeze away from old age. When he shook Auhl's hand, he did a double-take. 'Thought you'd retired.'

'They can't function without me,' Auhl said.

Karalis crossed swiftly to the autopsy table, spoke his name and the date into the overhead microphone, lifted the face mask over his nose and mouth and stared at the mess before him. A collection of grimy bones hung with scraps of cloth and dirt. The cheap trainers had fared better. He made a circumnavigation of the table, halting to peer at and lift a couple of bony limbs, noting succinctly his initial impressions of the body.

That done, he said, 'Now for a closer look.'

Under his supervision, the assistant removed the footwear and the cloth scraps, placing them on an adjacent table. The pathologist peered at them, straightened, said, 'They don't tell me anything in particular,' and ordered them sent for forensic analysis.

'Now for the bones.'

He stood over the skeleton with his hands on his hips and said, 'Trauma is present in the rib cage and L5 region of the spine. If one is an entry point and the other an exit point, then a downward projection is indicated.' He turned to Helen and Auhl. 'Was a projectile found with the remains?'

Auhl answered. 'No. He was buried in soil, under a concrete slab. No bullet or bullet fragments—no arrow head or spear-gun point for that matter—leading us to believe he was shot elsewhere then moved.'

'Pity.'

Helen Colfax said, 'So he was shot, Doctor Karalis?'

'That would be my opinion, yes. Certainly a projectile of some kind, and more likely a bullet than, say, an arrow.'

'Shot in the back?' Helen asked. 'The front?'

'Shot in the front, the projectile then nicking the spine on exit.'

'A downward trajectory,' said Auhl. 'A taller person?'

'Or the victim was on his knees?' said Colfax.

'If I had to put money on it I'd say he was face to face with a taller person when he was shot,' Karalis said. 'Now, age. The teeth are a useful indicator here. A cross-section analysis will reveal the age to plus or minus a year, but this young fellow had all his teeth and there is very little sign of wear. Second, the skull is not fully knitted, indicating a person in his late teens, early twenties.'

'Height?'

The assistant measured it: 172.5 centimetres. 'About five feet eight in the old scale,' Karalis said, 'but bear in mind the cartilage has contracted and the flesh on his skull and feet has decomposed, so he was slightly taller than that. Five nine? Not tall.'

'Ethnicity?'

'Caucasian,' the pathologist said promptly. 'The teeth tell us that.'

'DNA?'

'You're firing the questions today, Helen,' said Karalis mildly.

'Sorry, doc.'

'This is a *cold* case.'

'They're all hot to us, doc,' she said.

Karalis said, 'As to DNA, I should be able to create a profile from marrow in the long bones. But it will take time to do that and then see if this poor fellow's in a database.' He continued to examine the body, muttering, 'No further signs of injury...'

Auhl glanced around the room restlessly. It was an eight-bay lab, homicides, suicides, OD cases, accident victims, other reportable deaths. The bodies were stored on steel trolleys in refrigerated units. Even the gleaming steel added to the chill in the air.

A movement in the corner of his eye. Up in the glass-walled viewing room, standing at a rail, a couple of students. One waved at him with sly cheek. He nodded back to her. She grinned, nudged her friend.

'Okay.' Karalis had finished. He stripped off his gloves. 'I'll get the rest of the team onto the bones and teeth and DNA extraction. Obviously we can't do a toxicology examination. Do you have his wallet? Wristwatch?'

'No,' Helen said.

'We have a coin dated 2008,' Auhl said.

Karalis cast a brooding look at the bones. 'That would fit. Meanwhile let's hope the DNA gives us something. But he might not be in the system—he is on the young side to have a criminal record.'

He glanced at the clothing. 'The shoes might give you something, but they're everyday cheap runners.'

Helen Colfax had been staring into the distance. 'Certainly run the DNA, but that'll take weeks, I expect. It would be good if we could release a face to the media. Any chance someone here can whip up a digital reconstruction?'

'Whip up. I like that,' Karalis said. 'I'll need to see if anyone's available. Better yet, has the time. Better yet, has a case number and budget approval.'

'Come on, doc,' Auhl said. 'Haven't you got any tame PhD students in the building?'

The pathologist gave it some thought. 'Actually, yes.'

'They might get a kick out of joining the fight for justice,' Colfax said.

'They might get a kick out of a few dollars, too,' Karalis said, and Auhl could see him considering the paperwork, the budget, whom to sweet talk. 'I'll see what I can do.'

BEFORE THEY LEFT, Auhl spread the contents of the Elphick file across an empty autopsy table.

'Wondered if you could have a look at these, doc.'

'We could do this in more salubrious surroundings,' Karalis said, with a wink for Helen Colfax.

'Humour the bugger,' she said.

Karalis bent over the Elphick report, scanned it and said, 'My predecessor performed this post-mortem.'

'And reading between the lines,' Auhl said, 'he didn't want to go out on a limb about the cause of death.'

Karalis grunted. He picked up the file and read aloud:

'Depress fracture, left frontotemporal skull. Subdural haematoma, left frontotemporal skull. Lobe cerebral contusion, left frontotemporal skull.' He glanced at Auhl. 'The left frontotemporal skull took a fair old whack.'

'If you say so, doc.'

'Jaw fractures…abrasions, contusions and lacerations…a broken tooth…'

Karalis read the rest in silence, the icy air around him antiseptic. Somewhere a saw started. Auhl pictured the ripping of saw-teeth and winced.

'Third left finger fractured,' Karalis said, 'contusions and lacerations to the left hand, some bleeding with dirt and vegetable matter in the injuries.'

He looked at Auhl, who said, 'He put his hand out to absorb the fall.'

'What fall?'

'He was hit on the head,' Auhl said, 'and fell to the ground.'

Karalis grunted. He read on. He said, 'Crusted abrasions, both knees,' and turned to the photographs: the body, the fence, the ute, the ute's interior.

Auhl said, 'As you can see, doc, blood drops were found in various places between the fence and the ute, on top of the bonnet, and around on the other side of the ute, and inside the ute. It suggests a lot of movement while bleeding.'

'Entirely possible,' the pathologist said. 'He might have had a dizzy spell. It says here that blood, hair and skin tissue were found on the edge of the roo bar. He fell, knocked his head on the roo bar, got up, disorientated, then staggered around a bit. Falling, getting up again…'

'But if you look at the photos there's an injury on the *top* of his head.'

'If he was bent over and fell forward onto the roo bar, that would account for such an injury.'

'Yeah, yeah. Meanwhile there's also blood on the drivers seat and the drivers-seat headrest,' Auhl said. 'He got *into* the ute at one point.'

'And fell out again?'

'Or was pulled out. First he was hit on the head and fell, hitting the roo bar, then got up again and was chased right around the ute, trying to get away. Managed to get behind the wheel but was pulled out again.'

'That's one explanation,' Karalis said, gesturing at the photographs. 'There are others, equally plausible.'

'Account for the blood on *top of the bonnet*, doc.'

'Hmm.' Karalis was silent. 'Again, the guy fell, hitting his head on the roo bar, staggered upright, dazed, shaking his head. Flinging off blood drops.' He paused. 'But I'm not a blood-spatter expert.'

Auhl, faintly impatient, said, 'All I want to know is could someone have hit Mr Elphick on the head as he stood between the front of the ute and the fence. He fell onto the roo bar, got up again, tried to get away, eventually climbed behind the wheel, was pulled out again and given another whack on the head and fell to the ground, where he died.'

Karalis shrugged. 'It's plausible, no more than that.'

In the car on the way back to the police building Helen Colfax said, 'You heard the man.'

'Give me a couple of days, boss, that's all I'm asking.'

8

JOSHUA BUGG AND Claire Pascal had their heads down when Auhl and Colfax returned. Typing, making calls.

Helen Colfax headed straight for the whiteboard and announced, 'Slab Man, everybody.'

When they'd angled their chairs in a semicircle, she delivered a fast, concise update: the slab, the body, Auhl and Pascal's door-to-door, the pathologist's findings.

'So that's where we stand,' she said in conclusion. 'He was young, no older than early twenties, Caucasian, not tall, and probably shot. Shot elsewhere, then buried under the slab.'

Bugg said, 'Any idea where?'

She shrugged. 'Possibly an old house that was on the property, but it was pulled down some years ago.'

'Shame,' Bugg muttered.

'Yes.'

'Missing persons?' Pascal said.

'That's an obvious place to start. I want you on that, Josh. We have a possible first name: Sean. Start no earlier than ten years ago and no later than five. If that doesn't pan out, broaden the parameters.'

'Boss.'

Colfax turned to Auhl and Pascal. 'Some enterprising reporter's going to wonder who used to own or live at the property, so I need the pair of you to stay a step ahead. Certainly track down the daughter if she's still alive, but also search property records. And check utilities: phone, gas, electric. Who demolished the place? Do they remember blood on the floor, signs of struggle? Was there ever an old structure over the concrete slab? So on and so forth.'

'Real estate agents,' suggested Auhl. 'They always seem to know plenty.'

'Excellent. The place was a rental at one point, yes? Did any of the local real estate firms handle that?'

'And we need to find Donna Crowther,' Claire Pascal said. 'See if she can explain the boyfriend disappearing from her life.'

'Good, good, we're on a roll. Were Crowther and the boyfriend known to police?' Colfax continued. 'Not only domestic disputes, but were they dealing out of the old house, for example.'

'DNA from the bones,' Bugg said.

'There's a backlog,' Helen said. 'And he was a young guy— quite likely he's not on any database, so we're looking at releasing some kind of facial reconstruction to the public.'

'What about our other cases?'

Helen gave Bugg a smile devoid of pity. 'I expect you to continue to discharge your obligations in that regard, Leading Senior Constable Bugg.' She paused. 'You're working Bertolli?'

Antonio Bertolli was a Mildura market gardener, shot dead in 1978. He wasn't the only one of his profession murdered around that time, the common denominators being the Vic Market and the Calabrian Mafia. The case was reopened every few years. This time it had taken Bugg to Mildura for a couple of days, even though few of the original figures were still alive.

'Lost cause,' Auhl said, before he could stop himself.

'Words of wisdom from the old geezer, always much appreciated,' Bugg said.

'Children,' Helen said. She glanced at Claire. 'You're working *Waurn?*'

The desiccated remains of Freda Waurn had been found on her kitchen floor after she'd defaulted on her mortgage and her bank hired a locksmith to break in. He found a skeleton: she'd been dead for two years. Her hyoid bone was broken, every room of the house ransacked.

'Still looking,' Claire said. 'No spouse, no children, no siblings. She didn't seem to have anyone in her life.'

Helen turned to Auhl. 'Alan?'

'Well…Elphick, boss.'

'Backburner, all right? I want you on Slab Man.'

'Boss.'

Joshua Bugg was looking at him with an unfriendly grin.

'Got spinach caught in your teeth, Josh,' Auhl said.

LATE MORNING NOW. Auhl and Pascal strolled across the river to the Land Titles Office in the CBD. Expecting bureaucratic resistance, Auhl was pleased they were given quick access to the deeds related to the property where Slab Man was buried. Bernadette Sullivan and her husband Francis had bought the property in 1976. Terra Australis AgriCorp owned it between 2012 and 2015.

'So if Slab Man has been there for ten years, the Sullivans were still the owners when he died,' Pascal said.

Auhl said, 'The parents are dead, the daughter inherited.'

They examined the certificate of title, a stiff document smelling faintly of mould. At the top were the volume and folio numbers and the quaint address Blackberry Hill Farm…*being part of Crown Allotment 60A*. The owners were listed in two columns, with Bernadette Sullivan named as a Married Woman and joint proprietor with Francis Sullivan Fire Officer in 1976. Then in 1986 Bernadette was listed as Surviving Sole Proprietor. The property passed to Angela, her daughter, in 2011; she later sold it to Terra Australis, who sold it to Nathan and Jaime Wright.

'Next stop, Angela Sullivan,' Auhl said.

BACK AT THE COLD CASE Unit they were stopped by Helen Colfax. She gave Auhl an odd look. 'You remember Bluebeard?'

Auhl tried to read the look. 'He's killed wife number three? What's her name...Janine?'

'Not exactly. He's claiming she wants to kill him.'

9

BACK WHEN DR ALEC Neill's second wife died as mysteriously as his first, Auhl was the Homicide Squad sergeant in charge of the investigation. His team had never been able to prove anything but Auhl, convinced of Neill's guilt, had had a quiet word with Neill's new girlfriend, a hand therapist employed at one of Neill's hospitals: *Don't let yourself become murdered wife #3.*

'He'll get tired of you, Janine. He'll meet someone new and he'll fake a suicide or an accident.'

She'd given him a look of disgust and walked off.

Auhl recalled a slim woman, incensed, her gym-toned flesh tight over her bones, her lips a slash across her over-refined face. The way she'd stalked away from him on a tide of vanity and gratification that day in 2012. Auhl, keeping an occasional eye on the pair, heard that she'd gone ahead and married Neill, living half the week in East Melbourne and half on a hobby farm near St Andrews, less than an hour north-east of the city.

Worst case, Auhl thought he'd see Janine Neill on the mortuary cutting table one day. Best? Divorcing her husband—or even giving evidence against him to the Homicide Squad. The last thing he expected was Neill in fear of his life from her.

Colfax told him some of it as they walked upstairs to the victim suite, where Neill had been telling his story to Homicide Squad detectives. 'Apparently he found drugs hidden in her car yesterday, and he thinks she used them to kill his second wife—the one she replaced—and his girlfriend.'

'Girlfriend.'

'She died a few weeks ago. Suddenly, mysteriously.'

'*Before* he married her? That's new.'

'Keep an open mind, Alan. The man might be genuine.'

'Not this fucker,' Auhl said, remembering the well-groomed surgeon he'd questioned all those years ago. The slender bony nose steering a patrician, faintly contemptuous, face. The calm monosyllabic replies, Neill staring back across the interview table as if charting and storing the thoughts and feelings of his questioners.

They entered the victim suite, a soft, bland expanse of curtained windows and sofa, with books and magazines, a tea urn and a percolator. Forgettable landscapes and cute animals decorated the walls. Neill was seated at a long table with a crumpled-looking Homicide sergeant named Debenham, and went rigid when Auhl and Colfax walked in.

He pointed a trembling finger at Auhl. 'What's he doing here?' He turned to Debenham. 'Is this an ambush? I come to you with information about two murders, and you turn him on me?'

Debenham cocked his head at Auhl, who said, 'I questioned Doctor Neill a few times concerning the deaths of his first two wives.'

'Questioned me? You all but accused me. I got the distinct impression you would have liked to smack me around when no one was looking.'

You bet I would, thought Auhl.

Neill looked different. Still good-looking, well tended, but raw with emotion today. But then Auhl recalled that Neill had the ability to adjust to situations. Cold in interview, but when questioned at the coronial inquiry following his second wife's sudden, apparently suspicious, death he'd appeared anguished and self-flagellating. Upset that he hadn't been able to diagnose the illnesses that had taken each of his wives.

And here he was, upset again.

Neill swiped at his reddened eyes. 'I don't want that man here.'

Debenham patted the surgeon's arm. He seemed bored with Neill, as if he couldn't see why he should offer comfort, but knew he had a job to do. 'Alan isn't here to hassle you, Doctor Neill, he's interested in your accusations. Isn't that right, Acting Sergeant Auhl?'

'Absolutely,' said Auhl, ignoring Helen Colfax's warning touch on his sleeve.

Neill subsided, glowering.

Auhl and Colfax sat in the chairs opposite Neill and Debenham. 'The first sign you're investigating *me*,' Neill said, 'I'll call my lawyer.'

Auhl gave him an empty smile as Colfax introduced herself. 'Why don't you fill us in, Doctor Neill.'

'I've already told it a hundred times.'

'Not to us.'

Neill wore a sleek suit, with a white shirt and green tie. He loosened the tie, a busy man undergoing a harrowing experience, and placed his forearms on the table. He smelled faintly of antiseptic soap, and his moist, sorrowful eyes sought Colfax's. 'I'm frightened. I think Janine intends to murder me. I'm positive she murdered—'

'Let's take matters one at a time, shall we?' Colfax said. 'First, if you think your life's in danger from your wife, we can protect you. And until we can sort this out, you might consider avoiding all contact with her.'

'Do you think?' he sneered. 'I'm driving straight to our country place as soon as I leave here. Janine's staying in the city. She has a conference this weekend. Melbourne University.'

'Okay. Let's go back to the beginning. In 2004, your first wife, Eleanor, died of a mysterious illness.'

Auhl watched Neill's face. Bewilderment, then anguish. 'You're bringing that up? I thought we'd moved past that. Yes, El died. She got ill, and she died.' His fists were two earnest clumps near his heart. 'These things do happen.'

Colfax was soothing. 'I know they do, Doctor Neill.'

Of course, Auhl had looked into the death of Eleanor Neill while investigating the death of Siobhan Neill eight years later. The first Mrs Neill, a hospital admin secretary then aged twenty-seven and in the sixth year of her marriage to Neill, had suddenly begun to complain of vomiting and diarrhoea. A week later she was dead. Asphyxia—too sudden to get her to hospital.

Colfax said, 'And then in 2012 your second wife, Siobhan, died suddenly; also in apparent good health until that point.'

'That's correct,' Neill said, shaking his head at what life can throw at you. 'It was ruled a heart attack, in the absence of anything more compelling. At the time I thought it was a ghastly coincidence. Unfortunately that's not what the police thought.' He glared at Auhl. 'However, given the drugs I found yesterday in Janine's car, I now think Siobhan's death *was* murder. Except I didn't do it and it's time I was vindicated.'

Auhl stared at him steadily. Siobhan, aged thirty-two, had been found dead in her bed one morning. The post-mortem found no poisons in her system, no physical trauma, no signs of disease. But there were indications of a heart attack, and that was the pathologist's ruling.

Her parents were not satisfied. They approached the Homicide Squad and, making no effort to conceal their loathing for Neill, pointed to the sudden death of his first wife. Auhl's team weighed it up: one husband; two fit, young, healthy wives, one dying after suffering vomiting and diarrhoea in the days preceding death, the other of a possible heart attack. Neill had married Siobhan, the speech therapist with whom he'd been having an affair, less than six months after the funeral of his first wife. This was generally thought to be bad form, but no one talked about murder.

They started to when it was revealed that, at the time of Siobhan's death, Neill had been having an affair with the woman who became his third wife. Janine was also married at the time of the affair. When her divorce came through, a week after Siobhan's funeral, Neill sent her a hundred red roses. Seven months later, he married her.

Auhl recalled the coronial inquiry, Neill claiming he'd been Janine's friend, not lover, at the time of Siobhan's death. In a record of interview played to the court, he'd sobbed: 'You don't know what it's like to be viewed as a brilliant doctor yet unable to save the lives of those you love.' He'd gone on to say he'd thought long and hard about the events and, yes, was spending a fair amount of time blaming himself.

Now Auhl heard Helen say, 'Siobhan was murdered, and you think your present wife did it.'

'Yes.' Neill shifted uncomfortably. 'I know what you're thinking, you think I'm a serial womaniser, but things were shaky with Siobhan and I was flattered when Janine started to pay me attention. Then when Siobhan died, Janine was there for me and...I was weak, I admit it.'

'And history repeats itself and things get shaky with Janine and you find yourself a new girlfriend,' said Auhl.

Neill flushed. He turned to look at Debenham. 'Do I have to listen to this?'

'Sergeant Auhl apologises for his tone,' soothed Colfax, kicking Auhl under the table. 'Returning to Siobhan: do you think your present wife killed her so she could have you to herself?'

'Obviously.'

'Was Janine around when your first wife died?'

Neill was astounded. 'God, no. She would have been still at school.'

Auhl suppressed a snort.

'I've just about had it with you,' Neill said.

Auhl folded his arms. 'Have you been feeling ill recently, Doctor Neill? Vomiting? Diarrhoea?'

Neill looked at him. 'You'd like that, wouldn't you? No. Janine's drug of choice is sudden and undetectable. She used it to kill Siobhan, and she used it to kill Christine.'

'The bodies just keep piling up,' Auhl said. 'Who's Christine?'

Debenham, the Homicide Squad detective, gave Auhl a bleak smile. 'Christine Lancer, a friend of Doctor Neill, died suddenly a few weeks ago.'

Auhl opened his mouth but Helen Colfax kicked him again and said, 'Perhaps you could tell us about Ms Lancer, Doctor Neill.'

Neill said primly, 'Chris is, was, a physio at the Epworth.' He made a rolling motion of his wrist: 'Naturally I'm always conferring with physiotherapists in my line of work.'

'Naturally,' said Auhl, visualising Neill's type: pretty young blondes who looked about fifteen. And, crucially, blondes who were not doctors. Neill didn't want to shack up with an equal. Or, indeed, with someone who might recognise she was being poisoned.

The thought earned him another kick from the boss, who apparently could read his mind.

'How did Ms Lancer die, Doctor Neill?'

'I think my wife—'

'No, Doctor Neill, leave her out of it for now. How did Ms Lancer die?'

'It was ruled a heart attack.'

'Just like Siobhan.'

'Just like Siobhan,' confirmed Neill. 'Do you believe in coincidence? I don't.'

Nor did Auhl. 'Are you saying Janine used something in both

60

cases that mimicked the symptoms of a heart attack?'

Neill's moist eyes glittered. 'I am indeed, and I found the evidence. Sux.'

'Sucks?'

He smiled and leaned in. 'Succinylcholine.'

'How do you know she used that particular drug?' asked Colfax.

'Because I found her stash, hidden in her car.'

'That doesn't answer the question,' said Auhl. 'What makes you think she used it to kill anyone?'

'Because deaths from succinylcholine reproduce the symptoms of heart attacks.' A catch in Neill's voice as he said it, and he swiped at the leakage from his eyes.

Debenham gave him a look of impatience tinged with sympathy. Auhl sensed from Helen, too, not exactly sympathy but a willingness to hear Neill out. 'Tell me about this stash,' she said.

'Two ampoules, each twenty-five mils, one half-used, sufficient to kill several wives.'

Auhl said, 'Found in Janine's car? Why did you decide to search it? And when?'

Neill shot him a testy look. 'Yesterday I went out to buy wine. Janine's car was parked behind mine so I borrowed it. I was getting out some coins for the parking meter and dropped them—they rolled under the drivers seat somewhere. When I got out and started peering around, I saw this little Velcro bag.'

Neill took out his iPhone, swiped at the screen and placed the device face up on the table. Auhl leaned over to look: a dark but mostly clear image of the underside of a car seat, and a rectangle of fabric. Leaving the phone in place, Neill swiped again: the bag, open, showing a syringe and two ampoules, one full of fluid, the other half-full.

It was entirely possible that Neill planted the stuff, but Auhl let that go. He said, as though curious, 'It doesn't have to be refrigerated?'

'It's stable for a few weeks at room temperature.'

'Let me play devil's advocate,' Helen Colfax said. 'Let me be your wife's defence barrister. She's a hand therapist, right? Damaged tendons, other painful injuries? One day she's needed the succinylcholine for some reason—maybe an emergency procedure—but the hospital's run out, so to make sure that never happened again she stocked up. Hid the stuff under the seat of her car so junkies wouldn't steal it or whatever.'

Neill shook his head dismissively. 'There's no legitimate reason why a hand therapist would use sux. It's used in operating theatres.'

'But a skilled *surgeon* might use it?' asked Auhl, all innocence.

Neill scowled. 'Yes, I'm a surgeon, and yes, I'm skilled. Tendons, bones, sinew, nerves. Microsurgery when someone chops off a finger with a bandsaw, for example. But sux isn't used for that kind of procedure. Sux is a muscle relaxant used in emergency or critical procedures where it's necessary to intubate. It sedates and paralyses extremely quickly. In fact, the lungs stop working, but the patient then breathes by way of a respirator.'

He swung his head from one to the other: Debenham, Auhl, Colfax. 'If it's used in the absence of a respirator the result is immediate paralysis of the diaphragm. Breathing stops, followed by fatal brain damage. In a matter of seconds.'

'Let's say for the moment we believe you,' Auhl said.

Neill curled his lip. 'That's it, I want a lawyer.'

Helen Colfax said, 'I apologise for my colleague, Doctor Neill. But humour us for the moment. Alan?'

Auhl said, 'I merely wanted to ask where you think Janine obtained the sux.'

'She stole it from the hospitals she works in.'

'Wouldn't they have records? Wouldn't she be found out?'

Neill said, 'Not if a hospital is missing just one vial. It would be explained away as sloppy paperwork. But if *two* vials went missing, it would be another story. Thus, to avoid arousing suspicion, Janine took one from the Epworth and one from the Alfred—two of the hospitals she works in.'

Thus. Wanker. 'It's injected and acts quickly?' said Auhl.

'Acts in *seconds*.'

'Surely there are symptoms?' Helen said.

'Sux is the perfect killer. It's quick, not much is needed and the victim gives every indication of dying from a heart attack,' Neill said.

'There was a pretty thorough post-mortem when Siobhan died,' Auhl said. 'Why didn't it turn up anything?'

'Not even a good pathologist would think to test for sux. A specific urine test is needed, which isn't part of the protocol. And the results can be inconclusive.'

Auhl glanced at Debenham. 'Can we get the pathologist to have another look at this girlfriend of his?'

Debenham gazed back levelly. 'Cremated. And there was a family history of heart problems.'

'Convenient.'

Auhl watched Neill for...what? Smugness? Relief? 'We have two perhaps unexplained sudden deaths and photos of two tubes of some liquid. None of it is proof of murder.'

Except he knew there had been murder. *Murders*.

Neill said, 'I can tell from your face you don't believe me. Nor did Sergeant Debenham, at first. I'll lay it out for you, okay?'

'That's what we're here for,' Auhl said, earning another kick to the ankle.

'First, I admit I started an affair with Chris even though I'm still married to Janine. I was lonely. I hardly ever saw Janine and when I did she was cold and remote.'

Auhl opened his mouth but Colfax got in first. 'And Janine found out?'

'I left my phone in the kitchen and Chris texted me one day. Janine read it.'

'She tackled you about it?'

'No. But I could see she'd opened the message. It was pretty frank, you know, sexual. And her behaviour changed.'

'Changed how?'

'She became hard and vindictive and had this air of triumph, as though she'd thought it all out. Kill Chris like she'd killed Siobhan, then kill me.'

'Why kill you? Revenge?'

'Well, yes, revenge. And money, of course.'

AFTER NEILL HAD BEEN escorted downstairs, Colfax, Debenham and Auhl discussed tactics.

'At the very least we serve a search warrant on Mrs Neill,' Debenham said. 'If we do find she's stolen this drug, we can apply pressure regarding the other business.'

'You mean the murders,' said Auhl.

'Yes.'

'So you believe him. His present wife killed his previous wife and his new girlfriend.'

'Don't give me the shits,' Debenham said. 'An accusation has been made. We have to follow up. And you know it yourself, two sudden deaths.'

'*Three* sudden deaths,' said Auhl.

'Boys, boys,' said Helen Colfax.

Auhl wasn't finished. 'But what, realistically, can Homicide do? Wives number one and two are long dead, and the girlfriend was cremated.'

'We serve a search warrant,' said Debenham patiently, 'and we check hospital records. Maybe Janine's on camera with her hand inside the drugs cupboard.'

'*Shit.*' Helen Colfax twisted suddenly in her chair. Debenham and Auhl watched, fascinated, as she snapped her hand around to the back of her neck and dug beneath the collar of her shirt, a

64

new-looking candy-green item. 'Bloody tag's digging into my skin.' Tugging the fabric away from her neck, she said, 'But what if the good doctor planted the drugs?'

'At last someone sees sense,' Auhl said.

'Yeah, yeah. But our Homicide colleague is right, we need to obtain a warrant and have a word with the third Mrs Neill.'

'When?'

'First thing tomorrow morning.' She looked at Debenham. 'I'm suggesting a joint operation.'

'No skin off my nose,' Debenham said.

AUHL FINISHED AT 5.00 p.m. and decided to walk home. He was crossing Princes Bridge when his phone rang. 'I am wish to speak to Mrs Fanning, please.'

A mature female voice that seemed to reach Auhl from an echo chamber. 'This isn't her number. But I am a friend. May I ask what it's about?'

Then a hint of muffled sounds and urgent whispers.

'Are you Mr Auhl?'

'Yes. And you are…?'

'I am station attendant at Southern Cross. I have little girl here. She is cry very much.'

Then Pia was on the line. 'A. A.?'

'I'll come and collect you.'

'I tried to ring Mum and your house but I ran out of coins.'

She must have tried the only payphone left in the world, thought Auhl. Then: *We need to get her a mobile phone.* 'Your mum's at work, sweetie.'

'I didn't know what tram to get or what direction or anything,' and she was wailing.

Then the woman was on the line again. 'You come now, Mr Auhl?'

'Yes. Ten minutes.'

He found Pia standing with an African woman beside one of the ticket barriers. She hurled herself at him; fresh tears. Auhl knelt, and murmured, and patted, and finally stood to thank the attendant.

Who was wary. 'How you know her?'

'She lives with her mother in my house.'

'Where her mother?'

'At work.'

The woman didn't want to let Pia go yet. 'Where her father?'

Auhl explained: the access visit, a father who made things difficult for mother and daughter.

The station attendant began to unbend. 'You be smiling, little girl,' she said, with a gentle push to Pia's shoulders.

They walked to the tram stop. 'Thought you were coming back tomorrow.'

'Dad said he was too busy.'

Auhl nodded. Too busy for his daughter. His daughter an inconvenience. So he'd put her on the train back to the city without letting anyone know. Without even thinking about how she'd get home once she reached the other end.

10

SATURDAY. THEY TACKLED Janine Neill at 7.00 a.m. Found her awake. Dressed, but looking drawn and fatigued. Last night's conference dinner? wondered Auhl.

'What is this? Is this going to make me late? I'm delivering a paper at ten.'

She stood in her front hallway, frowning at Auhl, Colfax and Debenham on her doorstep, the uniformed search constables on the garden path behind them. Auhl regarded her. Still a classic Nordic blonde, dressed in a narrow skirt, snug jacket and court shoes. Showing plenty of the tall, shoulders-back certainty he remembered, but with a hint of bewilderment. And doubt...guilt concealed as bluster? Recognising Auhl, she said, 'Not you again.'

'I'm getting a lot of that lately,' Auhl said.

Helen Colfax shot him a look. 'Mrs Neill, we have a warrant to search your house and car, if you don't mind. May we come in?'

'I told you, I'm giving a paper this morning.'

'We'll be as quick as we can, Mrs Neill,' Debenham said, 'but you may have to postpone your talk.'

He handed her the warrant. 'The keys to your car, please, Mrs Neill.'

The driveway to the little 1890s house was narrow. Auhl confirmed one aspect of Alec Neill's story: there was room for two cars only if one parked behind the other.

'My car? Whatever for?'

'The keys, Mrs Neill.'

'All right. Come in.'

A dim cool hallway hung with small watercolours. Ornate ceiling fixtures, a long rug on polished floorboards. The hallway passed bedrooms and a sitting room, and opened onto a broad, sun-drenched, glass-walled living area: kitchen, dining room and lounge. The keys were in a glass bowl at one end of a long bench. Janine Neill picked them up, but her fingers seemed not to work and they fell to the bench. Nerves, thought Auhl. She stepped back and said, 'Help yourself. But why?'

Debenham ignored her and murmured instructions to the search constables. Two of them entered the hallway rooms and two went out to the car.

Meanwhile Janine Neill was pacing, glancing at her watch. She looked tentative now. She swung around on Auhl, squirrelly and apologetic. Closer to, she was beautiful, beautifully groomed. 'Sorry I was rude before. Just tell me what's going on.'

'Why don't we sit, Mrs Neill,' Colfax said, taking her arm gently and leading her from the kitchen to an area of easy chairs: two sofas, coffee table, armchairs.

When they were seated, Debenham, his scruffy bulk sinking into the far end of a sofa, said, 'Your husband has made certain allegations, Mrs Neill.'

She was astonished, bewildered. 'What? Allegations? About me? What allegations?'

Debenham put up a hand to silence her. 'But first I must advise you of your rights.'

'What? My *rights*? Why?'

Debenham delivered the spiel, then said, 'Doctor Neill came to us yesterday claiming that you have a dangerous hospital drug known as sux, or succinylcholine, concealed in your car and that he feared for his life. Is there anything you wish to say in regard to this matter?'

'What? *What*?'

Auhl could see that she was completely floored. 'As Sergeant Debenham said, Mrs Neill, you are entitled to have a lawyer present.'

Debenham shot him a shut-the-fuck-up look, turned to Janine again. 'Furthermore, Mrs Neill, your husband claims that you used this drug to murder his second wife, Siobhan. Is there anything you wish to say in regard to this matter?'

'What? Siobhan? No. Why? She died. It was a heart attack.'

'Finally, your husband claims that you used this drug just a few weeks ago to murder his friend, Christine Lancer.'

Janine went tight, putting her bewilderment to one side. '*Friend*. Is that what he called her?'

She'd started to look faintly unhinged to Auhl. She'd scooted to the front of her chair, knees together, her hands rubbing the tops of her knees. 'He was sleeping with her, the bastard.'

She turned to Auhl, another expression chasing across her face, a hard certainty. 'You were right,' she said, and the words tumbled out, how it all made sense to her now, the new mistress, the mystery drug... 'He murdered Siobhan so he could have me.'

Debenham sensed the interview getting away from him. 'Mrs Neill, kindly answer the questions I am putting to you.'

'I want a lawyer to sit with me while I answer your fucking questions.'

Debenham shook his head wearily, got to his feet—just as one of the uniforms entered, holding aloft a clear plastic evidence envelope containing the little Velcro bag that Alec Neill had photographed.

'Excellent,' Debenham said. 'You've logged it?'

'Yes.'

'And where was it found?'

'Under the drivers seat.'

'Photographed in place?'

'Yes.'

'Opened, contents photographed?'

'Yes.'

'Describe the contents.'

'Two small glass tubes, both labelled succinylcholine'—he stumbled over the word—'one full, one half-full, and a syringe.'

'Help the others search the house,' Debenham said. He turned to Janine. 'Your husband made serious allegations against you, Mrs Neill, and already we have confirmation of one of them. Can you account for the presence of this drug in your car?'

Janine Neill jiggled as if in panic. For a brief moment she seemed to zone out. She swallowed and blinked, looking pale, her face greasy with perspiration. She turned to Auhl. 'Alec must have put it there. You told me all those years ago he'd try to kill me. I'm sorry I doubted you.'

Auhl nodded.

She said, 'I don't feel too good. How does this drug work? What does it do?'

She swayed where she sat, her spine flopping against the back of her chair, then gathered herself, rose unsteadily and hurried to a doorway at the end of the room. Bathroom, thought Auhl, glimpsing white tiles.

She'd not shut the door. Auhl listened for retching. Meanwhile Helen Colfax smiled tiredly at Auhl and Debenham. 'We need to lay off now. Take her in for more questioning, yes, but no more of this.'

She entered the bathroom behind Janine Neill, the men heard murmured voices, and eventually both women re-emerged, Helen supporting Janine.

Who announced: 'I want to say a few things.'

She looked clammy, spent. 'You don't need to, Janine,' Auhl said, earning himself another scowl from Debenham.

'Context, okay?' Janine said.

'Okay.'

'On Wednesday, I served divorce papers on Alec.'

Auhl settled in to listen. 'Uh huh.'

'A while ago I learned he'd been having an affair with that Lancer person.'

'How?'

'His phone. It was on the kitchen bench, he was out in the garden. It buzzed: incoming text. From her. Christine. Sounding pissed off about something. I didn't touch the phone, let the screen go blank, went about my business. But when Alec was asleep I looked at his messages—he never deletes, the arrogant shit—and I looked at his emails. Dozens, hundreds, full of lovey-dovey stuff except that the more recent ones had become quite demanding. "When are you going to divorce her?" and "If you don't leave her soon I'm going to tell her what's going on" and "Unless you start divorce proceedings right now I'm going to tell everyone everywhere what kind of person you are." Et cetera, et cetera.'

'So you injected her with a drug you stole from the hospital,' Debenham said.

Silence while Janine shut her eyes and put her hands to her temple. She recovered and said, 'Don't be ridiculous. Don't you see what's happening?'

'Enlighten us. If we pretend for the moment that your husband stole the drug to get rid of *you* so he could marry *her*, why would he want to bump her off? He decided he didn't want her after all?'

'That's exactly what I'm saying,' Janine Neill said tremblingly. She fished for a tissue and dropped it. Stared at her hand in astonishment before picking it from her lap and delicately blotting her face.

'He changed his mind because of the inheritance.'

A strange calm settled in Auhl. He waited.

Janine took a deep breath, exhaled. 'Just recently I was told my grandfather's dying. Weeks rather than months, but you never know. The thing is, I stand to inherit quite a lot when he goes, being the only grandchild.'

'Your husband knows?'

'Yes. So now he needs me alive, not dead. So he bumps off the meddlesome girlfriend and gets all cosy with me, thinking of all that cash coming my way.' She searched their faces to see that they understood. 'Don't you see? He must've found out I'm going to divorce him.'

Debenham was sceptical. 'But you only told him a few days ago.'

'He'll have been snooping, knowing him.'

'He feared losing access to your inheritance if you divorced?'

'I'd say so.'

'And if you hadn't started divorce proceedings?'

'He would have continued the loving husband act. Bided his time until he could arrange an accidental death of some kind. Take me rock climbing. Shoot me or something.' She shook her head. 'It's clear to me now.'

'Or it's clear that he knew nothing of divorce and was having a great old time with his little love interest,' Debenham said. He placed a meaty hand over his mouth, stifling a burp. 'Meanwhile we have *you*—royally pissed off with your cheating husband and his little tramp of a girlfriend—stealing a hospital drug, knocking off the girlfriend, intending to knock him off. Whoops, bad luck, he finds your stash.'

'He planted it.'

'Why did you say your husband might shoot you?' Helen Colfax interrupted. 'Does he own a firearm?'

'He has this old twenty-two rifle. For shooting foxes. He can always stage something.' Janine shrugged. 'I don't know.'

Auhl said, 'There are foxes on your St Andrews place?'

She nodded.

Debenham was getting impatient. 'Mrs Neill, we just found a dangerous drug in your car. Probably stolen.'

'I gave you a good reason for that! He's framing me!'

'But why? Why not hide the drug and use it on you a few months or years down the track?'

'He's a very nasty man,' muttered Janine. 'And maybe he thought if I was in jail he'd have a claim on my estate.'

Colfax said, 'Did any of your work colleagues know about his affair with Christine Lancer?'

'Not that I'm aware of, but who knows? I do know he wiped his phone and his email history.'

Debenham said, 'You checked, I suppose.'

She gave him a long, unimpressed scrutiny, then seemed to swallow down a bad taste in her mouth. 'I found out he was cheating on me. So, yes, I checked.'

Auhl leaned in. 'Janine, where does your husband store the rifle?'

'In a metal box under a workbench in the shed. Why?'

'We may need to speak to him again and it's important we know that kind of thing.'

Debenham was fed up. 'Getting ahead of ourselves, aren't we?' But he did ask for the St Andrews address.

Janine Neill, watching his notebook, his ballpoint scribble, drawled, 'Don't sweat it, I know my husband and he's not going to shoot it out with you. For you, it'll be high-priced lawyers.'

She paused. 'How did he seem when he spoke to you? Emotional, right?'

They said nothing.

'It's an act,' Janine said, a hand over her eyes as if to bar the light.

Helen said, 'Let's say it wasn't. Would he ever self-harm?'

'You mean, shoot himself? The thought of how he'd look afterwards, all that blood and guts, would be enough to stop him. He's too pumped up with self-regard to hurt himself.'

Words to be engraved on many a headstone, thought Auhl.

11

DEBENHAM DIDN'T like it but accepted Colfax's suggestion to investigate further. Did Neill know that his wife intended to divorce him? Check hospital CCTV and drug-safe records. Talk to the pathologist who had performed the post-mortem on Christine Lancer. Check the syringe, glass vials and Velcro bag for prints and DNA.

And so Auhl was released from further duties that Saturday and took a tram home to Carlton. He felt weary, jostled, drowned in voices, ringtones, beeps and pings, yet Janine Neill's story was vivid in his mind, her words and accusations winding through his memories of the previous day's interview with her husband.

He alighted at the university and headed along Grattan Street. The spring air was mild, and the youth of Carlton were out in shorts, T-shirts and other scraps of lightweight cotton. Eyes were down, thumbs busy on devices. One young man in a Ned Kelly beard looked particularly self-absorbed. Auhl blocked the footpath. Juvenile, but fun.

No one seemed to be home, and meanwhile the noonday sun

was painting his backyard so he took a sandwich and the *Age* to the wrought iron garden setting and ate, read, dozed. Then he washed windows, picked trash from the front garden, cut off dead bits of jasmine from the laneway fence and later played backyard tennis at a friend's place in Northcote.

His turn to cook dinner—somehow, it usually was—Bec and Pia joining him at the table before Bec headed upstairs to her textbooks, folders and laptop and Pia eventually to bed. Neve was at work, evening shift. Who knew where the others were. Meanwhile Auhl hadn't heard from Liz. He wanted to call her. Didn't.

The evening deepened and the house creaked around him, and he read his event-free novel. That lasted until ten, when he closed the book and contemplated bed. Inertia defeated him. A deep silence suffused the house. It was a peaceful silence, a healthy silence. Nothing like the silences he knew the Fanning womenfolk had endured. He stroked Cynthia's black fur absently.

Just as he was wriggling free of his armchair, Neve returned from her cleaning job. She stood in the doorway, deeply fatigued, too tired to be shy or awkward. She hovered.

Auhl, used to her ways, knowing she'd speak eventually, took charge. 'Hungry, Neve? Plenty of leftovers.'

Into the kitchen: a bowl, cutlery, wineglasses, leftover pasta heated in the microwave. He poured two glasses of shiraz, grated some parmesan, served up. 'Dig in.'

She wolfed it down. She'd denied herself, he realised. He wondered how often she did that.

Finally, falsely unhurried now, she pushed her bowl away, the base bumping over the joins in the old tabletop. Eventually lifted her gaze to his. 'I'm worried about court on Monday.'

'I don't blame you,' Auhl said.

She gave him a pleading grimace, a woman used to disappointment. 'You're still coming?'

The arrangement was she'd spend Sunday night at her parents' and Auhl would make his own way down to the new Family Court building in Geelong. 'But all I can offer is moral support,' he said. 'I can't influence the outcome.'

He had no experience with the Family Court. The split with Liz hadn't troubled the legal or judicial fraternities. He sipped his wine, let Neve Fanning talk through her doubts. How her husband had money, a house, a good lawyer. How he was sure to come across as rich and successful—and meanwhile look at her, a cleaner, no decent clothes, represented by a Legal Aid lawyer who was rushed off his feet.

'And Doctor Kelso's report,' she said, hugging herself. The same tight body language she always displayed when she talked about her husband. Auhl wondered who this Kelso was and why he made her so tense. And why this tendency to withhold information, which he'd noted before? Shame? Carelessness? Maybe she didn't think he'd find it important.

'Who's Doctor Kelso?'

Neve gave him a faintly impatient look. 'The psychiatrist.'

'Right.'

'I was only with him about half an hour but he didn't like me,' Neve went on. 'He was kind of distant.'

'I'm sure you're wrong,' said Auhl inadequately. 'Did he interview Pia and your husband?'

She nodded. 'And watched Pia interacting with me and with him.' She shot Auhl a tormented look, about to speak, but thought better of it.

Auhl cocked his head. 'Maybe it would be a good idea if Pia attended court, too, and had her own lawyer?'

Neve drew herself up. Auhl sensed that, in this regard, she was very clear: 'I'm not going to put her through any more ordeals.'

'Right.'

Neve went to bed after that, and Auhl ran an internet search on Kelso. A psychiatrist experienced in medico-legal matters—meaning he was an authority figure, meaning Neve would be intimidated by him while automatically deferring to him. Among other things, Kelso was a 'single expert', one of a small number of specialists who might be called upon to assess parents and children caught up in fraught contact and custody issues. This required him to consider police and Child Protection evidence, interview the main parties and their friends and family, and report to the court.

Yawning, bone tired, too scattered to read more Google entries, Auhl shut his computer down, wondering what kind of impression Kelso had formed of Neve if he'd spent only half an hour with her. Let's hope the guy spent more time grilling the husband, he thought. And listening closely to Pia.

ON SUNDAY MORNING he checked his email.

A reply from Tasmania: the letter-number combination that John Elphick had scrawled in his notebook belonged to a 1997 Toyota LandCruiser registered to a Roger Vance, at an address outside Launceston.

Auhl called the older Elphick daughter, conjuring her in his mind. A leggy, horsey woman in loose pants and a check shirt, horses in the paddocks all around.

'Erica, don't get your hopes up, but there's something I need to check. Was your father in the habit of keeping notes?'

Sad regret in her voice. 'Poor Dad, he'd started to forget things. Not dementia exactly, but sometimes he'd be embarrassed when he realised he'd repeated himself or forgotten he'd spoken to someone the day before, that kind of thing. He started using a little notebook for reminders. What he'd done, who he'd seen, what needed doing. He'd check it all the time.' She laughed, a laugh ending with a sob. 'When he remembered to.'

Neither Auhl nor the daughter said the obvious, that a time would have come when John Elphick would have forgotten he had a notebook, let alone written in it or consulted it.

Next Auhl read out the numberplate. 'It's Tasmanian. Does that mean anything to you at all?'

'Afraid not.'

'No Tasmanian connection involving your father?'

'No.' A pause, then her voice vibrant in his ear: 'Wait! We had a trainer who moved to Tasmania. He and Dad had a bad falling-out, but it was, oh, years and years ago.'

'Trainer?' said Auhl.

'Horse trainer.'

'His name?'

Another pause. 'I'm thinking Vance, but I don't know if that's a first or a last name.'

12

ON MONDAY MORNING Auhl walked Pia to school then caught a train to Geelong. Neve was waiting on the steps of the new regional Family Court building. She looked presentable in a navy skirt, white blouse, grey cardigan, tights and black slip-on shoes, but a little makeshift, as though she was wearing someone else's best clothes. Her hair was a stiff, hairsprayed helmet and her face was gaunt. Auhl went to give her a bolstering hug, but she pulled away. Right, he thought: her husband or his lawyers might be watching.

A small huddle waited with her. Neve, still flustered, made the introductions. 'Alan, this is my mum and dad, and this is Jeff, my lawyer.'

'Jeff Fleet,' the lawyer said, shaking Auhl's hand.

He was young, more tired than fleet, wearing a threadbare gown over a sharp cheap suit and pointy shoes. Balding prematurely. Smeared glasses on the end of his nose. The parents, Doug and Maureen Deane, uncomfortable in their best clothes, ducked their chins shyly as they shook hands.

Auhl took Fleet and Neve aside. 'Did Neve tell you her husband sent their daughter back on the train by herself on Friday? No warning, no one to meet her, no one to keep an eye on her.'

Neve gave a little twittering laugh. 'It's what he's like.'

Auhl, faintly impatient with her, concentrated on the lawyer. 'Can we use it? If necessary I'll testify to it.'

The lawyer grimaced. 'Not today. I don't feel it would be appropriate, it would look desperate, especially if Justice Messer ruled it was too late. And plenty of children Pia's age ride the trains alone. No, today the psychiatrist is cross-examined on his findings, after which Justice Messer may or may not make a ruling, or decide to sleep on it for a week, and it might all be good news anyway.'

Auhl frowned at Fleet. 'Don't they give you time to prepare? How can you cross-examine if today's the first time you're—'

'Both parties and their lawyers were supplied with Doctor Kelso's findings a week ago,' Fleet said. 'It's required.'

Auhl turned to Neve, who wouldn't meet his gaze. Why hadn't she given him Kelso's report to read? He swung around on Fleet again. 'Well, what does he say?'

'I'm sorry but only the interested parties and their legal representatives are privy to that,' Fleet said.

Auhl shook his head, fed up. 'But you can and will cross-examine?'

'Yes.'

'Good luck, break a leg, whatever the phrase is,' said Auhl bleakly.

'Depends,' said Fleet, and Auhl wondered what that meant.

Neve was hugging herself. 'Lloyd's going to be sitting right there.'

'Don't look at him, Neve,' Auhl said. 'Deep breaths.'

THE COURTROOM WAS bland, an overall beige impression, the odours of new carpet and paint scenting the air. From his spot in the public seats, Auhl eyed the forces ranged against Neve. Lloyd

81

Fanning—looking confident, a well-cut suit concealing his bulk—sat behind his barrister, an older, thinner man with lazy-lidded eyes, who wore his gown with flair.

Auhl swung his head to the other side of the courtroom. In direct contrast to Team Lloyd, Neve, her parents and her lawyer sat low and nondescript in their seats as if not to attract notice.

The room stirred as a lanky man in his fifties swept in. Justice Messer: a small, neatly combed head, button nose and an air of busyness and grim despatch. As soon as he was seated, the court was called to order, its purpose announced: in a nutshell, that Mrs Neve Fanning had sought a formal variation to the existing arrangement vis-à-vis her husband's parenting time with their daughter, Pia, asking that it be conducted in a supervised environment and limited to one weekend per month and one week of each school holiday period. Given the contestable nature of the situation, Mr Fanning, and his lawyer, Mr Nichols, had requested an expert report assessment with the blessings of the other party and had borne his costs.

'This report is but one tool—albeit an important one—available to the court to help determine what orders should be made concerning the best interests of the child in this case,' Messer said, his gaze taking in everyone. He tapped papers together. 'I now call Doctor Thomas Kelso to the stand.'

Auhl watched a man in his sixties get to his feet. Lean, suave; full head of greying hair. Draped in a dark suit over a crisp white shirt. A natty rogue type, thought Auhl, watching the man flash a smile at a female court attendant as he was sworn in.

Nichols began, ascertaining Kelso's credentials and experience, then asking: 'You conducted interviews with Mrs Neve Fanning, her husband, Mr Lloyd Fanning, their daughter, Pia Fanning, and Mrs Fanning's parents?'

'I did,' Kelso said, the timbre of his voice deep, satisfied.

'Please explain to the court what matters an expert such as

yourself typically examines in cases of this nature.'

Kelso beamed as if glad to have been asked. 'I study the issues in dispute, past and present parenting arrangements, the parenting capabilities of each party in the dispute, the child—or children's—relationships with each parent and other significant persons, such as grandparents, the wishes of the child or the children, and potential risks to them.'

'Having studied these matters in regard to Miss Pia Fanning, is it your opinion that a reduction of Mr Lloyd Fanning's parenting time with her is warranted?'

'It is not.'

'You recommend an equal-time arrangement, going forward?'

'I do, with reservations.'

'Is it your recommendation that Mr Fanning's time with his daughter be supervised?'

'It is not.'

'Did you come to a conclusion regarding Mrs Fanning's ability to facilitate and encourage her daughter's ongoing relationship with her father?'

'I did. Mrs Fanning showed no openness, only reluctance, to the idea of a relationship between father and daughter.'

'Do you have a further recommendation regarding the conduct of the parties involved?'

Kelso lifted a thin bound report. Tipping back his nose to read through bifocals, he said, 'It is my recommendation that Mrs Fanning obtain regular counselling to help her accept and support an ongoing father–daughter relationship.'

Auhl felt helpless, fretful. He glanced at Neve, who seemed to sink in her seat. Fleet was toying with a ballpoint pen.

Nichols said, 'If it please the court, kindly explain why, in your expert opinion, Mrs Fanning should seek counselling in the matter of the relationship between her daughter and Mr Fanning.'

Kelso glanced at Messer, briefly out across the room, and then at his notes. 'As stated in my report, I question Mrs Fanning's ability to manage conflict and communication. She presents in a self-absorbed manner and, in my opinion, over-values the abuse she allegedly experienced at the hands of her husband. This led her to perceive bad parenting on his part.'

Neve shook her head, leaned against her mother and craned around to find Auhl in the audience. She shook her head again, as if to deny Kelso's statement. He gave her a full-on smile. She turned away, probably sceptical that smiles would be any help.

'Furthermore,' Kelso was saying, 'Mrs Fanning also presents as anxious and over-protective. It is my considered belief that she suffers from a psychosis.'

'No!' shouted Neve. She stood. Subsided again when her father gently tugged on her wrist.

Messer looked down his little nose at Neve, ready to be sympathetic this first time around, but not about to let her deliver another outburst. 'Mrs Fanning.'

Fleet stood. 'I apologise on behalf of my client, your Honour, it won't happen again.'

'Go on, Mr Nichols.'

Nichols nodded his thanks. 'Doctor Kelso, Mrs Fanning expressed a fear that the treatment she allegedly received at the hands of her husband would flow to the child?'

'That is correct.'

'What conclusions if any did you draw from that?'

'First, the operative term is treatment *allegedly* received.' Kelso looked around as if to acknowledge that, the courtroom being full of reasonable people, they must share his view, and returned to his notes. 'In my opinion, there was an element of strategy about Mrs Fanning's allegation.'

'You also interviewed Miss Pia Fanning?'

'I did.'

'And in the course of your interview with Miss Fanning did

you come to any conclusions in regard to her past and current interactions with her father?'

'I did. I found the child, who is ten years old, to be unconvincing. It is my belief that she was speaking from *suggestion* on the part of the mother, who is intent on the child rejecting the father.'

Auhl stared at the back of Neve's down-turned head. Why hadn't she said any of this to him? Had Lloyd started hitting Pia?

And just as Auhl swung his gaze back to Kelso, Neve sprang to her feet. *'Her name is Pia.'*

'Mrs Fanning,' Messer warned.

Neve subsided. Fleet stirred, as if to assess whether he was needed, but said nothing. Messer said, 'Please continue, Mr Nichols, Doctor Kelso.'

Nichols acknowledged Messer again and turned to his witness. 'Doctor Kelso, what opinion, if any, did you form of the child's— Miss Fanning's—interactions with her father?'

Kelso looked around again, making eye contact—a man with an unpleasant but necessary job to do. His gaze alighted on Lloyd Fanning, flickered over Neve and Fleet, alighted on Auhl. He faltered, seeing the hardness in Auhl, and returned to his notes.

'The child presented as guarded. This may be explained as torn loyalties. The child feels pressured by the mother to reject the father. The mother places demands on the daughter, plants ideas and fosters hate and fear, thus giving rise to anxiety expressed as guardedness.'

Neve was weeping quietly, head bowed, shoulders rocking. Auhl wanted to…Auhl didn't know what he wanted to do. But couldn't Jeff Fleet do something to stop the flow?

Meanwhile Lloyd Fanning sat with his arms folded over his well-clad chest. His barrister mirrored him. They sensed victory. Auhl pictured Kelso alone in a room with Pia and her father. He could see plenty of reasons other than torn loyalties for Pia's guardedness: that she didn't know Kelso; that she sensed his dislike of her mother; that she sensed his sympathy for her father; that she couldn't accuse her father of anything when he was right there in the room staring at her.

'Doctor Kelso, in your report you use the term "alienation" to explain the dynamics of the Fanning family unit. Would you elaborate on that for the court?'

Kelso ran his gaze around the room again, avoiding Auhl. 'Certainly. The alienation of one parent by the other is often, in my opinion, the most compelling explanation of the dynamics present in these situations. The wife—'

Finally, Fleet stood. 'If it please the court, Parental Alienation Syndrome has come into disrepute in recent years and should not be considered as grounds for making findings of any kind in regard to Mrs Fanning's request that her husband have limited time with their daughter.'

Messer gazed balefully at Fleet. 'Mr Fleet, I am well aware of the arguments for and against Parental Alienation Syndrome. But correct me if I'm wrong, Doctor Kelso did not make mention of the syndrome in his report, and isn't doing so now. Please continue, Doctor Kelso.'

Kelso took on the air of a man choosing his words. 'It is my considered opinion that Mrs Fanning, the wife in this situation, gave rise to a, to a, an *extreme alignment*. She…*influenced*…her child to denigrate and sideline her estranged husband.'

Getting into knots trying to avoid saying 'brainwashed' and 'alienation', thought Auhl, as Neve exploded again.

'I did not!'

'Mrs Fanning.'

'But sir, your Honour.'

'Mrs Fanning, I must warn you that my patience may soon be at an end.'

Fleet turned to Neve, whispered furiously; she sat. Standing abjectly, Fleet said, 'Your Honour, I apologise unreservedly on behalf of my client.'

86

'Mrs Fanning? Will you allow matters to proceed?'

Neve muttered something. It was accepted as consent. With a quick look at Jeff Fleet, Nichols said, 'Please continue, Doctor Kelso.'

'Studies have shown the enormous benefit that may result when a child is removed from the, ah, when a child is placed with the, ah, sidelined parent.'

Not allowed to say 'alienated', but still getting the message across, thought Auhl. Fleet seemed to notice it, too, but had his shoulders hunched.

Nichols said, 'But you are not recommending a wholesale removal of the child from the mother in this particular case.'

'I am not,' Kelso said, going on more smoothly now. 'I accept that Mrs Fanning has been her daughter's sole carer for the past eighteen months.'

Big of you, thought Auhl. He wished he'd looked more thoroughly into Kelso. He wished he'd met with Fleet before today. He wished he'd grilled Neve more comprehensively. She wasn't… worldly enough. It wouldn't occur to her to challenge or question Kelso, her lawyer or the system. She'd hold back out of a sense of politeness and shame.

So, had the situation with Lloyd been worse than she'd said?

'Doctor Kelso, your report makes a recommendation should Mrs Fanning not support a relationship between her daughter and her estranged husband.'

'That is correct,' said Kelso comfortably. 'If the mother is not able to support such a relationship, or raises further spurious or mischievous allegations, then it is my recommendation that she undergo psychiatric assessment and treatment and the child be placed permanently with the father.'

Neve sprang to her feet. '*He's* the one needs a psych assessment!'

'Mrs Fanning, please,' Messer said tightly.

'And I have a *name*.'

Both parents tugging at her hands now, Neve went on: 'Even if you take my daughter away from me, *do not give her to her father.*'

She slumped finally, collapsed into her seat with a sad, brief look around at Auhl, then leaned into her mother.

Messer waited. He waited for some time, making a point; he reminded Auhl of his Form Five maths teacher. 'Mr Nichols, please continue.'

But Nichols, looking satisfied, handed over to Fleet.

Fleet stood, busily rolled his shoulders in his gown, gazed at Kelso as if at another species. 'Doctor Kelso, in regard to Miss Fanning's guardedness, might not it have stemmed from abuse—abuse that she suffered, and abuse she saw her mother suffer?'

Take that, his tone seemed to say. Kelso smiled bleakly. 'I saw nothing in the child's demeanour to suggest recent trauma, and if *historical* trauma was present, it stemmed—in my belief—not from physical acts but the toxic relationship and attitudes of the mother vis-à-vis the father.'

'You are aware that Mrs Fanning took out an intervention order on her husband?'

'I am.'

Fleet waited, Kelso waited. Fleet said, 'Such orders are not applied for or granted on a whim.'

Nichols stood. 'With respect, your Honour, is Mr Fleet making an observation or asking a question?'

Messer looked at Fleet. 'Mr Fleet?'

'With respect, I am asking Doctor Kelso whether, in his opinion, Mrs Fanning's actions in taking an intervention order out against her husband, and later asking this court to reduce and supervise his parenting hours with their daughter, might reasonably stem from actual, historical and ongoing violence on his part?'

Auhl thought it a useful if wordy question. Everyone looked at Kelso. Kelso said, 'I stand by my report. Abuse allegations should be seen in the context of a convoluted and strained marital relationship.'

88

That's how it's going to go, thought Auhl. Clipped answers to take the wind from Fleet's sails.

Fleet changed tack. 'Doctor Kelso, are you aware that Mr Fanning currently lives some distance from his estranged wife and daughter, and has shown little to no interest in maintaining a relationship with the latter?'

'I cannot speak to where the parties may or may not live or how they might arrange future meetings and visits, but as I understand the situation it was Mrs Fanning and her daughter who moved some distance away from Mr Fanning and not the other way around.'

Fleet swallowed. 'In addition to the parents of the child in question, you interviewed her grandparents?'

'The maternal grandparents; the paternal are deceased.'

'The grandparents have a close, ongoing and supportive relationship with their granddaughter, wouldn't you agree?'

'I would.'

Fleet didn't know what to do with that answer. Kelso did. He added: 'But as I understand it they live some distance from the city, where Mrs Fanning and her daughter currently reside.'

Fleet waggled his mouth as if composing his next question. 'Mrs Fanning is, and has been, the primary caregiver?'

'As I understand it.'

'Always there, always available, compared to Mr Fanning?'

'As I understand it,' Kelso said, 'Mrs Fanning is currently employed as a cleaner and as such works long hours, including weeknights and weekends.'

As if desperate to regain some ground, Fleet said, 'Doctor Kelso, I imagine you've heard of the term Parental Alienation Syndrome?'

'I have.'

'Isn't it a fact that—'

Nichols stood. Messer waved him down. 'Mr Fleet, you did read Doctor Kelso's report, I take it?'

'If it please the court, I—'

'We will not discuss theoretical or other matters not related to Mrs Fanning's application and the report supplied by the single expert in the case, is that clear?'

Fleet bobbed. He turned to Kelso and said, 'My learned colleague asked you what matters a single expert such as yourself might typically take into account to assist the Family Court to make its recommendations?'

Kelso cocked his head. 'He did.'

'Parenting capacity, the extended family, and whatnot?'

'Correct.'

'Doctor Kelso, mightn't a single expert also consider past or ongoing domestic violence, drug and alcohol abuse, the parties' mental health and the views and needs of the child?'

Kelso paused. 'As I said in my report, it is my belief that Mrs Fanning would benefit from counselling.'

Didn't answer the question, thought Auhl, waiting for Fleet to pounce. But Fleet said, 'The wishes of the child, Doctor Kelso. She requested fewer hours with her father.'

'She did. She also is only ten years old.'

It was as if Fleet didn't know how to follow up. He asked a handful of further questions—all of them mild and inoffensive, to Auhl's ear—and seemed to run out of steam. And he'd asked nothing about Kelso's view of Lloyd.

Messer turned to Team Lloyd. 'Mr Nichols, do you have any further questions?'

Lloyd's lawyer stood, declined graciously, sat again. Auhl wasn't surprised. Why rock the boat?

'All right then,' Messer said, 'that concludes these proceedings. Court will adjourn until next Monday at 2.00 p.m., at which time I will deliver my ruling on the merits of Mrs Fanning's application. In the meantime, Mr Fanning is to enjoy equal and unsupervised parenting time with his daughter. That is all.'

Auhl eyed Lloyd as he edged out into the aisle. The man was smirking as he shook hands with his lawyer, a picture of reason and prosperity.

AUHL FOUND NEVE, HER parents and Fleet on the courthouse steps. Neve, splotchy with tears and bewilderment, said, 'Lloyd in his suit, looking all calm and rational, and look at me. Something the cat dragged in.'

'Hush, dear,' her mother said. Maureen Deane gave Fleet, Auhl and her husband looks of stubborn hostility, then placed an arm around her daughter. 'Let's get you home.'

Neve was to spend the afternoon with her parents. But she wasn't finished, and gently disengaged from her mother. 'Why couldn't the judge give his ruling today!' She hugged herself. 'I've got a bad feeling. It's like those people think an abusive father's better than no father.'

Auhl nodded. Pity you didn't have decent legal help, he wanted to say, but held his tongue.

He asked the lawyer, 'What's your take on it?'

Fleet shifted his feet, in a hurry to be off. 'As I told Neve, single-expert assessments are not uncommon when the situation is fraught.'

Auhl was impatient. 'But this is a guy who comes up with so-called in-depth and professional recommendations on the basis of a few half-hour meetings.'

Here Fleet winced. 'He is old school, I'll give you that.'

He touched Neve's forearm, said he had to be off, he'd be in touch, see her next Monday afternoon.

'Thanks, Jeff,' Neve called after him.

Thanks for what? Auhl wanted to ask her.

Saying his own goodbyes, he raced back into the courthouse and looked for a men's room. Up one long corridor and down another—stopping in his tracks when he saw Kelso with Nichols, Lloyd

Fanning's lawyer. They were halfway along, heads close together, and suddenly each man was tipping back his head to laugh. Kelso clapped the lawyer on the shoulder and then they were moving off in separate directions. Mates, thought Auhl, like the backslapping fathers he remembered from school sports and speech days, the senior officers at police HQ. Secret knowledge, secret connections. Secret deals and understandings reached—often without a word uttered or written.

Kelso was ambling towards Auhl. Auhl turned on his heel and up a flight of stairs and finally there was a men's room.

RATHER THAN RETURN to Melbourne just yet, Auhl stuck his head into his wife's office at HomeSafe, in one of the government buildings near the library. There were harbour views, but not from Liz's office. Auhl commented on that but added, 'I'd much rather look at you anyway.'

A misstep. He was prone to them around her. She glanced at her watch. 'Neve?' she prompted.

Auhl described the morning's events, finally saying, 'The husband had a high-priced lawyer with him and they both looked calm and prosperous and successful, whereas Neve looked kind of ratty and high-strung, which didn't help. Her lawyer didn't help much, either. But the prevailing atmosphere was: any kind of father, even one with a big question mark hanging over him, is better than no father at all.'

Liz snorted. 'Yes, that seems to be the guiding principle. I see it all the time with the women and kids who come through the agency. Unless there's clear evidence of violence—severe violence—it's difficult for the mother to cut the father out. And as for domestic violence and sex abuse training for judges and lawyers, forget it.'

'But you'd expect the shrink who interviewed Neve and Pia to have some experience or training?'

92

'Don't count on it,' Liz said. 'The system's stressed, under-funded and paternalistic. Nothing works the way you'd like.' She looked at her watch again.

Auhl got the message. He always wanted to hang out and chat with her, but that was gone now. She was no longer his chief conversation partner and sounding board.

13

AUHL WAS BACK IN the city by one-thirty. He headed straight for the police complex, upstairs and into the office of a friend who worked child sex abuse cases.

'Lloyd Fanning. Anything?'

'Hello to you, too, Al.'

Trina Carter was a senior sergeant, Auhl's age, with the gaunt look of someone on the prowl for prowlers. She got him to write the name on a slip of paper, checked the spelling, and typed, her fingernails clacking rapidly on her keyboard.

'Nothing.'

'Even if there were a whisper, would he show up in your system?'

'Not necessarily. Who is he?'

Auhl told her. 'But no one's said anything, I'm just checking.'

'Let me know if you turn anything up,' Carter said.

AUHL CONSIDERED HIS long to-do list. First, follow up on Elphick.

Working the phone for the next thirty minutes, he was shunted from one paper-shuffling desk drone to another as he sought

Tasmania car ferry passenger and vehicle records for the period before and after Elphick's death. In the end, he told a supervisor she was hindering his investigation into the long-term smuggling of drugs and handguns from Tasmania to the mainland by way of the ferry; that he was simply trying to stay a step ahead of reporters from the *Herald Sun*. He got the answer he was looking for fairly quickly after that.

Roger Vance had taken his LandCruiser on the ferry from Devonport to Melbourne one day prior to the death of John Elphick and returned to Tasmania on the evening of the day Elphick died.

Not enough for an arrest warrant. Would the department spring for a flight to Launceston, to question the guy? More to the point, was Vance still there? Auhl sent an email to the police station in Launceston then knocked on the boss's door.

'I thought you were taking the whole day off.'

Auhl shrugged. 'A quick hearing, final word next Monday.'

Colfax was aware of Neve Fanning's predicament. She told him once again not to let it interfere with the job.

'I won't.'

'Don't get too involved. Perspective.'

'Yup, good.' He was what, twenty years older than her? 'Meanwhile, further developments in the Elphick case.' He explained: a numberplate, a vehicle, a name, an address near Launceston, the vehicle on the *Spirit of Tasmania* just before and after the time Elphick died.

Patting her pockets for cigarettes, forgetting she was an ex-smoker, Colfax said, 'Do we know if he still lives in Tasmania?'

'Still checking that,' Auhl said.

Colfax gathered herself. 'Good. But Elphick can wait. Slab Man. Remember him?'

'Boss.'

'Get onto Angela Sullivan. I want you and Claire to interview her this afternoon.'

'What about the Neill case?'

'What about it? If Mrs Neill stole hospital drugs, it's not our case. If she recently murdered Christine Lancer, it's not our case. We're monitoring their movements. The good doctor's in the country, Janine's in the city. Leave it for now.'

MID-AFTERNOON BY THE time Auhl and Pascal had signed out an unmarked sedan and begun battling early peak-hour traffic to an address in South Frankston.

Auhl, driving, said, 'She knows we're coming?'

'Yep. She's agreed to dig out what records she can find.'

'Or she's our killer and you've tipped her off.'

'Cheers for that, Alan, but it's not as if she hasn't had advance warning.'

Slab Man had been all over the news since Thursday evening, the combination of snake, snake catcher, skeleton and murder proving irresistible.

They came to a small tan brick house tucked among others like it on a side street near Mt Erin Secondary College. The woman who answered Auhl's knock was about forty, her face, neck and upper arms tucked, pillowed, as though she'd lost a great deal of weight. Shoulder-length greying hair, old short-sleeved white shirt over cargo pants, sandshoes without socks.

'You must be the detectives. Please come in.'

Calm, gracious, but Auhl sensed tension in her. He mustered a smile. 'We don't intend to take up too much of your time, Ms Sullivan. A few questions, a quick look at any paperwork you've managed to dig up and we'll be out of your hair.'

'Call me Angie, please.'

They followed her into a small sitting room. Floral carpet, armchairs and curtains from another era. The late mother's taste? Hardly Angela Sullivan's, thought Auhl, eyeing some kind of native-art talisman on a leather thong around her neck, a strange but appealing hammered-silver ring on one finger, and hippy-market earrings. A woman slowly breaking away from her past?

She settled them onto the sofa and dashed to the kitchen, returning with a tray, a jug of water, three tumblers. Perched herself on the edge of an armchair and clapped her thighs: 'Now, how can I help?'

Auhl pointed to a photograph on the mantelpiece. 'Your parents?'

Sullivan glanced at it, swung her head back. Guarded, she said, 'Yes. Mum died a few years ago, Dad when I was only ten.'

'According to our records, your parents bought the property where we found the dead man in 1976?'

'That sounds about right. Mum was pregnant with me.'

'There was a house on the property?'

'Old fibro farmhouse.'

'Your father worked for the fire brigade?'

She was astonished. 'However did you learn that?'

Auhl and Pascal were practised at enigmatic looks and never-you-mind shrugs.

A little rattled now, Angela Sullivan said, 'He was stationed in Frankston, but he and Mum wanted to bring me up in the country.'

'It must have been hard on you and your mother when he died.'

Sullivan glanced down at her bony, veined hands as if they were not attached to her. 'Yes.' She lifted her head. 'But we had a spare room so Mum started renting it out to farmhands, anyone who wanted full board.' She paused, as if dismayed at the disclosure. 'You can't think the dead man was one of those?'

Claire held up a calming hand. 'We have reason to believe he was buried no earlier than 2008.'

Relieved, Sullivan said, 'Me and Mum weren't even living there then. I left home to get married but that didn't last long and Mum moved in with me after the divorce. That would have been almost twenty years ago.'

'So she lived here with you from the late 1990s until her death in 2011?'

'Yes.'

'Meanwhile renting out the old family home, where you grew up?'

'Yes. It was handy money for her. She didn't have much in the way of savings.'

'She could have sold it when she moved in with you.'

'She kept meaning to, but somehow the time or the price wasn't right. She saw the place as security, I think. Plus the house would have needed money spent on it to make it attractive to buyers.'

A harsh engine-revving outside and Sullivan rushed to the window. 'Little idiots.'

Auhl glanced at Claire. He stood and ambled across to join Sullivan. She'd yanked aside a drape of dusty, semi-transparent mesh curtain, and he could see two young men outside, wearing street-hoon caps and tatts, baggy jeans and studded belts, bent over the engine compartment of a hotted-up Subaru WRX. A third boy was behind the wheel, revving the motor, easing off, revving again.

'You could ask the local uniforms to have a word,' Auhl said.

Sullivan shook her head. She released the curtain and returned to her armchair. 'It's all right. I've known them all their lives. They're nice enough lads, just a bit inconsiderate. No jobs, not much education, too much spare time, you know how it is. Now, where were we?'

'Still working out the timeline,' Claire said.

Sullivan rattled it off: 'Okay. Bought in 1976, Dad died 1987, Mum moved in with me 1998, she died 2011, I sold a year or so later.'

'To the agricultural company.'

'The real estate agent handled all that.'

'Did the same agent handle the tenancy agreements? Collect the rent on your behalf, that kind of thing?'

Sullivan shook her head. 'They're all Scrooges, that lot. Me and Mum handled the rental side of things.'

'You kept records? Tax all squared away?' Auhl asked, wanting to show a degree of harshness now, sensing that Sullivan might turn vague.

'Now, where did I put that folder?' she said, looking about the room.

'Over there on the piano,' Claire said, sharing a glance with Auhl.

Flustered, Angela Sullivan gathered the folder, slapped it onto the glass-topped coffee table. Some of the contents slithered out and fanned across the surface.

'Perhaps you could take us through it,' Auhl said, gesturing at the paperwork.

Sullivan flipped open the folder and picked up the first sheet. She frowned at it, thrust it at Auhl. A name, monthly dates and amounts in smudged ballpoint.

'John Allard,' said Auhl, looking at Claire. 'He moved in in mid-November 1998, stayed…two years.'

'If that's what it says, that's what it says,' Sullivan said.

Claire scribbled the name and dates in her notebook. 'Do you know his whereabouts now, Angela?'

'You think it could be him?' She gave herself gentle slaps to the cheeks, one side, the other. 'No, can't be him.'

'Are you sure?'

'I saw him last year. He bought a place in Langwarrin. Can't be him.'

Auhl picked through the remaining rental records. Paltry, approximate, hand-scrawled. But he found Donna Crowther. 'A woman named Donna Crowther rented the house from Christmas 2001 until mid-2005.'

'Yes, Donna. That sounds about right.'

Claire said, 'Did she have a boyfriend?'

Elaborately vague, Sullivan said, 'I *think* so?'

With a shift in his tone, Auhl said, 'Angela, we talked to some of the neighbours. Donna had a boyfriend and they often argued, fought.'

'Yes?'

'We heard the boyfriend was there one day, gone the next.'

'I really wouldn't know. I didn't have much to do with them. They were tenants.'

'Do you happen to know where Donna lives now?'

'Somewhere in Carrum, I think.'

'Do you stay in touch with her?'

'No.'

'But you do have an address for her? Phone number?'

'No,' Angela Sullivan said, looking hunted.

Auhl said, 'Donna Crowther was your last tenant?'

Sullivan glanced up and shifted her jaw from side to side as if severely taxed by the question, before nodding, 'Yes.'

'Why? Your mother was still alive. Still needed the money. She let the property stay vacant from 2005 until her death, what, six years later?'

'Well, if you must know, the house was a wreck. Fibro, holes in the walls for the rats to get in. Rusty roofing iron. Badly in need of a restumping. Loose floorboards, you name it. We couldn't afford to fix it up and it wasn't in a fit state to rent to anyone.'

'So after Donna Crowther moved out, the house sat vacant for several years, then you demolished it to make the land seem more desirable to buyers?'

She whispered, 'Yes.'

'This is very important, Angela. You would have looked inside the house before it was demolished? Taken out any valuable fixtures, that kind of thing?'

'Don't really recall.'

'Angela,' said Auhl, disappointed.

100

'Okay, all right, I had a look through it. For the first time in years, actually. The fireplace surround was quite lovely, so I pulled it out and sold it to a dealer.'

'Did you see any signs of a struggle?'

She blanched. 'What sort of signs?'

'Blood on the floor or walls,' said Auhl with an edge to his voice. 'Fresh holes in the walls or floorboards. Or failing that, fresh signs that the place had been cleaned, painted, patched.'

Looking at her gnarled hands again she said, 'Nothing like that.'

'Who carried out the demolition?'

'Oh come on.' She shook her head, a little too emphatically for Auhl's liking. 'It was years ago. And I was still grieving the death of my mother, plus talking to the real estate people and I had debts to clear and my health wasn't that good.'

Auhl waited.

'Just a name on a flyer in my letterbox,' she said at last. 'Some man who advertised home maintenance and repairs. All I had was a mobile number. I didn't keep it.'

'A home maintenance guy demolished the house? How? Did he have the right equipment? Where did he take the rubbish? How did you pay him?'

'He said he'd recycle most of it. Lovely pressed-tin ceilings, wood mouldings, that kind of thing. Any wood that wasn't rotten he'd turn into kindling. It was a small house. I think he got some of his mates in and they stripped it and carted it all off in trailers.'

By now she was sounding confident. She had a story she was sticking to, and she was tired of them. She had nothing more to give them except repetition.

AUHL COMPARED NOTES with Pascal in the car afterwards, the sun beating against the glass, a sense that Angela Sullivan was watching them from her sitting room. Or maybe she was eyeing the boys

101

tinkering with their car. God, he was weary after a day of running around the state.

'Maybe the real estate agent saw something,' he said.

Claire was staring at the house glumly. 'She got twitchy a couple of times.'

'She did,' agreed Auhl. 'The house, or maybe the demolition. And Crowther.'

'The woman who told me about Crowther said she stayed on for at least a year after her boyfriend disappeared.'

'Pretty calculating to shoot your boyfriend, bury him next to the house and carry on as if nothing had happened.'

'Yes, but does the timeline work? And if she *did* shoot and bury her boyfriend and stay on in the house, she'd need to clean up, meaning it's pointless asking anyone if they saw blood or brains or bullet holes.'

'True,' said Auhl. 'Or Slab Man is not her boyfriend but a stranger, buried later, and she had nothing to do with any of it.'

Claire grunted.

They continued to muse. Auhl said, 'What if squatters moved in after Crowther moved out?'

Pascal groaned. 'That means talking to the neighbours again. Or Angela is lying.'

'Give her the benefit of the doubt first,' Auhl said. He lowered his window. Late afternoon air flowed through the car, faintly scented by petrol and exhaust fumes.

There was an explosive backfire, smoke wreathing the little Subaru. The street racers backed away from the car, waving at the fumes, casting embarrassed looks at Auhl and Pascal in the Cold Case car.

'Get a job,' Claire muttered.

14

EVENING NOW. AUHL at the kitchen table with his laptop, the house mostly silent around him.

He'd keyed in 'parental alienation syndrome', curious that Neve's lawyer, in a rare flash of animation that morning, had thought Kelso was drawing on the theory, and curious to know why it had been discredited.

PAS, he read, was the brainchild of an American child psychiatrist named Richard Gardner in the 1980s. The theory grew quickly in favour and influence, spreading from the US to the UK, Canada and Australia, and held that children affected by the syndrome had been brainwashed by one parent to denigrate, or allege abuse against, the other. Typically, such children used foul language against the accused or rejected parent, insisted their allegations were not coaxed, and were protective and supportive of the non-accused parent.

Auhl sat back. He hadn't seen, or heard, anything like that from Pia. She didn't talk about her father.

Or not to me, he thought.

He read on. According to Gardner, PAS was found mostly in custody cases where child sexual abuse was alleged. The solution: the child should be removed from the alienating parent—usually the mother—and placed with the alleged abuser—usually the father. Gardner went on to suggest that mother–child contact should cease for long periods and mothers who persisted in their abuse allegations should be jailed.

Not only that, he believed that most sexual abuse allegations were false. In a book published in 1992 he argued that hysteria attended such allegations in the context of an overly moralistic and primitive understanding of paedophilia. The tendency of a father to seek gratification from a child could be reduced, he argued, if therapists treating child sex abuse victims helped the mother become more sexually responsive.

Auhl was stunned. He poured a scotch and read on. Eventually Gardner was discredited. He'd never treated children and was accused of demonising women. Finally the Family Court in Australia disavowed PAS.

But were all judges and 'single experts' up to speed? Were some ignoring the shift? Dressing PAS up in softer language?

Neve hadn't alleged sexual abuse, though. So Justice Messer was justified in slapping down Fleet when he tried to suggest Kelso was arguing Parental Alienation Syndrome. But did Kelso believe PAS applied in all instances of abuse—including the plain old violent kind?

Auhl googled Messer. A Melbourne Grammar boy, educated at the University of Melbourne and later Columbia in the US. Resided in Brighton. Divorced, no children. Belonged to a couple of predominantly male business and social organisations and was a stern fixture in Anglican church circles.

Then Auhl dug more deeply into Kelso, finding a couple of less formal sites. Apparently the psychiatrist had no particular training in recognising or treating sexual abuse in children. Hadn't been obliged to reach a level of expertise before becoming a 'single expert'. Yet he'd been called on to evaluate several hundred families, and was regularly used in cases featuring highly contentious allegations of physical and sexual abuse. He'd been reported as saying that ninety per cent of the child sexual abuse allegations he'd assessed were false. Which didn't square, Auhl read, with the view of many of his peers that ninety per cent of such allegations in fact had substance.

A two-year-old newspaper piece quoted Kelso saying there'd been some differences of opinion about the efficacy of PAS but clinically it was a useful concept in some circumstances.

'Useful in all *your* circumstances,' Auhl muttered.

As the evening deepened, Auhl brooded. Men like Kelso, Fanning—Alec Neill. Their assumptions, cronyism, power, sense of entitlement. Pre-emptive strike kinds of men: they seized the advantage while the rest of the world was thinking things through. Like Neill with his accusations against his wife, thought Auhl. And as soon as we move against him he'll surround himself with lawyers and colleagues.

Auhl couldn't deny it, Neill obsessed him. Three deaths. The first wife might have died naturally, but he doubted it. Her queasiness, gradually getting worse over several days? It indicated some kind of poison. Not the same kind that killed Siobhan and Christine. But then, although arrogant, Neill wasn't stupid. He wouldn't use the same drug three times in a row.

Quite suddenly, a deeper unease settled in Auhl. Saturday morning. Janine Neill, pale, dizzy, uncoordinated. She had speculated blithely that Neill might shoot her or push her off a rock, but what if he'd poisoned her? Surely he couldn't be *that* arrogant? But he'd succeeded three times before. Maybe he thought he was untouchable.

Auhl phoned Janine, mobile and landline. No answer.

He sat and thought very carefully, then dug around in an old sleeping bag for one of the protective clothing packs he'd scrounged over the years, working crime scenes. He dressed in dark clothing, backed his elderly Saab out of the garage and headed across to East Melbourne, heart jumpy and mouth dry.

Parking against a dark, leafy kerb a few blocks from the Neill house, he checked for surveillance. Was unsurprised to see none—the department hadn't the resources for around-the-clock watches on the Neills—but he entered the property via the laneway at the rear anyway. He tested the back door and found it unlocked, as if Janine were at home and not yet in bed.

Except there were no lights on.

At that moment, however, Auhl had no need of lights. He was familiar with the odours of sickness and death. And whatever slimy stuff he was treading in, he was thankful he had forensic overshoes on his feet.

15

ALAN AUHL DIDN'T GO home. Didn't call anyone. Midnight, a brilliant moon. He drove Janine Neill's Jetta north-east out of the city, taking minor streets and roads as much as possible. He couldn't avoid all of the CCTV cameras but it wasn't his car, and he had the sun visors down, a cap over his brow. Even so, he made a wide loop, through Eltham and Yarra Glen and the farmland around Kinglake, north of St Andrews, before turning south. A play of tricky light and shade across the roads, the moon striking through the trees. A distant red flicker that proved to be a dying bonfire in the middle of a harrowed paddock. Further heaped pine trees and branch litter awaiting the match.

Finally the maps app on Janine Neill's phone took him to a driveway on a region of wooded hills and dirt roads. He drove past for a kilometre. Parked behind an abandoned fruit and vegetable stall. Deleted maps from the phone.

He'd ditched his first forensic suit in a builder's skip. He pulled on another, all but the gloves and overshoes, pocketed a small torch, and walked back to the Neill driveway. The hour of the fox, he thought. He still didn't know what he was doing. Knew enough for self-preservation, however: thinking of the driveway, of powdery dirt holding shoe impressions, he parted fence wires and slipped onto the property that way, crossing a lightly wooded slope to the house. Good: the garage door was up. Fitting the overshoes to his feet, the gloves to his hands, he entered.

He felt around under the workbench. No metal box. The rifle was not where Janine Neill had said it would be.

And then Alec Neill said, 'This is harassment.'

His voice was a squeak. He was as scared as Auhl—but he was armed and Auhl wasn't.

'I saw you. Got up for a glass of water and there you were, glowing like a light bulb in that white suit.'

Auhl said nothing. Kept his hands where Neill could see them.

'Any reason you're dressed like that? You look like you've got something…messy in mind.'

Neill was in the shadows beside his car, a black Porsche Cayenne. Auhl darted a glance out at the moon-soaked slope of land leading down to the road. He could run. He could get shot in the back if he ran. Or he'd make it out safely and Neill would call the local cops. Or Debenham, Colfax. Either way, Auhl was finished.

His mouth was dry. 'What did you use on Janine? Same poison you used on your first wife?'

Neill stepped into a patch of brighter light. He wore pyjamas, paint-spattered blue Crocs on his feet. His hair was askew from his pillow and the rifle shook minutely in his hands. He held it as if he didn't know what it was—but you don't need to be an expert to shoot an old .22, thought Auhl.

'Where are the others?' Neill said, the rifle absently turning away from Auhl as he risked a quick look out at the empty night.

Before Auhl could act, man and rifle swung back. In that short time, Neill had gathered himself. His voice was steady, laced with undisguised, sardonic amusement as he said, 'It's just you, right?'

'Just me.'

Neill grinned. 'This is going to be good,' and his eyes were aglow. Auhl saw the madness there at last.

'What is?'

In reply, Neill motioned with the rifle, a busy, get-a-move-on, up-and-down jerk of the barrel. 'Inside.'

Inside, where he'd call the police. Shoot Auhl, the intruder. Auhl didn't move.

'*In*, I said.'

More gesturing. Impatience when Auhl didn't move. But Auhl was watching the rifle, timing his move. He'd need two seconds and suspected he had only one. *The barrel tip is trained on his chest, then it's bisecting his face, it reaches the ceiling, and now it's tracing a downward arc.* The action repeated again and again, expressing contempt and pure arrogance.

'I'm not fucking around, Sergeant. Move.'

Another gesture and Auhl charged, covering half the distance before the rifle barrel was fully up, slamming into Neill as it came down. The men grappled, the rifle trapped between them, Neill trying to push him away with it. Neill was strong, wiry. Auhl, despite his morning walks, was the older man. Then Neill slipped on an oil patch and Auhl followed him down, tangled and desperate as their sweaty hands fought for control of the little rifle and then it was at an awkward angle and then it went off.

AUHL SPRAWLED PANTING on the floor, waiting for his senses to return. Neill had toppled onto his side, the rifle tangled under him, his cheek on the cement, revealing his jaw, the entry wound. No exit wound, not with a little .22; and not much blood yet. But it was leaking down inside the collar of the man's pyjama top; it would stain the cement soon. Auhl moved at last, badly panicked. He ran to the bench, ran once around the interior of the garage, trying to think.

A painters drop cloth, still in its cellophane wrapper. He tore it open, spread it on the cement floor, rolled Neill onto it. Wrapped him in it, finally, and carted him outside onto the lawn.

He listened. He hadn't seen other houses nearby, and the barrel had been pressed under Neill's jaw, muffling the shot. What next? His actions seemed inevitable: like everything he'd done this evening, aimed at concealment. The hour of the fox, he thought. The hour when a hobby farmer might take his .22 rifle to henhouse marauders. Or shoot himself because his wife was leaving him. Or because he was a killer and couldn't stand the guilt a moment longer.

Auhl was improvising here.

He went with the fox.

Auhl, the old Homicide cop… It was instructive, carting Neill's body by the light of the moon. To understand at last the weight of the human body, its lumpen intractability in death.

He skirted a broad, neatly plotted area of rosebushes at the rear of the house and crossed a patch of grass to a barbed wire fence separating the Neill property from empty paddocks and distant trees. He choreographed the death of a man who had gone after a fox in the night-time and overbalanced while climbing a fence. A man with his right foot tangled between the first and second wires and his torso on the other side, his shoulders on the ground and his face staring blankly at the sky. Barbed wire tears on his calf, arms and torso. A rifle near his outstretched right hand. The wound under his jaw.

Then Auhl stood back. He'd constructed a narrative: what narrative would investigators construct? Auhl didn't admire his work but eyed it critically. He asked himself the questions a man like Debenham would ask. The length of Neill's arms, the length of the rifle. Was he right- or left-handed? Whose gun?

Satisfied, he crossed back to the house, entering via a connecting door in the garage. A faint odour of curry and human habitation. Working as rapidly as he could and using thirty years of police experience, he searched every room. Behind the bathtub skirting, behind power points, under the toilet lids, inside shampoo bottles and lumpy packs of frozen peas, the floor space under bottom drawers…

He found two ampoules of succinylcholine inside a laser printer. One labelled Cabrini, the other Peninsula Private.

Pocketed one, left the other where it would be found in about two minutes.

AUHL STOPPED AT THE unknown neighbour's bonfire on his return trip. Burned the forensic clothing and the drop sheet and cellophane and walked gingerly back to the car with his shoes in his hands, trouser legs rolled, socks in his pockets. A clever forensic technician might trace the soil on his feet to this paddock, but Auhl hoped to have showered multiple times before that happened.

A fast run back to the city, his nerves jangling, waiting for something to happen. An abrupt swamping of guilt. Sirens. The alarm going off, time to wake up.

He tried to search his feelings. Remorse? Shame, glee, fear, chest-thumping sense of righteousness? None of the above. But the jumpy nerves meant something. That he'd killed a man? More than that: *he didn't want to get caught*. He'd covered his tracks. He was careful, oblique, a shadow slipping in and away again.

Bundle of nerves, though.

Thirty minutes later, he was swapping cars and heading for Carlton, thinking inexplicably of Liz. He hadn't expected the break, but he hadn't been surprised by it either. And he hadn't argued. There was no fighting or bitterness, just acceptance tinged with regret.

He wondered what Liz would think if she ever learned about the night he'd just had. She'd always thought him slightly inert: under-motivated, content with his own company, absorbed in his own thoughts. Would this change her opinion?

Couldn't tell her about it, of course. Couldn't tell a soul.

16

TUESDAY.

Auhl did not vary his routine. He walked; he took the tram to work and made calls and checked records. A picture of diligence. But as the morning progressed, he found himself controlling external indicators of stress: shoulder tension, jaw clenching, his right leg jiggling. Every time footsteps passed the Cold Case main door, or anyone entered the office to check a matter with Bugg, Pascal, Colfax, he believed the sword of judgment was about to fall.

Hadn't the bodies been found yet?

He'd already checked his private and work emails. Clumsily worded offers of anal sex with beautiful Russian women; unmissable deals from online store sites he'd never visited. Nothing from Tasmania. No recent suspicious deaths in East Melbourne or St Andrews.

Half an hour later he checked again, and some of the anxiety lifted. A new message: Launceston police had visited the address listed on Roger Vance's LandCruiser registration papers. According to neighbours—who continued to stay in touch, forwarding the occasional letter—Vance had moved out four or five years earlier. Lived in Victoria now, an address in Moe.

Not so far from the late John Elphick's farm.

A familiar and welcome sensation replaced the anxiety: the hunt. Auhl thought about Vance, forming a mental picture. A man who hadn't bothered to take out Victorian registration on the Land-Cruiser because it was an effort, an irritation. A man who didn't look far ahead. Wouldn't factor in the risk of attracting police or bureaucratic attention. Vance was the kind of killer who'd drive around with broken tail-lights and a body wrapped in a blanket.

Auhl made a series of phone calls. Roger Vance still lived in Moe. He was deeply in debt; on a community service order for drug possession; finding occasional work as a farrier, in horse country where farriers were thick on the ground.

Knocking on the boss's door, poking his head in, Auhl said, 'I've found the guy who might have killed Elphick.'

Colfax, about to make a phone call, replaced the handset. 'Where?'

'He lives in Moe now. Moved there a few years ago. I'd like to question him.'

'Moe? Christ, that's halfway across the state,' she exaggerated.

'Until we have a face for Slab Man, we're at a standstill,' Auhl said. With a sudden dryness in his mouth he added, 'And the Neill business has nothing to do with us until Homicide finish with it. So I'd like to move on Vance before his old Tasmanian neighbours tell him we've been sniffing around.'

Helen waved a hand at Auhl, wincing as if the action hurt her head. 'Okay, okay, made your point.' She patted her pockets absently for cigarettes. 'Not entirely at a standstill. You still need to find Donna Crowther.'

Auhl said nothing, let her stew on his request.

Finally, looking at her watch, she said, 'I don't want you going down there by yourself. Take Claire or Josh with you, and contact the local station and see if they'll provide a couple of uniforms.'

'A wise boss is a revered boss.'

Helen was still looking for her non-existent smokes. 'Question him at the local station in the first instance.'

'Deeply revered.'

She sighed. 'Alan, just piss off, all right?'

AUHL CALLED MOE POLICE, arranged backup, signed out a car and by late morning he and Pascal were heading east. They rode in silence, Auhl driving, the motion of the car and the growl of the tyres encouraging reflection. No spring light today, only a dank and sunless sky.

Claire looked over. 'Is anything wrong?'

Auhl realised he had the steering wheel in a death grip. He breathed in and out and let some of the tension drain away. The bodies would have been found by now; forces must be moving against him. He cleared his throat. 'I'm fine.'

'In that case, how about you give me a bit more detail about this excursion instead of sitting there as if you'd rather be some-where else.'

Rebuked, Auhl outlined the backstory: Elphick, Vance, the LandCruiser, the ferry trip.

Claire chewed on that as the landscape unfolded. 'But you don't have actual proof of anything.'

Auhl shrugged. 'The elegant neatness. It all comes together.'

'All he has to do is deny.'

'He can't deny the numberplate, clear as mud on the cover of a notebook kept by a man he'd fallen out with, who died violently.'

'You know what a lawyer will do with that. There's no way of proving *when* the numberplate was written down. It could date back to when this Vance character worked for him.'

'You're a bit of a killjoy really, aren't you?' Auhl said.

He said it lightly, with humour, which he thought was an

achievement given the state he was in. They rode into Moe on a tide of muted goodwill.

ROGER VANCE LIVED IN a block of flats, three up, three down, at the edge of town. A short, sad, overlooked street behind a timber yard, the kind of place where trees were a blight and weed-clearing was someone else's job. At the kerb, a police divvy van. Glimpsed in the cramped residents' parking at the rear, a Holden ute with a built-in metal canopy, stencilled *Horse Sense Farrier*.

'Let's hope he hasn't got any,' Claire muttered.

'Let's hope he's home.'

They parked and got out. The police van was empty, but Auhl could see the local uniforms now, on the doorstep of a bottom flat. He could also see what they couldn't: Roger Vance in the side yard, scurrying for his ute. Claire grinned. 'You go one way, I'll go the other.' She paused. 'If you're up to it.'

'I'll throw my Zimmer frame at him.'

Claire sprinted the long way around, passing the local police, calling, 'Quick and the dead, boys.'

Auhl took the shorter route, down the side path. By now Vance had reached his ute but—panicked by police knocking on his door, the running footsteps behind him—was fumbling his keys. He dropped them, bent to retrieve them, couldn't find the right key. Gave up on all of that and darted a crazy look over his shoulder at Auhl. A pouchy face full of aggravations. Red hair and eyebrows and sallow skin, as though he'd walked off a dustbowl farm. Shorts, a T-shirt, runners with trailing laces.

He turned from Auhl, tensing to bolt the other way. The sole of one shoe stepped on a lace from the other and Claire was there, blocking his exit, placing a palm flat against his chest.

'You going to behave?'

Vance reversed direction, as if he might dodge around Auhl. The same shoelace messed with that.

115

'You want to smarten up before you leave the house,' Claire said. 'Didn't your mother teach you that?'

'Fuck you.'

'Also, language?'

'Fucking bitch.'

Auhl said, 'Settle down. Are you Roger Vance?'

'Who wants to know?'

Name and rank, then Auhl said they needed to ask him a few questions. 'At the police station, please.'

Vance had been born sullen. His disappointments were gathered on his face and in his voice. 'What about?'

The Moe uniforms appeared finally, unhurried. The older one saying, 'Guess you didn't need us after all.'

'If you could transport Mr Vance to the lockup,' Auhl said, 'we'll follow.'

'That's all we're good for,' the Moe cop said, grinning.

A MOE POLICE STATION interview room, Vance sulky. 'I don't know what's going on. I don't even know if I'm under arrest.'

Across the table from him, Auhl shifted to get comfortable in an unsafe plastic chair. 'We simply want to ask you some questions.'

Vance was a twitchy mess. 'So I can like, go if I want to?'

Claire, in a similar chair beside Auhl, was bored and contemptuous. 'Look at it this way, Rog. Roger. Roger the Dodger. The moment you leave this room we arrest you for resisting arrest and—'

'You said I wasn't under arrest!'

'—and assaulting a police officer.'

'That's a fucking lie.'

'Or,' said Auhl, 'no big deal, you answer a few questions regarding a case we're working on and we take you home.'

Vance was pale and clammy. Hadn't showered or shaved and a dank murky odour gusted from the neck of his shirt.

'Up to you,' Auhl continued.

116

'This is bullshit,' Vance said.

Some years had passed since the murder and it was entirely possible he'd forgotten it, shelved it, and was thinking of a more recent crime. A minor theft. Speeding. The weed hidden in his bedroom. He shot glances at the two detectives as if trying to decide what was worse: Auhl's unreadable mildness or Pascal's hostility.

Auhl came in hard. 'On the thirteenth of October 2011, you overnighted on the car ferry from Devonport to Melbourne. On the fourteenth you drove to Drysdale and murdered John Elphick. You caught the return ferry later that same day.'

'What?' Vance reeled. 'What are you saying?'

'Records have you on the *Spirit of Tasmania*, Roger. You came over on the thirteenth, left again on the night of the fourteenth. Quick killing trip. We even have a digital CCTV image of you on the ferry.'

'What?'

'Let's go back to a period *before* your little trip. Life was hard. Plus, you were always fucking up. Do a bit of work, fuck up, get the sack. After you got the sack from John Elphick you decided to give it a go down in Tasmania. Of course, you came a gutser there, too...'

'...and so eventually you got it into your head that it was all Mr Elphick's fault,' Claire said.

'We're not unreasonable, Roger,' Auhl said. 'As we understand it, Elphick could be a bit of a prick.'

'You can say that again,' Vance said.

And now Auhl knew they had him. 'Arrogant, would you say? A perfectionist. Always having a go at something. Even his family hated him.'

Auhl had no idea if that was true, but it resonated with Vance. He flicked his tongue over his lips, swallowing. 'Totally unfair what that arsehole done to me.' His eyes narrowed, a look of calculation chasing away the wounded air. 'But I never laid a finger on him.

Never went near the bastard. I come over to Melbourne to see a mate.'

'You knew Mr Elphick had died, though.'

A shrug. 'Heard it somewhere.'

'Perhaps on the news?'

'I guess so. I'm not much of a news person.'

'You came over to see a mate. This mate have a name? Phone number?'

'I think he's gone back to the UK. We sort of lost touch.'

Claire Pascal said, 'Why would you want to stab Mr Elphick?'

'I never stabbed him,' Vance said with a touch of scorn. He gathered himself to put her right on the details, remembered where he was, shut his jaws with a click.

'He taped it,' Auhl said.

'What?'

'Taped the whole thing on his phone. You shouting at him like a whiny kid, him telling you to piss off, the sounds of a struggle. No problem for the lab to match the voice print of this interview to his recording.'

All bullshit. But they hadn't arrested him yet, so—no caution. And no lawyer present.

Auhl slid a photograph across the chipped table surface. 'And to top it all off, here's a note he made of your numberplate. He saw an unfamiliar vehicle pulling alongside the fence, wrote down the plate number.'

Vance stared at it. Auhl nudged it closer. Vance reared as if it might strike.

'Go on, look closely.'

Vance worked his dry mouth. He looked for a way out. His eyes filled.

'Fucking ruined me, that cunt.'

17

AUHL DANGLED the car keys at Claire. 'You drive.'

But before she could turn on the ignition, her phone pinged with an incoming text. Auhl waited, a part of him certain the caller was Debenham or Colfax, ordering her to arrest him. He could see tension rising in Claire. They were telling her to watch her back.

Then, as the seconds lengthened and she didn't move—simply stared at her phone—he said, 'What? Something wrong?'

She blinked awake. 'Nothing. Look, would you mind driving?'

'Sure,' Auhl said, getting out. Whatever had unsettled her, it didn't seem to relate to him. Something personal?

He walked around the front of the car, Pascal the rear. She looked pale, suddenly. Drained of energy. When he was strapped in behind the steering wheel, he said, 'Claire? Tell me.'

She said miserably, 'My best friend just texted me.'

'Okay.'

'She says my husband's having an affair.'

'Hell,' said Auhl.

He reached out to touch her arm. Saw the hideous ridged scars where her cuffs had ridden up and thought better of it.

Pascal didn't move. Her hand was white-knuckled around her phone. Auhl reached for it. 'May I?'

She didn't resist. He read the screen:

Darls, thought you shd know, Michaels shagging Oxley. Call me ok? Love you Jess—followed by a string of emojis: sad face, wailing face, puzzled face, red angry face, green sick face.

Auhl shook his head. The best friend relates some earth-shattering news by *text message*? 'I'm really sorry,' he said. Pause. 'Have you known Jess for long?'

Distracted, Claire said, 'Since primary school. She wouldn't... she's not playing games.'

No, she's really there for you, thought Auhl sourly. He didn't understand modern etiquette. He handed back the phone. Claire took it, still shocked, teary, bewildered.

'I knew he was up to something.'

'Who's Oxley?'

'Deb Oxley, a friend of ours. Former friend.'

Auhl started the car. 'Late afternoon by the time we get back. Why don't I take you straight home?'

Claire slapped her hands to her cheeks. 'For me to do what? Wait for Michael to walk in the door? I'm not ready for that. I can't think.'

'So, back to the office.'

'No. I mean, yes. No. I don't know what to do.'

'Could you stay with this Jess person?'

Pascal gave an empty laugh. 'She lives across the street. And no, I don't like her boyfriend.'

Lives across the street, Auhl thought, but too much trouble to walk a few metres and give Claire the news in person, along with a comforting hug.

'Look, I have a spare room. Come and stay with me until you sort out what you want to do.'

She blinked at him. 'That's kind of you, but I couldn't.'

'No, no, it's a huge old place in Carlton. My daughter lives there, various international students and odds and sods in need of a temporary roof over their heads.'

Claire Pascal was distracted enough to say, 'Really? I had this image of you as…as…'

'As a sad old bastard in a bachelor flat,' Auhl said. 'But actually I'm a sad bastard with a spare room in a big house.'

A long pause. 'Can I think about it?'

'Deal,' Auhl said, putting the car in gear.

Presently he said, 'What does he do, your husband?'

'He's in IT.'

What can you say to that? Auhl drove.

And finally, breaking a silence that had lasted until they were crossing the eastern suburbs, Claire Pascal said, 'Is your spare room still available?'

'Last time I looked.'

First a quick stop at her house.

Claire directed Auhl to a narrow sloping side street in Abbotsford, a tight squeeze between residents' cars on either side. 'Drive past,' she said, ducking below the sill of her side window.

Auhl glanced at the house as he steered along the street. A cream weatherboard with a Brunswick green door and window frames, a few shrubs in the pocket handkerchief front garden, an empty carport.

'He's not home yet,' Claire said, sitting upright. She pointed to a house across the street. 'That's Jess's driveway. Pull in there, she won't be home yet either.'

Auhl guessed this was a street where you knew your neighbours' business. He barely knew who his neighbours were. Drummond Street was broad, with big houses and busy lives and a fast turnover of students in houses like his own.

'Want me to come in with you?'

She shook her head. 'Toot if you see a white Golf pull into my driveway and I'll slip out the back.'

She was quick, five minutes, returning to the car with a stuffed gym bag and a suitcase on wheels bumping over the bitumen's cracks and erosions.

Auhl said, 'Toothbrush? Comb? Phone charger? PJs? Spare... things?'

Claire looked at him. She was ready for some lightness and humour, but she'd also just walked out on her husband and was wound tight. And Auhl was a much older man, a work colleague she barely knew, taking her to a room in his house. Second thoughts chased each other across her face.

Auhl stopped teasing, gave her a sad, sweet smile. 'Ignore me. All set?'

'As I'll ever be.'

THEY RETURNED THE CAR to the police garage and caught a tram along St Kilda Road and up through the city to Carlton. Early evening now, the city streets teeming with people knocking off work or heading to evening classes or pre-show meals in Chinatown. Claire, lulled by the tram, fell silent. She stared out, registering nothing.

They alighted outside the university and walked across Carlton to Auhl's house. Claire stared. 'You live here?'

'In all its glory.'

'I mean, it's yours?'

'Yes.'

She gave him a look. 'Are you rich?' She caught herself, shook herself. 'Sorry, none of my business.'

'Inherited the place when my parents died,' Auhl said. 'Not rich. I might be comfortable if I sold it, I suppose. After giving my wife her share.'

Claire stood her wheelie case upright on the footpath while Auhl patted his pockets for his keys. 'I somehow thought you were divorced.'

'Separated, but friends.'

'Where does she live?'

'Here. Part of the time.'

Claire glanced doubtfully at the house, at Auhl. 'I don't know, Al.'

'Look, it's fine, no tension, nothing to worry about.'

'If you say so. But isn't it weird, her living here too?'

'It's only some of the time,' Auhl said.

Claire Pascal's expressions were fleeting: pity, puzzlement, sympathy, what-have-I-got-myself-into?

Acceptance, finally, which was okay by Auhl. He could see, though, that he would never be quite the same man in her eyes.

'Whatever works, right?' she said.

'Whatever works.'

She grabbed her suitcase handle and squared her shoulders. 'Anything else I should know?'

'Like strange pairings and weird fetishes?'

'For starters.'

'There's a cat named Cynthia.'

'I can cope with a cat. Not sure about the name.'

'Meanwhile the human population is quite normal. My daughter sometimes has a boyfriend to stay. A couple of postgrad students, including a married couple from Sri Lanka, live here. And a woman and her daughter who need somewhere to doss down during a custody battle.'

'And me,' Claire Pascal said. 'A pathetic workmate running out on her husband.'

'You wouldn't be the first one,' Auhl said, finding the correct key. Noticing the crack in Claire's voice, the slump of her shoulders, he gave her a brief hard hug and showed her into Chateau Auhl.

THE FIRST THING TO happen was Pia charging down the corridor to greet him, skidding to a halt when she saw Claire.

'Hello.'

'Hello,' Claire said, shooting Auhl a glance. Then, sensing Cynthia winding around her ankles, she looked down. 'And hello to you.'

'That's Cynthia,' Pia said. 'Are you allergic?'

'No.'

'What's your name?'

'Claire.'

'Are you A. A.'s girlfriend?'

Auhl looked on with interest.

'No,' Claire Pascal said. She paused. 'We work together.' And, 'We're friends.'

'Bub, show Claire to the spare room.'

'He calls me Bub,' Pia said, clattering away down the corridor to the junk room. 'There's the bathroom, there's the kitchen, that's upstairs,' she said, pointing.

'Okay.'

Auhl relieved himself of wallet, keys and jacket, changed into jeans and a T-shirt and headed for the junk room. Pascal was sitting on the bed, texting. 'I'm just...'

Just texting the husband. Auhl moved boxes of junk into the corridor and left her to it. Presently Bec came downstairs in a pre-exam-cramming daze, Neve appeared, still in her cleaner's overalls and Tiv and his wife walked in with meat and vegetables from an Asian grocery and announced they were cooking. It was as good a start for Claire Pascal as Auhl could have hoped for.

18

WEDNESDAY. AUHL walked, showered, and by 7.00 a.m. was reading the *Age* as he ate his muesli and listened to the ABC news. According to floor thumps and gurgles in the pipes, Neve and Pia were showering. Bec would emerge at 9.55 to start work at ten o'clock in GewGaws Gifts, around the corner. Tiv and Shireen were flying to Sydney for a conference. Auhl didn't know when he'd see Liz again. The doctoral student in the room next to his had crept in late last night, out again at dawn. He hadn't clapped eyes on her for a month. Thus was his life.

That left his newest waif or stray, and she entered the kitchen tentatively, hair damp, scowling. 'I drank too much last night.'

'There's muesli. Eggs in the fridge.'

Claire shuddered.

'And coffee in the pot.'

Another shudder, possibly of relief. She sat at the table with him and sipped coffee, reviving in stages, life coming into her face, eyes, neck, hands. Not much joy, though. Suspicion, if anything, suspicion in the hard look she gave Auhl, as if waiting for a particular response.

Wondering what, if anything, he'd done wrong, he said, 'What?'

'This is weird for me.'

Auhl pushed cereal bowl, *Age* and radio aside and folded his arms. 'Okay…'

'Makes sense for us to go to work together.'

'It does.'

'But that feels weird, Alan. I kind of think we need to travel separately. You've let me stay a night and I appreciate it, but we need to maintain a professional distance.'

He could see from her face that she was uncomfortable with the term, but had used it for want of another. 'Whatever makes you feel comfortable,' he said.

'Yet it's logical to travel together.'

'Uh huh.'

'But it's not as if we're friends or, heaven forbid, in a relationship.'

Auhl said, 'I'm guessing a tiny corner of you is wondering what my intentions are.'

She blushed.

Auhl held his arms wide. 'You've seen the place, the people who live here. You're the latest in a long line. I've not had a relationship with a single one of them. I don't imagine you'll stay long, but I'm pleased to be able to offer you a roof over your head while you decide what it is you want to do. If you want to stay on, then I'm happy to rent the room to you. Dirt cheap, by the way. Look,' he said. 'It's a big house, and a real waste to leave rooms empty when they're so scarce in the inner city.' He paused. 'You can always lock your door at night.'

She shot him a hard look, then saw the glint in his eye. 'Yeah, yeah.'

Auhl returned to his breakfast and news gathering, and presently Claire said, 'Michael's in a mess. Keeps texting me. Calling me. It gave him a shock, me not going home last night. But I'm not ready to see him just yet. I don't want to race back and make him

126

feel better. I just need to think for a few days.'

If the job allows, Auhl thought. He wondered what sort of mess the husband was in. A genuine mess, or an expedient one—a mess to tug at his wife's heartstrings? He said, 'Okay by me, Claire.'

Claire glanced around the kitchen helplessly. 'I should help with the food and cooking I suppose.'

'Claire, get yourself some breakfast for God's sake.'

She winced. 'Okay if I have some porridge?'

'Go for your life.'

'I hate muesli.'

'So have some porridge.'

'This is a ridiculous conversation.'

'Yes.'

Claire looked away, back down the kitchen to Doss Down, then up at the ceiling, as if divining the floors, bedrooms and people above. It occurred to Auhl that she might already have formed a connection to his house. She'd had fun last night, the food and wine and odd company. He didn't know if that would be a good or a bad thing for her.

THEY TOOK THE TRAM TO work and as soon as they neared the main doors to the police building, she said, 'Fuck.'

'What?'

'It's Michael.'

The husband was a solid, athletic guy in his thirties. Narrow suit, neat hair but full of hard stares, sullenness and sour coffee jitters. 'Who's the boyfriend?'

'Michael, please.'

Auhl took a step back, scorched by the guy's fury. Then stepped forward, sticking his hand out. 'I work with Claire.'

Michael Pascal ignored him, his face breaking in a spluttering display of grief. 'Please, Claire, I can't stand it. Please come back.'

Claire's shoulders slumped. She stepped closer to her husband,

127

patted him reluctantly, cast Auhl a complicated look: *I've got this* and *I wish you hadn't seen him like this* and *Don't worry about me.*

Auhl nodded and went upstairs to the Cold Case office.

'DON'T GET COMFORTABLE,' Helen Colfax told him, 'you're coming with me.' She paused, looking around the main office. 'Where's Claire?'

'Not in yet.' A tense little fist clenching in his gut. 'Where are we going?'

'St Andrews.'

Auhl tried to work moisture over his tongue as he followed her to the lift. 'Is this about the Neills?'

Helen pushed the button for the garage. She'd had a haircut. It was softly shaped and feathery around her face but didn't suit her. Her body seemed to thrum, ready for action, impatient with the lift. Auhl said again, 'Boss, the Neills?'

She gathered herself. 'Janine is dead. Her sister found her this morning after failing to get hold of her yesterday and last night.'

'Dead how?'

Still needing a distraction, Colfax compared her sleeve lengths. One was midway along her forearm, the other to her elbow. She rolled the longer one up and said, 'Good question. How dumb do you think the husband is?'

'Not dumb. But arrogant.'

'Exactly. The first indications are she'd had a seizure of some kind.'

'Poisoned? Succinylcholine?'

Colfax shook her head. 'She'd vomited and her body was twisted from the seizure. Not like a heart attack, according to the preliminary examination.' She looked at Auhl. 'And not quite the symptoms of the first wife, either. But would Neill really try three different methods? Would he be that stupid?'

'He'd use something very difficult to trace,' Auhl said.

128

They found the car, an unmarked white Holden, and Helen drove. Where Claire Pascal was nervous at the wheel, Colfax was brisk and fast. Auhl said, 'Does Debenham know?'

'He's meeting us there. I want a crack at Neill before it's taken away from us. I want to watch his face.'

'Crocodile tears?'

'Probably.'

Auhl's tension began to ebb. 'We need to check his browsing history.'

Colfax shook her head. 'Alan, the guy's a surgeon, surrounded by books and academic papers and fellow experts and access to drugs. We're not going to find out he's keyed in *How to kill my wife with an undetectable poison.*'

'Still…'

'How did it go in Moe yesterday?'

'He confessed,' Auhl said.

'Really?' She peered over. 'Good on you. So you're clear to concentrate on Slab Man now, okay? Josh thinks he's tracked down an address for Donna Crowther.'

'If she's not involved we'll need to release his face to the media,' Auhl said.

'Almost ready, apparently,' Colfax said. 'Possibly tomorrow.'

The car rolled through the northern suburbs and eventually to an area more rural than urban. 'Do you have a search warrant for Neill?'

'Debenham does. Turning up mob-handed with a search warrant, maybe the good doctor will fold quickly.'

'Not a chance,' Auhl said. 'He'll clam up and refuse to speak without a lawyer.'

'A girl can dream.'

THEY PASSED THE BONFIRE paddock. Nothing but an ash pile and a thread of smoke now, and Auhl felt a kind of giddy elation and terror. What if this was an elaborate trap? He'd been caught on a security camera he'd failed to spot. Or Neill was still alive. The sunlight was vivid, the spring colours burning bright as if he'd entered a parallel universe. And then they were climbing the driveway and he glanced at the grass, thinking his footprints might show in the dew, but there was no dew and the grass was vigorous, never trodden on.

He stopped thinking about the landscape when Debenham and a second plainclothes detective stepped out of an unmarked sedan parked on the white gravel turning circle in front of the house. He was followed a moment later by three uniforms who'd been waiting in a patrol car.

'Local uniforms,' muttered Helen. About to get out, she added, 'No one's jumping for joy.'

She was right. Solemn expressions all round. 'Maybe Neill's done a runner.'

They got out, shook hands, then the local uniforms retreated a short deferential distance, leaving it to the detectives. Hiding a yawn indifferently, Debenham said, 'Hate to be the bearer of bad news, esteemed colleagues, but you might have made a wasted trip.'

Auhl let Helen ask the questions. 'Doctor Neill not home?'

'He's home, all right.'

'And he's got a lawyer with him?'

'Oh, he's way past caring about his rights.'

'Jerry, cut the crap,' Helen said. 'What's the story?'

'He's dead.'

Helen glanced at Auhl, then swung back to Debenham with the whisper of a philosophical shrug. Receiving bad news, receiving late news, false news—all part of the game. 'Murdered?'

'Hard to say.'

'What can you say?'

'Looks like he shot himself by accident.'

'In the house?'

'Nope.'

'Spit it out, Jerry.'

A little testy now, Debenham said, 'When no one answered at the front or the back, we had a scout around. Neill is tangled in a wire fence over there.' He gestured lazily. 'Still in his pyjamas.'

'Weird,' Auhl said.

'Looks like he shot himself,' Debenham said. 'Climbing through a fence with a loaded firearm, it's happened before.' He paused. 'But what do I know.'

'Dead,' Helen said.

'As in very dead,' Debenham said. 'Small creatures with sharp teeth have already had a go at him.'

'Have you asked for—'

'Helen, I know my job. Crime-scene techs are on the way.'

'But is it suspicious, or isn't it?'

Debenham was impatient, as if he wanted a cigarette, a coffee and more sleep. 'See for yourself.'

'And it's Doctor Neill?'

'In his pyjamas, large as life—so to speak.'

He took Auhl and Colfax down along the left side of the house to the garden at the rear. Auhl shivered. So far, so good, but was this all still part of the trap? Strange, seeing the place in full sunlight. Neat beds of roses close to the veranda, looking out over a mowed slope of grass and young native trees beyond, with side and rear fences separating the property from neighbouring farmland. All of it drenched with colour: reds, yellows, pinks, greens, and the blue-sky canopy streaked with clouds.

Staring glumly at the body, Helen said, 'I see what you mean. Checked inside the house?'

'First thing we did,' Debenham told her. 'Soon as we saw this'—he gestured languidly—'we called it in and had a quick look inside. No one.'

'What about the search warrant?'

'All done.'

Debenham treated her to his complacent, half-lidded smile. Fished in his pocket, brought out an evidence bag, shook it in their faces. 'More of that drug he said his wife had stolen.'

Helen glanced at Auhl. 'Might as well wend our way home.'

'Leave me to pick up the pieces,' Debenham said sourly.

'We deal with cold cases,' Auhl told him. 'This one's still almost warm.'

'Arsehole.'

Auhl followed Helen back to the car. The garage seemed to watch him. There was the Porsche, the spartan interior, brand new paint tins, unused tools hooked in graduated sizes to a pegboard, the concrete floor looking clean, polished. But to Auhl it looked blood-spotted and he hurried past, trying not to recall Monday, the midnight darkness.

His own retributive darkness.

19

THEY DROPPED OFF the car, walked to Southbank and picked up lunch for four, mesmerised by the river glittering in the mild sunlight. Back at the police complex, Helen shut herself in her office while Auhl delivered tandoori wraps to Claire Pascal and Joshua Bugg. Claire gave distracted thanks, wouldn't meet his gaze. Bugg was suspicious.

'How much do I owe you?' He stared at the meal, as if reluctant to accept it.

'My shout,' Auhl said.

Bugg was uncomfortable. 'Thanks.'

Auhl returned to his desk, demolished his wrap, saw the others eventually munch away. And then Bugg was pulling up a chair in front of Auhl's desk, straddling it. 'Good sanger. Thanks.'

Eyeing him warily, Auhl said, 'My pleasure.'

'Two things,' Bugg said. 'One, Donna Crowther is known to police.'

'Okay.'

'Not for dealing or anything like that. Assault in 2005.'

A neat result, Auhl thought—the body shaping up to be the boyfriend, Crowther shaping up to be the killer. 'Charged, jailed?'

'Suspended sentence,' Bugg said. 'It seems she liked to belt the boyfriend when she was on the piss. One day it put him in casualty and so he took out an intervention order on her. Not renewed. Nothing after that.'

'Thanks, Josh. Let the boss know.'

'Will do. Meanwhile, young missing persons named Sean?' Bugg said. 'Quite a few more than you'd think.'

A popular name at the time? wondered Auhl. Maybe young men named Sean had more wayward tendencies. 'How many?'

'In that time range? Seventeen aged between fifteen and twenty-five. Of the seventeen, I've accounted for fourteen. They've either come home or made contact with home recently. Of those, three later died. I'm waiting to hear about the remaining three. I've left messages.'

The most animated and friendliest Bugg had ever been with Auhl. He glanced across the room to exchange a glance with Claire Pascal, but she was busy on her phone. 'Thanks, Josh.'

Bugg said, a twist in his face, 'My brother pissed off for a year. No one knew where he was.'

'He's back?'

'He's back and he's touch and go,' Bugg said, a finger to his temple.

Schizophrenia? wondered Auhl. 'I'm sorry.'

'My parents went through hell,' Bugg said, getting to his feet, turning the chair around to return to his desk. 'One thing: the seventeen missing Seans are all from Victoria. If our guy's from interstate or overseas…'

'That much harder to identify,' Auhl agreed.

After that he called the Century21 agent who'd handled the sale of the Pearcedale property to Nathan and Jaime. She confirmed that the vendor was an agricultural company, which had bought from the Sullivans. The agri-business had since folded. However, her agency had had a change of ownership and name since she'd joined as a young agent. No one on staff had knowledge of the property when it was in the Sullivans' hands.

Meanwhile Donna Crowther had been traced to an address in Edithvale. Claire Pascal said little to Auhl as they drove there. Her husband was a bit upset, that's all. She would be staying in Carlton again tonight, if that was all right with Auhl.

'Fine by me,' Auhl said. The car seemed superheated in the late afternoon sun. He ran the air conditioner.

The GPS took them to a huddled brick house with yellowing grass between the front door and the street, and the woman who answered the doorknock clocked them instantly as police. She stepped onto her porch, plump, tough, with spiky hair, piercings and tatts. Thirty years of belligerence on her face. Agreed that she was Donna Crowther. Agreed to answer some questions. But other than that, it was clear she wasn't in a hurry to help anyone, anywhere, anytime soon.

'You and a boyfriend named Sean once lived in an old fibro farmhouse near Pearcedale,' said Auhl flatly.

She snorted. 'That's what this is about? The body under the concrete?'

She lit and drew on a cigarette, her head, hand, cocked hip and the cigarette itself posed in a ghastly facsimile of sophistication. A crusty stain on her T-shirt.

'A real dump,' she went on. 'Good place to bury someone.'

'You moved out in 2005?'

'If you say so.'

'Because the house was a dump?'

'That's what I said. Roof leaked, rats getting in. Not a straight wall in the whole place.' She flicked her cigarette onto the parched front lawn. 'Why? You talking to everyone who lived there, is that

135

it? God knows who the old bag got in after I left. I kept on at her to fix the joint up.'

'Bernadette Sullivan?' checked Claire.

'That's who we're talking about, isn't it?'

'She died. We heard about you from Angela Sullivan, her daughter.'

Crowther's face softened a little. A mix of regret, confusion and old memories. 'Angela. God. How's she doing?'

'Were you two close?' said Auhl.

'I wouldn't say close,' Donna said slowly, looking back over the years. 'But we got on all right. Her bitch of a mother, though...'

'But you did spend some time with Angela,' Auhl persisted.

'Not a lot, no. I was closer to one or two of the neighbours, cleaning and babysitting and that.'

'What did Sean do?' Claire said.

The abrupt shift startled Crowther. 'What's it to you what he did? Me and Sean were good tenants.'

'Do you remember a concrete slab, Donna?' asked Auhl, watching closely.

'Nup.' She was emphatic. 'No slab. Not while me and Sean lived there.'

'No old chook shed, garden shed, pigsty near the house?'

'Told ya: no.'

Claire said, 'Did you have a fight with Sean? Is that why he left?'

Auhl came in hard, too: 'We understand things were pretty tense between the pair of you.'

'Enough for Sean to take an order out on you.'

They were mistaken if they thought she'd collapse under the blows.

'You cunts,' she said cheerfully. 'Pardon the language.'

Her amused sneer turned bleak as she opened wide her front door and gestured for them to step inside. 'After you.'

A dim hallway bisected the house. Closed doors and, at the end, a step down into a tacked-on sunroom. Hot, medicinal air heavy with urine odours, a man in a wheelchair with a rug over his legs.

'This here is Sean,' Crowther said. 'Seanie, say hello to the nice police persons.'

A livid, knitted scar ran from the man's left forehead and across the temple. His left ear was a knob of flesh and gristle, his mouth in permanent rictus. His eyes, slowly registering Auhl and Pascal, were dull.

'Sean came off his Harley. No helmet, no leathers, pissed out of his brain. Now he's pretty much a vegetable. Satisfied?' A sad hostility, her heart barely in it.

'We're sorry,' Claire said.

'I never killed no one. I never buried no one. Me and Sean never killed no one. Wouldn't have a clue *who* you found at our old place, all right? Would've happened after we moved out.'

A photograph on a little side table of a man—presumably Sean—astride a big Harley, Donna riding pillion.

'We had to check, Donna,' Auhl said. 'People were saying Sean left you. Disappeared.'

'Yeah, he did. After he took the intervention order out on me he pissed off and I didn't hear from him for nearly two years. Then I got word he come off his bike over in WA. I mean, I wasn't going to just wash my hands of him. Me and him were best mates since high school.' She gave a minute shrug. 'His family's useless.'

Feeling obscurely that he didn't match up to the goodness in anyone, Auhl shook hands, thanking her. They returned to the car, Auhl choosing the passenger seat.

'I'll drive, shall I?' Claire said.

'There's no steering wheel on this side,' Auhl said, leaning against his door and closing his eyes.

They laboured through the traffic. Returned the car, reported to

137

Colfax, went downstairs again and left the building. Early evening now, a queer half-light, some motorists running on headlights, some on sidelights, the others yet to make up their minds. Claire Pascal scanning the street for her husband.

20

WHEN THE HOUSE FELL quiet around him later that evening, Auhl sensed rather than heard Neve Fanning's tense presence in the sitting-room doorway. He was glad of it. Without distractions, the St Andrews moonlight and the struggle for the rifle and the shot itself and the tangling fence kept echoing in him. He said, as he always did, 'Hungry? Help yourself to leftovers.'

Stir-fry cooked by Claire. Auhl sat with Neve while she ate, polishing off the rest of an Elan merlot. Presently she pushed her plate away and said, 'Lloyd wants Pia to stay with him this weekend.'

'Does she want to go?'

'Not really.'

'Do you want her to go?'

'No.'

'But...?'

She was a woman of shrunken options. With great weariness she said, 'He's playing a game. He senses victory and he's rubbing it in. He doesn't care one way or the other about Pia coming to stay, he knows I won't object because we go back to court on Monday and he thinks I won't do anything to jeopardise the result. And it makes him look good.'

'And a corner of you thinks if you do win in court on Monday, and his time is reduced, you were at least magnanimous about this weekend.'

She grimaced. 'Something like that.'

'So what are you going to do?'

She shrugged. 'I spoke to Mr Fleet. He thinks it's a good idea.'

Auhl said nothing.

THURSDAY, AUHL WAS barely settled at his desk when Helen Colfax jangled car keys at him.

'You're coming with me. Slab Man has a face.' Today she wore a faded belted denim tunic over Lycra cycling pants, managing to look rakish and reckless as she drove in her expert manic way across town to the Forensic Science Institute. 'By the way, Doctor Berg called with a preliminary time of death for Alec Neill. Sometime Monday night.'

Auhl swallowed. 'And Janine?'

'Harder to ascertain. She was at work Monday morning, but went home, saying she felt ill. She'd felt ill all weekend, according to people who saw her at the conference. So, sometime Monday.'

'Was she poisoned?'

'The results aren't in yet.'

Auhl sighed and hoped it sounded philosophical, not edgy. 'At least we can wipe that one from the books.'

'Unless a third party was involved,' his boss said, and he stiffened, his muscles and tendons locking up as the car rolled relentlessly along the streets.

AT THE INSTITUTE THEY were shown to the forensic anthropology office and a man named DeLisle. Hearing his accent, Auhl thought: American. Amended that when DeLisle said 'out'. Canadian.

DeLisle ushered them into his lab and introduced two of his PhD students. 'Tin Kyaw is from Burma,' he said, beaming, 'and Lily from Scotland.' The women shuffled awkwardly, but DeLisle wasn't finished. 'These young ladies have worked all weekend, and I think you'll agree they've done a very fine job.'

The Burmese woman gestured. She'd made a clay model of Slab Man's head. The Scottish woman also said nothing but indicated a large computer screen, where a 3-D head turned constantly. Suddenly she announced, 'I can give him long or short hair, facial hair, any colour you like.'

There was another figure in the room, a slight woman with piled-up red plaits, glasses perched on the end of her nose. She'd been working at a corner desk but now wandered over. 'As you can see, there's a remarkable similarity between the two reconstructions, despite the different techniques.' Anna Weston, according to her ID tag.

'Our consulting artist,' DeLisle said, beaming again. 'When she's not painting portraits for a living.'

Weston shrugged. 'It's not really a living.'

After the handshakes, Auhl studied the facial reconstructions. Slab Man had a narrow head and a strong, bony nose and jaw. A face that probably commanded attention rather than indifference. A strange warmth came from the clay model, as if from living flesh, but the eyes were dead. Conversely, the eyes in the computer-generated reconstruction were lively enough but the flesh looked flat and unconvincing.

Auhl glanced at Helen Colfax, who gave him a tiny nod. 'The TV stations and daily papers won't know what to do with too much art,' he said. 'I'm suggesting you show them the clay model with short dark hair, the digital model with a shaved head, with a beard, and with long hair. But perhaps release a wider range of alternatives on YouTube and Facebook.'

'That can be arranged,' DeLisle said. 'When?'

Auhl deferred to Colfax, who said, 'We'll schedule a media conference for the weekend.'

She wandered towards a quiet corner, fishing out her phone. Auhl heard her say, 'Media office, please,' and then Weston, DeLisle and the students were drifting away, leaving him to wait with the reconstructions. He stared, trying to dream his way into the skull of the dead man.

Colfax came back. 'All set. I'm afraid you're going to be swamped by cameras and reporters.'

DeLisle beamed. Auhl doubted it was for himself or the students. It was for the science, the chance to talk about it.

KARALIS WAS WAITING for them.

'I've sent a sample for DNA profiling, but that will take time. Meanwhile one of our lab assistants wants a word.'

He took them to meet a kid in dreadlocks and a lab coat who gestured at a metal table covered in bits of concrete. 'Behold, the slab.'

Helen Colfax was impatient, her hair getting wilder as the morning progressed. 'What of it?'

'You were puzzled why the slab looked so old, am I right?'

Seeing the impatience on Helen's face, Auhl said, 'You found something?'

Dreadlocks invited him to peer at the largest chunk of the slab. 'I'm thinking dirt and grit were sprinkled over the surface before it dried.'

Auhl straightened, began to nod. He had a sense now of a shadowy mind at work. 'To age it?'

'To give the *appearance* of age. To give a weathered appearance.'

If you were unfamiliar with the property—a policeman, say—and saw what looked like an old slab, you'd think it had been there for years and had once served some kind of farm function. The floor of a shed, say.

The Sullivan women hadn't been in the habit of visiting. If they had visited, and seen an old slab in the grass, they might have wondered why it was there, or doubted their memories. Anyway, who wants to dig up a slab?

'No pristine fingerprint in an unadulterated corner of the cement?' Colfax asked.

The tech grinned. 'Live in hope.'

As they left the lab, Auhl remembered to ask Karalis about the dental findings.

'Nothing to tell you. A young man with healthy teeth, that's all.' He walked them to the car. 'I'll need a report for the coroner eventually.'

The coroner's task—with assistance and information from the police and the forensic science experts—would be to ascertain Slab Man's identity, the cause and circumstances of his death, and the particulars needed to register his death. As things stood now, the hearing would be brief.

'All in good time, doc,' Helen Colfax said.

In the car she said, 'Now we wait.'

21

AUHL SPENT FRIDAY contacting hospitals where Alec Neill had worked, requesting drug storeroom records and CCTV footage. Then report writing, Vance arrest paperwork, more calls to real estate agents in the Pearcedale area.

After work, he met Neve and Pia in the Bourke Street Mall, ~~Neve~~ *Pia* wearing a little backpack for her weekend with her father. He took them to a phone repair shop on Elizabeth Street and bought Pia a used iPhone, case and charger, along with a cheap monthly plan.

Neve gave Auhl a teary hug then knelt before her daughter. 'Sweetheart, it might be a good idea if you...'

Her voice trailed away. Pia finished for her: 'Don't tell Dad about the phone.'

'Exactly!'

'Avoid a shitload of grief,' Auhl said.

'You said "shit".'

'Shit, did I?'

He accompanied them to Southern Cross, saw them onto the

Geelong train. Poor old Neve—as soon as Pia had been delivered to her father, she'd have to travel back again. But, as she said, she didn't trust Lloyd to be there at the other end.

THEN, AS ARRANGED, Auhl met Claire at a rooftop garden bar above a tiny boutique hotel on Flinders Lane. No one else was over forty. Designer wear, emphatic conversations, expensive handheld devices. Friday evening, but it was quiet. Music that barely registered with Auhl.

'I stick out like a sore thumb.'

'Who cares? No one's looking. They're all trying to pull.'

Claire seemed then to realise what she'd said. She blushed. 'I chose it because I knew it wouldn't be crowded yet.'

He grinned. 'That's okay, you can go on the pull if you like.'

They got quietly sozzled, talked shop, talked marriage and love and the dying and death of love.

'Getting back to your wife,' Claire said.

'To be exact, estranged wife, sometimes resident under the same roof,' Auhl said, wondering if he'd risk visiting Liz in her office again after court on Monday.

'Do you have a type?'

Auhl swung his head around, searching the room. 'Not some youngster in a pickup joint, anyway.'

Claire swiped at his shoulder. 'You use jokes as a way of avoiding questions you don't want to hear. I've told you all about Michael—now you can tell me about what went wrong with your wife.'

'I wasn't paying attention,' said Auhl after a while. 'It seemed to happen while I wasn't looking.'

Claire Pascal weighed that up. She probably found the answer insufficient, but didn't pursue it. She said, 'Michael wasn't paying attention either.'

'Or not to you.'

'Exactly. He claims his fling was a one-off, but does anyone ever believe that? Even if he never sees Bitchface again, he's now more likely to try it with someone else.'

'But you'll give it one more go?'

'Probably. Maybe.'

Auhl looked around at the bar again and guessed it was the kind of place her husband took her to. Maybe she was trying to reassess that part of her past. Her phone pinged. Again, Auhl realised. At least half-a-dozen times now.

Claire saw the look on his face. 'Michael's love-bombing me.'

'He wants you to go home.'

'Yes.'

'Will you?'

'Undecided.'

Auhl said, 'Is he...' He trailed away.

'Is he unhinged? Violent? Would it be a terrible mistake? No.'

'Okay. What do your friends say?'

'Oh, everything: give it another shot, dump him for good, trial separation.'

'Helpful.'

'I'll say.'

SOME MADDENED FOOL fist-pounded Auhl's front door at six-forty-five on Saturday morning, then rapped the brass knocker a few times, the sound snapping like shots along the hall and into the far reaches of the house.

Auhl, just back from his walk and intent on a shower and breakfast, caught the brunt of it.

He flung open the door. 'What?'

Michael Pascal, weaving blearily. 'You're fucking my wife.'

'Deja vu all over again,' Auhl said.

Pascal blinked. 'What?'

His eyes were bloodshot, shirt untucked, face a mess of rasping overnight whiskers, broken capillaries, vomit flecks. Auhl took a step back from the smell. 'Go home, mate. Stand under the shower for a few years then sleep it off.'

'I said, you're doing my wife.'

'No,' Auhl said. 'Claire needed a room while she sorts out what she wants to do. Now go home.'

'Fucked if I'm going home till I—'

Claire was there at Auhl's shoulder. 'Michael, what the hell do you think you're doing?'

She'd padded silently along the corridor from the bathroom, wearing tracksuit pants and a T-shirt, her hair turbaned under a blue towel. The neck and shoulders of the shirt were damp. Auhl had a powerful sense of shower-damp recent nakedness close beside him. He wanted to say, 'I'll leave you to it,' but neither the hour nor the husband were civilised enough for him to risk shutting them out on the footpath.

'Claire,' begged Pascal, 'for fuck's sake, Deb doesn't mean anything to me. It was just a one-off thing.'

'Have you been up all night?'

'So what if I have? You just piss off and leave me, won't even talk about it. I need you, Claire. I'm under a lot of pressure, you know that. I've got this huge project to complete and I, er...'

The words trailed away as if he'd lost track of the subject. After a while a ghastly besotted expression suffused his face. 'Claire, we're a team. Mate. Come on. Please. I'm begging you. I'm suffering here.'

It was like a bad movie. Claire flinched, flicking Auhl a sidelong apology. 'It's okay, Alan. I'll talk to him. He'll calm down in a tick.'

So Auhl dragged the hall table and a couple of kitchen chairs out onto the veranda, fuelled husband and wife with coffee and toast, and went to have his shower. He heard murmurs on the other side of his window as he finished dressing, the voices fading as he walked down the hallway to the kitchen for breakfast. There was no shouting. Presently Claire re-entered the house and ran lightly up the hallway, where Auhl heard her call a taxi from the landline. He heard the front door open and close again. Then, as he was rinsing his cereal bowl, Claire was there in the doorway again. 'I sent him home to sleep it off.'

'Okay.'

'Jeez, I need a coffee.'

LATE MORNING, AUHL left to play tennis, coming back mid-afternoon to find his newest tenant seated at the kitchen table with Neve, Bec, Shireen and Tiv. The table was a mess, full of lunch plates and empty bottles; faces full of sleepy goodwill.

'Lunch is almost over,' Claire said.

He frowned at her in confusion. 'Which one are you? Visiting professor? Uni dropout? Parolee?'

'Ha ha.'

Auhl bent to kiss his daughter's forehead. 'Er, exam pressure?'

'I've only got one more. I'm allowed to unwind a little.'

One by one they drifted to other parts of the house. Auhl, dead tired, sprawled in his armchair and fell asleep with Cynthia curled against his hip.

THE HOUSE FELT EMPTY, composed of silence and closed doors, when he awoke. His daughter, his tenants, they might well have been nearby, pecking away at laptops or watching TV, but there was no human ripple in the air that Auhl could discern.

He chopped onions, ginger, garlic, snow peas, bean shoots, capsicum and broccolini and sliced chicken for a huge stir-fry, and watched the news while it marinated. A brief marination. He was starving.

Claire Pascal wandered in as the sports round-up started. 'Sorry about this morning.'

Auhl waved that off. 'There's enough stir-fry if you're interested.'

She shook her head. 'I'm still full after lunch with your other tenants.'

She was idly kicking at the furniture, so Auhl said, 'Spit it out.'

She said in a rush, 'I think I'll stay at my place tonight.'

Auhl nodded. 'That's fine.'

'I need to hash things out with Michael.'

'I understand.'

She kicked a table leg. 'But can I come back if it's a disaster?'

'The room's yours, any time,' Auhl said.

THEN SHE WAS GONE and Auhl walked up to the Nova Cinema. A local film and, not for the first time, he had a sense of actors acting and accents broadly, unnaturally Australian. He didn't speak like that. Knew no one who spoke like that.

When he got back, Neve was watching TV, still wearing her work outfit. She turned it off guiltily. 'Sorry.'

'What's mine is yours, Neve,' he said.

So they sat there and stared at the dead screen. 'About Monday,' Neve said.

'You're worried?'

'Yes. What if Justice Messer cuts my hours instead of Lloyd's?'

'He's not going to do that. But he might enforce equal time.'

She bit her lip and shortly afterwards said goodnight and wandered through to her room.

A HAND SHAKING AUHL'S shoulder and a voice hissing at him. 'Alan. *Alan.*'

The queer glow from the streetlight leaking around his bedroom blind, the murky darkness and the aches in his bones, and Neve Fanning, a spectre leaning over him. He thrashed awake. 'What. *What?*'

She wore threadbare cotton pyjamas and her face was creased. 'I have to get Pia. Can I borrow your car?'

Auhl shook off the bleariness. 'Sorry, start again?'

'*Pia called me. She wants to come home.*'

That sharpened Auhl. 'Did Lloyd do something?'

Neve's turn to be confused. 'What? No. She said the house is full of drunk people and loud music and she's scared and can't sleep and please can she come home.'

'I'll drive,' Auhl said.

They dressed and piled into Auhl's old Saab. He reversed crookedly at speed, skittling a rubbish bin, then straightened the car, and they shot across the city to the West Gate Bridge. Friday night, a steady stream of homeward-bound traffic leading to and over the bridge, and eventually they were on the awful endless snarling highway in the buffeting slipstream of heavy trucks. The moon and stars blotted out from the sky but brake lights and neon flaring greasily as they headed south from the city.

Neve agitated beside him, almost levitating in raw need.

Finally Geelong and the sedate streets of Manifold Heights, Neve directing Auhl to a sprawling house set back from the road. He parked between streetlights and they walked up the driveway.

Heard the music now, the heavy bass beat enough to shake windows and buckle the ground. But mostly what drew Auhl's cop-gaze were the vehicles: two black Range Rovers with tinted windows, a sports Mercedes, an Audi TT.

He knocked, no answer. 'Key?'

Neve shook her head. 'He changed the locks.'

They went around to the back. In through a sliding glass patio door. Bottles, dirty plates and glasses in the kitchen, porn flickering on a massive TV in the sitting room. An assortment of shapes asleep on sofas, beds and floors. Bottles, a couple of ashen joints, discarded clothing.

'Lloyd does drugs?' Auhl said.

Neve shook her head. 'Not really.'

But a bit? More often than he used to? wondered Auhl.

A quick run-through of the house; no sign of Pia. Then Neve clenched her fists, cross with herself. 'I know where she'll be—where she used to hide when Lloyd went mental.'

A built-in wardrobe of an upstairs junk room, Pia asleep but stirring when Neve reached for, lifted and carried her. When she was secured in the car, Auhl said, 'I'll be right back.' He returned to the driveway, aimed his phone, photographed numberplates. Re-entered the house and photographed faces and bodies and the party dregs.

22

EVEN AFTER HIS interrupted night, Auhl woke at six and walked. Bought a bag of croissants for the household on his way back, as he did every Sunday morning, then showered, dressed and yawned over the *Age*. Listened to the house stir around him, Cynthia winding about his ankles.

Neve appeared first, her hair damp, cheeks hollow. With coffee and a croissant before her on the old kitchen table, she kept picking up and putting down her phone. 'I don't know what to do. When Lloyd wakes up and realises Pia's not there, what's going to happen?'

Auhl, rinsing his cup and plates at the sink, suddenly froze. If he hadn't been dazed with tiredness he might have seen the legal ramifications of the night's events. Seated again he said, 'You need to text him right away. The last thing you want is his lawyer accusing you of abduction, or denying him contact with Pia. Keep it mild, don't make him feel you're accusing him, just tell him that Pia felt ill and didn't want to be a nuisance so she asked if you'd come and fetch her.'

'I *hate* this,' she spat, surprising him. 'I hate bending over backwards for his precious ego. What about me, me and Pia? When do we come first?'

Auhl clasped her forearm briefly. 'Tomorrow afternoon, with any luck. In court. Meanwhile let's put everything about last night in writing, together with photos, for your lawyer to look at.'

Neve clasped herself tightly, with the effect that she seemed even smaller and easier to defeat. She stared at the dead screen of her phone as if finding the words. She'd had a lifetime of finding the right words with her shit of a husband, Auhl thought.

Then his own phone pinged. *OK if I stay tonite and Mon, dept. meetings? Liz x.* A feeling crept through him. She would brighten his existence briefly, and he would let her—even though she was a lost cause and he knew it.

Something to be said for habit, though. For the familiar.

IT WAS A HOUSE OF stunned souls and Liz didn't arrive and didn't arrive and didn't arrive. Then, early afternoon, his phone pinged again. John Elphick's daughter, Erica: *Apologies for the late notice: Brunettis in five?*

He texted back: *I'm on a diet.*

Ha ha.

Five minutes later he told the sisters, 'You've already thanked me.'

An effusive phone call, a bottle of Bollinger couriered to the office, an elaborate card.

'But not yet in person,' Rosie said.

The sisters hadn't been to town for weeks, months, they told him. 'We thought,' said Erica, waving a cream-smeared fork at him, 'why not deal with the cake withdrawal and thank you at the same time.' She'd ordered cannoli, Rosie an almond croissant, and both were nursing large lattes. As Auhl watched, each woman gave a little exploratory tongue-flick, seeking traces of powdered sugar. To be sociable, he ordered green tea.

'You must have something to eat.'

He patted his stomach. 'I'm stuffed with croissants.'

'Alan,' Erica said, her expression saying he could do better than that.

He sighed and admitted that the cannoli looked good; both women beamed at him. Confident women who'd grown up with horses and were faintly anachronistic here, among the smart, inner-urban crowd. Well, so was Auhl, tired and greying.

He gave the sisters a troubled look. 'There's still the trial. You might have to appear.'

Rosie said, 'Oh, we can handle that, don't you worry.'

Erica, wily but half-serious, said, 'Will you miss our annual phone call?'

The annual conference call, the pair of them ganging up on him. 'I probably will,' he said.

'Liar.'

He stayed awhile, then, amid enormous goodwill and vague promises to keep in touch, he pecked their cheeks and left them to finish their pastries.

STILL NO LIZ. Early evening, Claire Pascal returned bearing Chinese takeaway. Telling Auhl, 'Don't ask,' she called his ragged household to the table. They ate, the others drifted away, then it was time to wait for Slab Man's face on the evening news.

He appeared at the ten-minute mark, the clay version, then the digital. In the latter he wore short hair, then a shaved head, long hair, a beard. A minute later he was dropped for another drive-by shooting in Lalor.

'Short but sweet,' Claire said.

'There's always tomorrow's papers.'

Claire took their empty bowls to the kitchen and returned with her iPad, settling beside Auhl on the sofa. Her fingers tapped and swiped. 'It's getting more play on social media.'

Auhl peered at the Slab Man images. 'Good.'

'I suppose you want to know how it went with Michael.'

'None of my business. Except I think he'd like to flatten me.'

'He's a bit upset, that's all. I told him you were just a colleague. But what I want to ask is can I stay here a few more days? I need more time.'

'Sure,' Auhl said.

That was his life, stretched by competing demands, pissing off some people, helping others. Then the front door banged and footsteps sounded and Liz appeared with her suitcases, saying a brisk hello, she'd already eaten, she had a ton of work to do for tomorrow's meetings. Then like a whirlwind she clattered upstairs and Claire was murmuring, 'That was the famous, mysterious wife?'

'It was.'

'Kind of gorgeous.'

'I wouldn't know.'

'Yes you would,' Claire said, with a touch of sympathy Auhl purely hated. Upstairs there were shouts as Liz and Bec said hello.

23

BEFORE TAKING THE lift to the Cold Case office on Monday morning, Auhl and Pascal poked their heads into the media room. The half-dozen night-shift constables assigned to field the Slab Man hotline were half-asleep, feet up, talking football and sex and waiting for the 8.00 a.m. shift change.

'Much action?'

They looked at one another and shrugged. 'Usual ratbags and psychos. Sorry.'

'You've noted the likely ones?'

Yawns, back stretches, bleary red eyes. 'As per instructions.'

They said their thanks and went upstairs. Conscious that in four hours he'd be catching the Geelong train, Auhl quickly read emails, drew up action lists, made online searches and fielded Slab Man calls forwarded from the media room. These proved to be useless or mischievous.

'Yes, about the reward?' someone might ask.

Auhl would close his eyes, open them again. 'Reward?'

'The man found buried under the concrete.'

Usually a male voice, drunk at nine-thirty in the morning.

'Do you know the name of the victim?'

'Depends on the age, right? A lot of Serb war criminals came to Australia. Some of them carried on what they were doing when they got here.'

'Thank you for your help,' Auhl would say.

Or sad, haunted people would hope a male friend or relative had been found, and Auhl would tease out the story and learn the father, brother, uncle, son or family friend had been forty when he vanished, or decades had passed.

Or they'd confess. 'That guy you found. The one under the slab.'

'What about him?'

'I done it.'

'What gauge shotgun did you use?'

A silence. 'You're not getting me that way. I'm onto you. *You* tell *me* what kind.'

Then, mid-morning, her hand masking her landline phone, Claire called out: 'Alan, Josh, you need to hear this.' She spoke into the phone. 'Bear with me, madam, I'm just going to put you on speaker, okay? Now, two of my colleagues are here in the room with me and I need you to repeat what you just told me.'

They listened. A woman, her voice young, hollow. 'The dead man is Robert Shirlow.'

'Spell that for me, please,' Claire said. That done, she asked, 'And how do you know this person?'

'I can send you pictures. I'm his sister. Carmen.' There was a pause, and she said, in a rush, 'It's definitely Robert, and I always knew something bad happened to him. I knew he didn't murder anyone.'

BEFORE AUHL COULD run a search on the name, Jerry Debenham walked in, trailed by a younger Homicide Squad detective.

Debenham jerked his head. 'Quick word.'

Neill, thought Auhl. He coughed to give himself a moment, then shrugged on his jacket, wondering if they'd keep him long. Claire was watching curiously. He said, his voice sounding unnaturally loud in his ears, 'Can you see if we have anything on Shirlow?'

She looked worried. 'Will do.'

Debenham took Auhl through to his sergeant's cubicle in the Homicide Squad office. 'Pull up a pew.'

And so Auhl sat against one wall, the other two facing him. The younger detective was named Vicks and she said nothing. Just watched, her face mask-like.

'We're doing the paperwork on the Neills,' Debenham said.

'Okay.'

'Dotting i's, crossing t's.'

'Okay,' Auhl said, his mouth dry.

'Ironing out anomalies, things like that.'

Auhl didn't know how to answer, but knew he had to, and heard himself say with forced innocence, 'All I can say is it seemed to me Neill was trying to set up his wife.'

'But why not leave it at that? Why kill her?'

'Is that what the pathologist thinks?'

Debenham shrugged. 'Still waiting on the toxicology.'

Hearing the contrivance in his own voice, Auhl said, 'I understand there was vomit and diarrhoea? His first wife died of what was thought to be some kind of stomach bug, so what if he used the same method again, knowing we'd be on the lookout for that other drug, the whatchamacallit...'

'Succinylcholine,' Vicks said.

Auhl nodded, conscious that he'd been babbling and determined to shut up now.

'It's possible someone was there when she died,' Debenham said.

My footprint in the vomit...

'Well, Neill, I suppose,' Auhl said—too promptly.

Debenham cocked his head and waited a beat before saying: 'I checked with Senior Sergeant Colfax. Like me, she recalls Mrs Neill showing signs of illness the other day. Remember?'

Auhl nodded. 'Yeah, she did look a bit pale. Like I said, maybe Neill used the poison he used on his first wife. Slow-acting.'

'Except the first wife wasn't ruled a poisoning,' Debenham said.

He was looking at Auhl, as if to trip him up. Auhl said nothing.

'Did you ever go to the St Andrews property, Alan?'

They have me on camera, Auhl thought. But I wore a hat and glasses. I was in Janine's car. He didn't know how to answer, but knew he should and heard himself say, 'Before we met you there last week? No.'

'Not when wives number one and two died?'

Now Auhl felt on firmer ground. 'The first death wasn't seen as suspicious. The second was ruled cause undetermined, from memory. But Neill didn't have a place in St Andrews in those days. He lived in South Yarra.'

Debenham clapped his hands. 'Well, thanks for your time, Alan.'

Was that it? Was that going to be the end of it? Auhl stood to leave. Knowing he sounded faintly desperate, he said, 'A long shot, but I've asked for CCTV footage of the drug storage in the hospitals where Neill was on staff.'

But he was mistaken if he thought they'd be grateful. 'Doing our job for us, Alan?'

'Didn't mean to double-up,' Auhl said, and got out of there.

24

ONE-FORTY-FIVE NOW, the steps of the Family Court in Geelong, Jeff Fleet addressing Auhl and Neve with a severe expression on his young face. 'Mrs Fanning, it's come to my attention that you collected your daughter from your husband's house halfway through her weekend visit?' Waiting a brief, cool moment, he added, 'I received a phone call this morning. From Mr Fanning's lawyer.'

Auhl was still jittery from the session with Debenham, the strain of reading between the lines, sensing traps, so his voice was not quite under control: 'They're going to play dirty?'

Fleet nodded, his glasses slipping. He thumbed them back. 'It was made clear to me that they'll raise the issue of abduction if they have to.' He turned to Neve. 'That means no outbursts, Neve, all right?'

'But it was a *rescue* mission. She wanted to come home. Lloyd was having a party and the house was full of people who were passed out on the floor and watching filthy DVDs and taking drugs. I was *protecting* her.'

'I've got photos,' Auhl said.

'I don't care. At this stage, I don't care. Even if you swear blind you had good reason and can present a stock of photos to prove it, what if Mr Fanning or his lawyer complain to the police? My advice is simply let events take their course this morning. Justice Messer will rule, a mere formality, over and done with quite quickly. Then we can all go our merry ways.'

Auhl was frustrated. 'That's it?'

'Can't rock the boat, Mr Auhl. We've already run the risk of Neve appearing to be a no-contact mum, i.e., hostile and vindictive. Last week was the hearing, today's the ruling, so it's not the place for raising fresh allegations. We need to be realistic, or we risk Mr Fanning getting substantially more time with the daughter and Neve substantially less.'

'I'm wondering why you didn't go in harder last week.'

'Mr Auhl, let me do my job. I'm run ragged enough as it is.'

Neve was touching Auhl's sleeve warningly. He took a deep breath, told himself to calm down. 'What are Neve's chances?'

'Oh, I'm sure it will all be fine. Neve just needs to be aware that she made a bit of a poor impression the other day. Softly, softly, Neve, okay? Worst case scenario, your parenting time is reduced.'

'The mind boggles,' Auhl said.

'Not permanently,' Fleet went on, rolling his shoulders in his tatty gown. 'Just for a while, after which the situation would be reviewed.'

THE SAME COURTROOM, bland pale wood, grey industrial carpet and off-white walls. Neve seated behind her lawyer, Lloyd Fanning behind his. Fanning looked competent, patient, successful. With Neve were her parents. No sign of Kelso.

Then Justice Messer swept in, and after the rising, the sitting, the formal announcements, he said: 'The purpose of these proceedings was to decide upon the matter of Mrs Neve Fanning's application to formalise and limit her husband's time with their daughter,

Miss Pia Fanning. To assist the court, and in the best interests of the child, Doctor Thomas Kelso, an experienced psychiatrist and single expert whose specialty is difficult Family Court situations, conducted interviews with the three parties, and I have given his testimony close consideration. Doctor Kelso found Mrs Fanning to be anxious and over-protective and possibly to have suffered a temporary psychosis. In his assessment, she placed demands, planted ideas and fostered hate, fear and anxiety in her daughter. Indeed, he saw no indication in the child that she'd been mistreated by her father or was at risk of mistreatment, going forward. Although the child presented as guarded in her father's presence and unresponsive with Doctor Kelso, these behaviours should be seen in the context of the mother fostering a toxic attitude towards the father. The mother had presented in a self-absorbed manner to Doctor Kelso and over-valued the notion of risk to the daughter.'

Never respect a man who says, 'going forward', thought Auhl sourly.

Messer looked around the room, down at his report again. 'Furthermore, Doctor Kelso went on to say that Mrs Fanning's accusations of domestic violence may be seen in the context of a convoluted and strained marital relationship.'

Auhl felt himself shrink and, watching Neve, saw her helplessness, her chin against her chest. Lloyd Fanning sat calmly, head high, as though saying that at last someone was speaking sense.

Everyone else in the room looked bored. Courtroom hangers-on, staff, young lawyers and legal clerks, they'd heard it all before. Auhl wished Fleet could object.

'Which brings me to my decision in this matter,' Messer said. 'I find that there are insufficient grounds to reduce Mr Fanning's parenting time with his daughter.'

Neve tipped her chin up. 'But he just ignores her! He doesn't care about her!'

Maureen Deane touched her daughter's forearm. Messer shot

them a glance, went on: 'The consequences of denying the daughter a relationship with her father are, in the court's view, serious indeed.'

Auhl shook his head. Messer continued: 'It is a shame, Mrs Fanning, that you sought to make the ancient history of alleged domestic abuse a part of these proceedings. You are urged to put aside your resentment and prioritise your daughter's interests.'

He stared at her and the room was still and silent apart from a nervy cough somewhere, a fidgeting from a bored courtroom attendant in a doorway.

'May I suggest that you obtain regular counselling so that you might support your daughter in her relationship with her father?'

Neve had leaned forward to whisper in Fleet's ear, her upper body quivering. Fleet was shaking his head. Auhl's back and backside ached. The seat, the tension. He shifted futilely.

Suddenly Neve was getting to her feet. She stood at rocky attention. 'I am *not* the vindictive person you're portraying me as. I'm telling the truth.'

She pointed at Lloyd, who smirked. Her parents tugged on her arms. Messer said, 'Mrs Fanning, please, these histrionics do you no good at all.'

Neve said, 'Do you know what happened on the weekend? Pia was staying with him and she—'

Lloyd Fanning's lawyer stirred. Seeing that, Fleet turned to Neve and her parents, spoke sharply, and Neve subsided. Fanning's lawyer subsided. Then Neve was turning to find Auhl in the courtroom, her face showing betrayal and loss. Auhl made a tiny useless reaching-out gesture as if his arm were ten metres long and his touch might bring reassurance. She faced front again, vibrating with suppressed emotion while Lloyd Fanning sat calmly, a picture of parental responsibility.

Justice Messer gathered his reports. 'That concludes these proceedings.'

Neve stood. She looked down at the top of Fleet's head. He didn't turn around but tapped folders and papers together. She turned to her mother, who embraced her. Auhl waved goodbye but no one saw it.

25

AUHL RACED BACK TO the city in time for a four-thirty briefing.

'To get you up to speed,' Helen Colfax said, 'we were emailed these photos by the woman who claims Slab Man is her brother.'

She turned her iPad screen around. Auhl, clustered with the others, said, 'Uncanny.'

'Perfect match,' Colfax agreed. 'Meanwhile Josh found separate confirmation. He ran the name, and a Robert Shirlow was indeed tied to a murder. This was in the file.'

She slapped a small, passport-size portrait on the briefing table. A young man, full of grinning vitality. Again, a match to the Forensic Institute's mock-ups.

'The murder victim was a young woman named Mary Peart, and this was inside a wallet found with her body. Josh?'

Bugg read from a file. 'Mary Naomi Peart, aged twenty, found shot dead behind the wheel of a Corolla in a parking bay overlooking a lake in Wilson Botanic Park near the Princes Highway in Berwick. Ninth of September, 2009.'

Auhl began to snap out his questions. 'Shot in the car?'

'Possibly. The forensic team couldn't say for certain.'

'Was it her car?'

Claire shook her head. 'Registered to Shirlow. The address: the Pearcedale property owned by Angela Sullivan and her mother.'

'Presumably they were interviewed at the time?'

'Yes.'

'When we spoke to Sullivan the other day, she didn't say anything about Shirlow. In fact, I got the impression no one rented the place after Crowther.'

'You and Claire better have another crack at her,' Colfax said.

'Shirlow and this girl were in a relationship?'

'Living together.'

'And he was suspected of the murder?'

'Yes.'

'What do we have on him?'

Claire Pascal read from a separate file. 'Robert McArthur Shirlow, born August 1987, father dead, mother and sister living in Cranbourne at the time of the murder but later moved to Brisbane.' She looked up. 'Shirlow was questioned, but never charged, in relation to a bit of dealing and handling in 2007 and 2008.'

'Then in September 2009 his girlfriend dies,' Auhl said. 'Are we thinking he was killed at the same time?'

'Or he killed her and was then killed by someone else.'

Auhl nodded gloomily. 'It's always a joy to have an unknown third person.'

Claire continued: 'Anyway, the car led police to the house. It was empty, cleaned out, as if no one intended to return, so they assumed Shirlow killed the girlfriend and did a runner, and all the time he's buried under a slab.'

'Anything in the house to indicate they were both shot there?'

Claire shook her head. 'Locked, curtains drawn, swept and vacuumed and wiped clean. The fridge empty and switched off with the door open. It gets better: someone had put a stop on Australia

Post and *Herald Sun* deliveries and the landline was cancelled.'

'Personal possessions?'

'Plenty of the girl's, but nothing of Shirlow's. Very few prints, but no match to any database and neither kid had ever been printed.'

'Someone was being slow and methodical. Doesn't sound like a twenty-two-year-old kid,' Auhl said.

'But that's who got the blame when his girlfriend was shot dead and he dropped off the radar. According to his bank and mobile phone records, he was in Sydney soon afterwards. A text from his phone was sent to his mother and sister, saying, *I did something bad and I won't be coming back*, and his card was used to buy a Lonely Planet guide to Thailand in a Glebe bookshop and a fish dinner in Watsons Bay. Then nothing.'

'Except the rumours,' Josh Bugg said. 'He was having an affair, he was running from creditors, he had mental health issues.'

'But no way of knowing who made the whispers or how much credence to give them,' added Colfax.

'The official line?'

'The official line was Shirlow murdered his girlfriend and went into hiding. We raked over the coals a couple of times in recent years, but nothing turned up.' She smiled at Auhl. 'Except the gun.'

Auhl felt the old tingle. 'Okay.'

'Read about it,' Colfax said, handing him a file.

Auhl read the summary. In early 2010, a twenty-year-old apprentice mechanic had been sent by his boss to a Langwarrin wrecking yard to strip the dashboard gauges out of a 2007 Suzuki Vitara that had sat in the yard since the end of 2009. Tucked behind the glove box, partly held in place by the wiring loom, was a 9 mm Ruger automatic. In due course the pistol was test-fired at the Forensic Science Institute and the test slug was matched to the bullet found in Mary Peart.

The Suzuki itself had been reported stolen at the time of the murder, but from an address some distance from the Berwick nature reserve and so the Homicide Squad hadn't, until later, made the connection. Just another stolen vehicle, assumed to have been torched or chopped—until, just before Christmas 2009, a semi-trailer loaded with hay crested a hill on a back road near Tooradin and rear-ended it. Empty, abandoned, no petrol in the tank. Declared a write-off by the owner's insurance company, which had already paid out on the theft, the Suzuki was towed to the Lang-warrin wrecking yard.

The gun was tested for prints. Two sets, none in the system and no match to any found at the old house or in Shirlow's car. A forensic team, sent to examine the wrecked Suzuki, found dozens of useless smudges.

'We need Shirlow's mother and sister to come in,' Auhl said.

'The mother's dead,' Colfax said, 'but the sister's arriving on Thursday. She lives in far north Queensland. Can't organise to get here any sooner.'

Auhl nodded. 'Meanwhile it would pay us to speak to Sullivan again, the team who investigated the Peart murder and the owner of the Suzuki.'

'Excuse me, who's boss here?' Colfax said.

'*You* are, oh esteemed leader,' Auhl said.

'Don't forget it.'

THAT NIGHT THEY HELD a kind of wake and celebration at Chateau Auhl. No more exams for Bec, a fuck-the-system piss-up for Neve and Pia. Three giant pizzas, cheap plonk, bodies sprawled on the sofa, the armchairs, the kitchen chairs, the carpet. Cynthia winding among them, hoping for a dropped anchovy. Liz, arriving late, looking tired, seemed removed from everyone.

'Lloyd gave me this look, like he'd won for good,' Neve said, with a glance at her daughter as though wondering if she'd said too much.

Pia seemed to hunch her shoulders. 'Do I have to go to his place this weekend?'

Neve was looking at the wall clock. She had an evening shift at the university. 'He didn't say anything about it.'

'I'll run away if I have to go.'

Neve gave her daughter another look, then, aware that everyone was watching her, said, 'A step at a time, love.'

She left the room, changed into work clothes. On her way out of the house she came to stand at trembling attention before the sofa, where Auhl sat—a metre from his wife that might as well have been ten.

'I want to thank you both for all your help.'

'It's not the end of it,' Liz said.

But Neve shook her head. 'I'm too tired to fight anymore.'

26

ON TUESDAY MORNING Auhl and Pascal started with Osprey Auto Marine in Keysborough. Auhl drove, Claire navigating, out along Dandenong Road and south onto Springvale Road. Springvale took them past a stretch of Vietnamese shops and restaurants, past some modest housing and finally to the section they wanted. A pricey private school, ugly mega-churches, and businesses for cashed-up bogans: car yards, garden centres, boatyards.

Osprey Auto Marine sprawled between a funeral director and a building named the True Gospel Congregation Church. Speed-boats and aluminium runabouts on trailers crowded the main lot, with separate smaller sections for kayaks, inflatable dinghies and jet skis. The auto section consisted of a handful of used SUVs with trailer hitches. Plastic bunting thrummed and snapped in the wind.

'Not exactly a marine environment,' Claire observed.

But the environment of people who wanted to park a huge boat in the driveway and join a clap-hands-for-Jesus church, Auhl thought.

They entered the showroom. Motorboats dwarfed them, racks of outboard motors and paddles, safety gear, ropes, anchors, display stands of men with beautiful teeth and women in bikinis. And, in contrast to the mercantile gleam, a depressed reception desk, one woman chewing gum and flipping through a *New Idea*, the other chewing gum, staring at a computer and talking into a bluetooth headset.

The first woman swallowed a yawn, eyes watering. 'Sorry,' she said. 'May I help you?'

Pascal took the lead. 'Mr Osprey is expecting us.'

An avid glint in the woman's eyes now. She leaned towards them, whispered: 'You're the police that called?'

'We are.'

'Just a moment.'

She swung her chair around, stood and retreated along a short corridor. At the end she glanced back at Auhl and Claire, then tapped on a door. Waited, opened, went in.

Then she was back. 'Mr Osprey will see you now. Would you like to come through?'

REX OSPREY WAS TALL, about fifty, wary, wiry, with the air of a busy executive. He wore steel-rimmed glasses, tan trousers and a white shirt, the sleeves rolled to reveal strong forearms.

He slid a file across the desk. Addressing Auhl he said, 'That's all I could find on the matter.'

Auhl pulled the file onto his lap, flipped through the contents: the Suzuki's trade-in papers, registration and insurance papers, a letter from the insurance company detailing the payout.

He passed it to Claire. 'Do you remember the event, Mr Osprey?'

'Not well. It was years ago. And four-wheel drives and utes and SUVs pass through my yard all the time. As people trade their watercraft up or down, they trade their towing vehicles up or down.' Spoken as if he'd stumbled upon a vital commercial truth.

Auhl, polite but beginning to harden, said, 'But this one was stolen. Do you get many thefts?'

Osprey shrugged. 'Smaller items from time to time.'

Auhl glanced around the office. Plain walls, apart from a small tapestry Bible verse. Filing cabinets. Photographs of Osprey and his family: wife and daughter in plain dresses, two sons brushed and scrubbed in dark suits and neck-pinching ties.

Claire had opened the folder. Resting a forefinger on one of the documents she said, 'Mr Osprey, it says here the building wasn't broken into.'

'That's correct.'

'And presumably the keys to the vehicles are locked away in a drawer somewhere?'

'They are.'

'So the Suzuki was hotwired, do you think?'

Osprey stiffened, as though he felt challenged. 'I imagine so. I have no other explanation.'

Auhl asked Claire for the folder, found the document he wanted. 'Mr Osprey, you reported the Suzuki stolen on the eleventh of September 2009?'

'If that's what it says.'

'But you have no memory of the theft. Could the vehicle have been stolen some time before the eleventh?'

Osprey shifted in his seat. 'It's possible. See, our business is concentrated mainly on the marine side of things. We didn't notice the Suzuki was missing until someone came in asking to test drive it.' He paused. 'We had it listed online and in the local newspapers.'

'You immediately informed the police and your insurance company?'

'We did, yes.'

Auhl mused on the timing. The Suzuki was reported stolen on the eleventh, yet Mary Peart was found on the ninth. The vehicle then disappeared until rear-ended near Tooradin five months later, a handgun concealed behind the dash. Peart and Shirlow were probably shot dead the same day. But was the Suzuki stolen purely for the killings? Stolen the same day, or earlier? If earlier, where was it stored? Auhl supposed it wouldn't necessarily have attracted attention if parked on a street or in a driveway or garage for a couple of days, but surely someone clever enough to commit two murders and a cover-up would also be clever enough to torch the Suzuki afterwards? Maybe it was stolen from the killer.

He said carefully, 'Mr Osprey, we believe the Suzuki from your yard was used in the commission of a serious crime. We need to see a list of everyone who was employed by your firm in 2009.'

Osprey drew himself up. 'I can vouch for everyone who has ever worked for me. Most have worked here for *years*. They are like family, they'd never steal from me. They would never commit a crime of any nature.'

Claire scratched at the scars under her sleeve. 'Would a warrant make things easier for you, Mr Osprey? It might help you explain to people why you were obliged to give their details to the police?'

Osprey had struck Auhl as a women-need-to-know-their-place kind of guy, and was intrigued to see him respond to Claire's smiling tact.

The scowl easing a little, Osprey said, 'That won't be necessary. If you could give me thirty minutes?'

Auhl looked at his watch, impatient. Anxious to head down to Frankston and have another shot at Angela Sullivan. But Claire Pascal saved him. With the sweetest of smiles she said, 'That would be perfect, Mr Osprey. We'll find somewhere for coffee.'

As they left, Auhl asked, 'Did Robert Shirlow ever work for you, Mr Osprey?'

Osprey was bewildered. 'Who? I don't know that name.'

The confusion was genuine. Auhl nodded and they left to find coffee, settling on a weak but acrid brew in the local service station.

ARMED WITH THE employee list half an hour later, they headed east on the Frankston Freeway. Claire, keeping up a phone commentary with Josh Bugg, finally completed the call and said, 'Josh says every-one's clean. Osprey, all his staff.'

'It was a long shot.'

'You didn't tell him about the gun in the Suzuki.'

Auhl said, 'Too soon, and we probably won't need to. But a useful lever if we ever make another run at him.'

'Guess so.' She didn't sound convinced.

ELEVEN A.M. AND Angela Sullivan was in a Chinese-dragon-patterned dressing-gown over pink satin pyjamas. Strong, shapely bare feet with chipped red nail polish, untidy hair, and clear fluid in the tumbler in her right hand. Not drunk, but intending to be, thought Auhl. And somehow, he didn't think she usually started her days like this.

'Are you worried about something, Angela?'

They were seated at her kitchen table. A single woman's kitchen, cereal bowl and cup and saucer draining on a rack beside the sink. An older-style fridge, business cards under magnets. A toaster on the bench. A glass stovetop, a black, glass-fronted oven. A tiny vase on the sill above the sink, one rosebud. Small, sad touches of a lonely life.

'It must rake up old memories, a body found on the property where you grew up,' prompted Claire.

Sullivan drew the dressing-gown closer about her torso and shrugged.

'Have you had reporters here?' asked Auhl.

'Not yet.'

'But you will,' Claire said.

'All kinds of people might crawl out of the woodwork,' Auhl said.

Sullivan jerked to her feet and shot the contents of her glass into the sink. 'Look, what do you want? I haven't got all day.'

'We thought you might want to help us find who killed Robert and Mary,' Claire said.

'Who?'

'Your tenants. The people living in your Pearcedale property in 2009. The young people paying you rent money.'

Sullivan gave them a ferrety look.

'One of whom was murdered,' Auhl said, 'and the other blamed for it. Are you really telling us you don't remember?'

Sullivan sat again and stared despondently at the tabletop. She wet a fingertip and rubbed at a spot; said in a low voice, 'I'd rather forget that period in my life.'

'Well, you can't, Angela,' Claire said. 'Not at the moment. We need to know all about Robert and Mary.'

Sullivan looked up at her, swung her face to Auhl, back to Claire. 'I barely knew them.'

'Angela, was this rent income you weren't declaring? We're not interested in that. That's ancient history. We need to know something about the backgrounds of these two kids and who they hung out with and what you saw and heard. Anything at all.'

'Okay, okay. But like I said, I barely had anything to do with them. Robert used to do a bit of general maintenance in the district and I was at Pearcedale one day, mowing the grass, and he called in and said did I have any handyman work for him, and we got talking and he said he was looking for a place to rent and I said why not this place. It was a bit of a dump, but anyway, he moved in. Later I saw him there with his girlfriend, and I knew they wouldn't stay long. *He* might have if he'd been single, but no woman would've put up with it.'

'How long were they there?'

Sullivan shrugged. 'Six months?'

'Did you ever chat with Mary?'

'No.'

'Did you ever see other people there?'

'No. Like I said, I left them alone.'

Auhl said, 'What did the police tell you at the time?'

Anguished, Sullivan said, 'That maybe Rob wasn't such an angel. He might have been dealing from my old house and he probably killed Mary. It made me queasy, if truth be known. I couldn't wait to pull the place down.'

27

HALF-FEARING DEBENHAM would detain him for another 'chat', Auhl left work at five. He boarded a crowded tram on Swanston Street, jostled and clenched in stale, sick air. A solid toecap clipped his ankle and Christ, it hurt.

And he found Neve Fanning on the edge of an armchair in the unlit sitting room, rocking her torso. She glanced up at Auhl, tear-streaked. 'Now Lloyd's put in an application.'

After a moment, Auhl understood. 'Family Court?'

'He *rang* me, gloating. His lawyer has already filed the paper-work. He's applying for Pia to live with him, and me to have limited time with her.'

'On what grounds?'

'I'm unfit. I need counselling, to quote Doctor Kelso and the judge. I removed Pia from his legitimate right to have time with her.'

'I'll call Fleet.'

FLEET LISTENED AND said, 'Look, I'm about to leave the office. What is it you think I can do?'

'Jesus Christ, a challenge of some kind. Lloyd's behaviour, the drunken party, et cetera, et cetera.'

Auhl could picture Fleet at his desk, his all-encompassing, ineffectual regret: 'It's not that clear cut. You were there—without stating it outright, Kelso argued that Neve planted suggestions in her kid, and Justice Messer seemed to buy it. And Mr Fanning's legal team can play nasty with that abduction business.'

Auhl could have strangled the guy. 'It wasn't an abduction.'

'A small step at a time would be my advice,' Fleet said. 'But I'll tell you what I'll do, I'll talk to my colleagues and get back to you.'

HE GOT BACK HALF an hour later. 'I'm afraid Legal Aid cannot commit to further representation of Mrs Fanning.'

'Why not?'

Fleet sounded like a recorded message. 'Our resources are over-stretched as it is, and I'm afraid we are not satisfied as to the merits of representing her further. I'm sorry, Mr Auhl.'

Auhl said sourly, 'If you can't help, tell me who can. A good lawyer. Family violence.'

'Mrs Fanning can afford to pay a lawyer?'

'Don't be a prick. I can,' Auhl said, hanging up on the man.

As if reading his mood, Cynthia stepped onto his lap, circled his crotch, stretched her forefeet up onto his chest and stared at him, purring thunderously. 'You wouldn't let me down, would you, Cynth.'

He glanced at his watch and called Liz.

'A good lawyer?' she said, her voice sounding as far away as always when he used the landline. 'Georgina Towne. We were at Monash together. I'll get back to you.'

She called late evening: Georgina Towne would see him first thing in the morning.

AT 8.00 A.M. WEDNESDAY, Auhl and Neve alighted from a tram at the bottom end of Collins Street. The city rang to the sounds of traffic and shoe leather. Everyone looked trim, combed and a little bleary.

Towne occupied a small suite of offices near the corner of Collins and Russell. The reception desk was unoccupied, but the lawyer appeared in the corridor behind it as soon as Auhl and Neve stepped through the door. She was slight, guarded, dressed in a white long-sleeved shirt and grey skirt. Combed, trim, not bleary at all.

She came forward, shook their hands, looked steadily into each of their faces, made some small talk about Liz, then indicated that they should follow her to her office.

With Auhl sometimes prompting, Towne sometimes interrupting with a penetrating question, Neve outlined her predicament. Gradually Auhl relaxed. There was something reassuring about Towne. She had authority and calmness. Her face was serene, close to austere. The only expressions he saw were fleeting: scepticism, anger, pity, calculation.

'Did Doctor Kelso use the term Parental Alienation Syndrome?'

'Too clever for that,' Auhl said, 'but if that's the theory behind his thinking, Justice Messer didn't quibble about it.'

'They might not like their words quoted back to them, however. Do we know why a single expert was brought in rather than a family report writer?' Seeing Auhl's puzzlement, she explained: 'A social worker or psychologist selected by the director of counselling and mediation.'

Auhl said, 'No, I don't know,' but had an inkling: that encounter he'd witnessed between Kelso and Nichols.

'Anyway, it's done now,' Towne was saying. 'Meanwhile let's set the legal machine in motion. Alan? Ask around, see if Mr Fanning's lawyer has in fact made an allegation of abduction to police.'

Auhl winced, but nodded.

'I thought if Pia and I went away for a while,' Neve said, 'where she's safe and...'

Towne shook her head vigorously and stiffened her expression. 'Don't on any account do something like that, Mrs Fanning. Let the court process follow its due course. Meanwhile, legally, you continue to have significant time with Pia and are the primary caregiver. If you get arrested on an abduction charge, you're looking at a custodial sentence and probably a psych evaluation and your daughter placed with your husband.'

'Not with my parents?'

'Possibly. Or possibly with your husband's parents, have you considered that?'

Neve shook her head. 'Lloyd's parents are dead.'

'The thing is, let's tackle this in court. Be patient.'

Neve was sobbing. 'It's so unfair. The system's against me.'

'Well, let's see what we can do about that. I'll get things started today.' She paused. 'You might think about separate legal representation for your daughter.'

Neve sniffed, straightened her shoulders. 'No, thank you.'

Towne glanced at Auhl, gave him a minute shrug.

AUHL TEXTED COLFAX that he wouldn't be in until mid-morning and walked Neve back to Carlton, that simple act helping to calm her. They found a table at Tiamo's, drank strong coffee. Quite soon, Neve lapsed again, a stunned, mute presence opposite him. He found himself doing most of the talking. It was a strained, bereft hour. A part of Auhl wanted to shake her, ask why she hadn't played it smarter; another blamed himself for not hiring Georgina Towne much earlier.

But after a while he was aware of tension in her upper body, the slight movements of each arm, the way she kept glancing at her lap...

'Neve, what are you doing?'

She looked up. 'What?'

'Who are you texting?'

She shrugged, avoiding him.

'Neve, are you texting Pia?'

'It's just to send my love. I'm not doing anything wrong.'

'Please be careful what you say. What if Lloyd checks her phone and finds texts he can use against you in court?'

'He doesn't know she has a phone.'

Auhl derived no comfort from that. 'But he sounds to me like someone who'd search her things, looking for ammunition to use against you.'

Neve snorted. 'He barely knows she's alive. He's just playing mind games with me, this whole parenting time business.'

Auhl wanted to yell at her to wake up. 'Have you told Pia to delete your texts?'

'Yes.'

Auhl thought it unlikely. 'Tell her again. And *you* delete everything.'

'Yeah, okay,' she said.

Auhl derived no comfort from that, either.

28

LATE WEDNESDAY morning. Auhl heading out, with Bugg this time, to Warrandyte in the hills north of the city. Bugg drove like he was watching TV, sprawled in the drivers seat, one hand on the wheel. The unfolding road was in some way soothing to Auhl, but there was also Neve: he continued to feel uneasy about her state of mind. And Warrandyte was not so far from St Andrews. His mind kept flashing back to the struggle in Neill's garage, the stumbling walk to the back fence. Flashing on Debenham, an old cop like Auhl himself, preternaturally suspicious.

Bugg's phone directed them to a house surrounded by gum trees on the kind of precipitous slope that would funnel a bushfire if the conditions were right—like today's hot northerly wind, a taste of the summer ahead.

The house was owned by a retired inspector named Rhys Mascot. He'd been the lead detective in the Mary Peart murder investigation.

Auhl and Bugg were expected, a bustling woman greeting them at the door and taking them to a sitting room where a lumpish, greying man sat with a pen in his mouth and a newspaper open at the form guide. A vast glass wall overlooked the canopies of hot, wind-gusted gumtrees. Auhl felt nervous, more trapped in Mascot's house than he ever did among the towers of Collins Street.

After the handshakes the woman left the room and Mascot ushered them onto a three-seater sofa. He took an armchair on the other side of a coffee table; darted a look at the file in Auhl's hands. 'Mind if I have a squiz?'

Auhl placed it on the coffee table and the old cop leaned over and turned the pages. 'This takes me back,' he said. A gingery, weather-beaten character, his legs bony in faded khaki shorts, his chest small and belly large. A loose thread in the V-neck of his faded Lacoste shirt. Auhl itched to get out the scissors.

Mascot glanced keenly at Auhl. 'You were Homicide? I don't recall you.'

'It would have been after you moved to Traffic,' Auhl said.

Mascot winced, and Auhl wondered if the move to Traffic had been some kind of punishment. He said, 'Back then the theory was the boyfriend did it.'

Mascot nodded. He frowned through a couple of pages and then his face cleared. 'Shirlow, that's right. Robert Shirlow.'

'Well, he's surfaced, so to speak,' Bugg said. 'Last week, out near Pearcedale—the body under the concrete slab?'

Mascot raised his eyebrows. 'You're kidding.'

'We're not a hundred per cent sure. An anonymous tip gave us the name, which gave us the Peart case and the contents of Peart's wallet, including a photo that matches the facial reconstructions we had worked up by the lab.'

'So he kills the girlfriend and then someone kills him?'

'Or someone killed both of them,' Auhl said, 'but constructed a scenario that had us chasing the boyfriend.'

Mascot cast him a darkly dubious look. Auhl almost welcomed

183

it—Mascot's sitting room, like his wife, was over-fussy, a mess of flowery fabrics. It needed the salty corrective of cynicism, suspicion, doubt.

'We didn't find a "third man",' Mascot said, his fingers supplying the quotes. 'The little shit was into a bit of low-level dealing and thieving, but the people he hung out with didn't seem to be the type to commit a double murder and cover their tracks. Not a bright spark among them.'

'But you were ready to believe *he* was bright enough to pull it off?'

'The theory was he'd struck it lucky somehow. Ripped someone off bigtime and wanted it all for himself. Killed the girlfriend so he didn't have to share. Or the girlfriend got cold feet or wanted to turn him in or had become a millstone...'

'You had no reason to think he might have been a victim too?'

Mascot gestured at the folder of reports and statements spread over his coffee table. 'You know all this. You trying to catch me out? Someone—and to our thinking it had to be Shirlow—cleaned out the house, cancelled the newspaper and mail deliveries, emptied the fridge, et cetera. Gone to Sydney, where he used his credit cards and phone a couple of times before going off the grid.' He shook his head. 'Looks like you've got one smart cookie here, taking the time and effort to stage all that.'

Sooner you than me, Mascot seemed to be saying. I've got my retirement house and my golf and my superannuation and *you* have a major headache.

Auhl said, 'Files are always suggestive. You sometimes get a sense of undercurrents. But they're also devoid of...flesh, so to speak. I was hoping to hear if you had any doubts or wild guesses you couldn't put down on paper.'

It was cop speaking to cop. They each knew what it was like to entertain private hunches about old cases, even those apparently done and dusted. There was always more to be said. There was always a sub-strand not followed because a newer, hotter case had come along or the budget was tight.

But Mascot grimaced. 'Wish I could help you. The kid didn't have a violent history, wasn't even in the system, but there were rumours. You know what these kids are like. Blameless and harmless until they start using and dealing, then they run up against harder types, so they become hard just to survive. They take risks, arm themselves. Become suspicious and paranoid, often with good reason. They also start looking for the big score—but so is everyone else, and they can't *all* win.' A shrug. 'Maybe that's what happened here.'

Auhl nodded. The police image of Shirlow was always going to differ from the sister's. 'Now that you know both kids were murdered, is there anything about the time or the place or the people that puzzled you back then but makes sense now? For example, one of them was the intended target, the other collateral damage?'

Mascot shook his head. 'We found *her* body, not his. Everything pointed to him killing her and then covering his tracks. As for why he wanted to kill her, I've already told you what we thought back then. Not that there appeared to be any logic to it. She seemed pretty harmless. Her parents were dead, she and her sister were taken in by someone—friends of the family—and she got itchy feet and ran off to be with her boyfriend. Eventually he killed her, end of story. But given that *he* was also murdered, I wouldn't know where to start. Who knows what drives people? Best thing you can do is look at whoever they both spent time with.'

Mascot seemed a little defensive, so Auhl changed tack. 'You spoke to his mother and sister?'

'The sister was just a kid, from memory. Lived with her mother in Cranbourne? Neither of them knew what the boy was up to.'

'According to a Cold Case follow-up five years ago, they moved to Brisbane,' Bugg said. 'Fresh start.'

'We treated them both with kid gloves.'

185

'I don't doubt it.'

Mascot's wife came in with a tray. Shortbread biscuits on a plate, coffee in a plunger. A small jug of steaming milk, a bowl of sugar, three mugs.

'Thanks, love,' Mascot said. She bobbed at him, at Auhl and Bugg, and left the room.

Mascot eyed the coffee plunger. Reached out a hand, withdrew it. 'Better give it another couple of minutes.'

He usually drinks instant, Auhl guessed, reaching for a biscuit. He was starving. 'Anything linking Peart or Shirlow to the nature reserve?'

'Remind me.'

'Mary Peart was found shot dead in a car owned by Shirlow, parked at a botanic reserve near Berwick.'

Mascot's face cleared. 'Right. Yes, I was always of the opinion she wasn't shot in the car. She was shot elsewhere and driven to where she was found—a location that's not often teeming with people, incidentally. The house she shared with Shirlow? We didn't see any indication it happened there, but then again, we didn't luminol the place either. We saw it had been cleaned and emptied and that's as far as we took it.'

He shook his head, self-critical. 'If I were you I'd test for blood. Might still be able to lift something from some of the surfaces.'

'Can't,' Auhl said. 'The owner pulled it down.'

Mascot shook his head again. He depressed the coffee plunger, poured, offered milk. Auhl took his and sipped. Lukewarm. Weak.

'How do you factor in the gun?'

Mascot frowned. 'What gun?'

'The murder weapon.'

'A mystery to me, pal.'

Of course: Mascot had been transferred to the Traffic Division soon after the murder. Apologising, Auhl told him how the gun was found. Handed him the report.

'Ah, prints,' said Mascot.

'But not in the system,' Auhl said.

Mascot looked up at him with a fatalistic cop look. 'Let's hope he fucks up sometime soon.' His lips pursed slightly. 'Or she, of course.'

BACK TO THE COLD Case office, where Helen Colfax called a briefing.

Auhl recounted the conversation with Mascot. 'If we work on the assumption they were both shot at the same time, then there's a good chance the house was the murder scene. Both victims lived there, Robert Shirlow was buried there. Set back on a quiet road, no one around to see or hear anything.'

'And it had been thoroughly cleaned,' Bugg said.

Claire Pascal said, 'But think of the time it all took. Shoot two people, drive one to a nature reserve *in the boyfriend's car*, get back to the house and dig a hole and pour concrete over it, clean up blood and brain matter, stage a disappearance.'

'You're thinking the killer had help?'

'Reckon they'd need it.'

'Which would indicate Shirlow pissed off an *organised* crew,' Josh Bugg said.

'Or someone with time and nerve and patience,' Auhl said.

'Speak to the Drug Squad,' Colfax said, 'see who was active in the area back then. Also, dig deeper into Shirlow and the girl-friend. Parents, friends, relatives, work colleagues. Work history. The murders mightn't have anything to do with drugs or organised outfits. An awful lot of elaborate effort was involved. I mean, why not simply shoot the pair of them in their house or wherever and leave them there?'

She sorted the Mary Peart crime-scene photos into a sequence: distant shots, mid-range, close-ups. 'Something about this bothers me. Look at the left hand.'

Mary Peart behind the wheel of her boyfriend's car at the nature reserve. Her torso blood-soaked. Her head resting against the steering wheel, staring sightlessly down at her knees. Hands in her lap.

'What about it?'

'The ring finger of her left hand looks broken. And look at the abrasions,' Colfax said.

They passed the photo around. Claire said, 'She was wearing a ring, someone ripped it off her finger.'

'You could be right,' Auhl agreed. 'Valuable?'

'Enough so that two people had to die? Hard to see.'

'So, opportunistic, maybe? She's dead, the killer sees she's wearing a nice ring...'

'Or it was special to someone. Like a family heirloom,' Claire said. 'What do we know about the Pearts?'

'Nothing much from the original investigation. I don't think Mascot's team looked too closely. The parents were dead, that's all I know.'

'Start from scratch,' Helen said. 'The family backgrounds of each kid.' She fished inside her shirt, pensively adjusted a bra strap. 'Track down Peart's sister, see what she has to say, talk to the people who took the girls in when their parents died. And so on.'

But before Auhl could get started, his phone rang.

29

NEVE'S MOTHER, sounding hysterical, launching straight in. 'What are they saying? We would *never* defy the court.'

'Hold on, start at the beginning,' soothed Auhl.

'I phoned your house and someone there gave me your number.'

'Please, Maureen,' Auhl said, 'tell me what's wrong.'

'The police were just here. And Lloyd and that lawyer of his.'

'What about?'

'We would never run off with Pia. We're her *grand*parents!'

Wouldn't be the first time, thought Auhl. 'Of course not. Just tell me what happened.'

She took a breath. At last some reason entered her voice. 'It seems Neve took Pia out of school and they think she's run off with her and we're involved.'

Auhl closed his eyes. 'Who contacted you first? The police?'

'Yes.'

'What exactly did they say?'

'They wanted to know where Neve and Pia were. They even searched the house.'

'Has Neve spoken to you?'

'No. And she's not answering her phone.'

'The police said she took Pia out of school?'

'They said she assaulted one of the teachers.'

Auhl was bewildered. A parent collecting a child from school wasn't uncommon. The teacher tried to stop it? Why?

Then Auhl thought he knew. Neve in Tiamo's this morning, texting Pia—she was alerting her daughter: *Get ready, I'm coming to fetch you.* And maybe, like an idiot, calling Lloyd? Telling him he'd never see his daughter again?

Lloyd—or his lawyer—would immediately have informed the school. That's why a teacher had confronted Neve. And Lloyd or his lawyer would have informed the police: *She's unstable: a danger to her daughter.*

Auhl muttered some unconvincing reassurances and ended the call.

Pascal touched his sleeve. 'Anything wrong?'

Auhl explained, she listened, at one point rubbing his back briskly, telling him not to worry. Except that she asked a cop question, one Auhl had already asked himself: 'She's not suicidal, is she?'

Auhl was truthful. 'I don't think so.' He looked squarely at her and added, 'But she's not thinking straight.'

He dialled Neve's number. Voicemail. Dialled Pia. Voicemail, her high little voice inviting him to leave a message.

Next, Chateau Auhl. Bec answered; he told her what had happened.

'Check their rooms, will you, sweetheart?'

Bec came back. 'It looks like a lot of their stuff is missing. Clothes, toiletries.'

'Okay, thanks. Let me know if she calls or shows up.' Auhl paused. 'Did she say anything to you?'

'I was at the shop all morning. I didn't see her.'

*

BACK IN THE OFFICE, he called Georgina Towne.

'This is bad, Alan,' she said.

'What's she looking at? Abduction?'

'Worst case scenario? Definitely. Look, can you put out some feelers? Friends, family, is she travelling by car? Has she bought tickets to Timbuktu? I'll do what I can, but a custodial sentence is definitely on the cards. Even if she's not prosecuted for abduction, the Family Court might want to lock her up on the grounds of non-compliance.'

'Let me know if she contacts you,' Auhl said.

But the line had gone dead. Auhl checked his phone for messages, sent another text, read reports dispiritedly.

Finally Neve called him, her voice and mood muted. 'Don't be cross with me. Did you get my note?'

'What note?'

'I left a note on the table.'

'Neve, I've been at work. Come back, will you, please? Everyone's worried. Your poor parents have been hassled, I'm probably next on the list. Let Georgina deal with it. She's a good lawyer, she'll fight for you. But the longer you stay away, the harder it's going to be.'

Auhl could hear traffic in the background, a truck grinding through the gears. A hill? A traffic light somewhere? 'Where the hell are you?'

'Somewhere.'

Auhl took a breath. 'Please, Neve, don't do anything stupid.'

She began to cry.

'Neve, come back, go home, go to your parents'. I'll join you later and we'll sort something out.'

'I'm sorry about the kitty money.'

The Neve and Pia Fanning Emergency Fund. 'That's okay.'

191

'And I promise to look after your car.'

She'd taken his car? Christ, it hadn't occurred to him to ask Bec to check. 'Neve, think about it.'

She shrieked the words. 'I have thought about it!'

'Don't do anything stupid. Just come back and we'll talk later.'

Claire was watching him, sympathetic, reading his panic and powerlessness.

'Please, Neve.'

'There's no alternative.'

'Neve.'

'I phoned Lloyd and gave him a real earful, and he said I was mad and he'd prove it in court and I'd never see her again.'

Auhl felt no satisfaction in knowing he'd guessed right. 'Neve, the police are involved.'

'Just a road trip, okay? I'll leave your car somewhere safe.'

When she was gone, he sat staring at his phone. Claire Pascal looked at him sadly. 'And?'

He told her. She shook her head. He called Neve again, sent texts: *Please go home* and *Don't be rash* and *We'll work something out.*

FOUR-FORTY-FIVE. Helen Colfax called him into her office.

'Close the door,' she said, before he was barely over the threshold. 'Sit,' when he'd closed it.

He sat. She watched him. 'Alan, I've just been on the receiving end of the mother of all tongue-lashings.'

'About?'

A rasping chill in her voice now. 'Don't piss me about, Alan, please.'

Auhl waited, clenched tight.

His boss said, 'Your friend with the custody woes…'

Auhl's mind raced. 'Okay…'

'Did you abet her? That's the question being asked. Did you put this woman up to snatching her kid?'

'Come on, boss.'

'She used your car.'

Feeling disloyal, Auhl said, 'I didn't give her permission to take it.'

Colfax leaned over the desk, her upper body inclined towards him, her shoulders straining a collarless pink striped shirt. 'So, theft of a car, child abduction and assault.' She sat back, folded her arms. 'Suicidal?'

'I just spoke to her. She didn't sound it. I don't think she's suicidal.'

Colfax exploded. 'Christ, Alan, where is she? Did you tell her to come in?'

'Yes, I told her. And I have no idea where she is.'

She shook her head, collapsed against her seat back again. 'The fact remains you're in the shit, Alan. She was living in your house— were you sleeping with her?'

'Fuck off.'

'She was living in your house and your car was used and you attended her court appearances and apparently you and she fetched the daughter from her husband's house without permission recently.'

'Oh for God's sake,' snarled Auhl.

'That's how it's going down, you know that.' Colfax checked her watch. 'Professional Standards want a word with you in five. They may or may not suspend you, who knows. If they don't, I want you working Slab Man, twenty-four seven. No more interruptions.'

'Boss.'

A PROFESSIONAL STANDARDS officer named Inger Reed grilled Auhl for half an hour. Feeling obscurely ashamed, as though he were saving his own skin and throwing Neve to the wolves, he showed Reed the texts he'd sent since lunchtime. 'It all came as a shock to me.'

Reed, stony-faced, let him fret and babble for some time, until a transfiguring smile lit up her face. 'Don't get your knickers in a twist. Mrs Fanning has already admitted she took your car without your knowledge.'

So you thought you'd have some fun at my expense, thought Auhl. 'You've got her? She's under arrest?'

Reed shook her head. 'She called to explain.'

'Called the police?'

'Yes.'

'When?'

'After the disturbance at the school.'

'But she's still out there somewhere?'

'I was hoping *you* might tell me where she is.'

'I have no idea. Look, I don't want her charged with car theft.'

'She's in enough trouble,' agreed Reed. 'But your insurance company might not be so understanding.'

'What happened?'

'Briefly, she side-swiped a teacher's car.' Held up her hand: 'Minor damage, no one hurt. But how well do you know her? Is she suicidal?'

Auhl shifted uncomfortably. 'Everyone keeps asking me that. I wouldn't say so.'

Reed changed tack. 'I put it to you that you were in a relationship with Mrs Fanning. Do you have anything to say in regard to that matter?'

Fuck's sake, he thought. 'It's not true.'

'You were seen attending Family Court in support of Mrs Fanning.'

Information that probably came from the husband or his lawyer, thought Auhl. 'Nothing should be read into that. I was there as a friend.'

They stared at each other, Reed expressionless, Auhl trying to match her. Then Reed said, 'What's it like, coming back after retirement? Finding yourself on the back foot?'

'Do I have anything to say in regard to that matter?' asked Auhl. 'No.'

Reed gave him a crooked, humourless grin.

'You need to be looking at the husband,' Auhl said.

'Not me, I'm Professional Standards,' Reed said.

AUHL RETURNED TO his desk, finding the others gone for the day. Claire had left a note: friends were taking her to dinner, she'd be late. So Auhl dragged himself home, and checked Doss Down before doing anything else. The bed was stripped, sheets and pillow cases in a neat pile. The wardrobe and drawers mostly empty. No luggage. Checked the garage: no car. Checked the kitty: no money.

He prepared and ate a pesto desultorily, and was slurping wine, chasing a pasta spiral up the side of his bowl, when he noticed the envelope. It was at the end of the table, amid the permanent nether-world of bills, receipts, flyers and takeout menus. Pink, unstamped, addressed to him.

Perhaps it had been propped against the radio and one of the tenants had knocked it down, tossed it with the stuff Auhl rarely got around to sorting. He reached for it and, recognising Neve Fanning's handwriting, her broad, immature loops, felt a return of his dread.

'Dear Alan,' she had written.

> You are the kindest, most supportive man I have ever known.
> It's been a privilege. You stood by me. You gave me hope.
> You were there for me. But now I have to do the rest alone. I
> wish you happiness. You deserve to find someone. You need
> to break out on your own. With the deepest love and regard,
> Neve.

She's giving me relationship advice? thought Auhl.
Unbelievable.

30

THURSDAY MORNING, Auhl breakfasting glumly in the backyard. Shafts of early sunlight striped the wrought iron table and chairs, showing up dust and old winter mould. Bees in the jasmine that choked the back fence. The pavers leading from kitchen door to alleyway gate were green, cracked. Someone had thrown a Hungry Jack's bag over the fence. And the certain knowledge that Lloyd Fanning would be given sole custody of his daughter, and his wife would go to jail.

Claire Pascal stepped from the house and blinked at the sun. 'Christ,' she muttered.

Marginally cheered, Auhl said sweetly, 'Hard night?'

'Could say that.'

She sat with him in the sun, not fully awake. She reached down for Cynthia, who wriggled to the ground, tail twitching. 'All right, suit yourself, cat.' She gave herself a little shake. 'Anything from Neve or Pia?'

Auhl shook his head.

More glum silence. They stared at nothing.

Claire said, 'Alan?'

A tone in her voice. Auhl said, 'You're going to move back in with your husband.'

'How did you know? Anyway, yes. My friends think I'm mad.'

'If it's worth trying, it's worth trying.'

'But if the timing's bad, what with the business with Neve and Pia…'

'I'm fine,' Auhl said.

'I'll stay till the weekend, if that's okay.'

With the back door open, they both heard pounding at the front door. The knocker rapping like hailstones.

It was an official kind of knock; Auhl felt it in his bones. *They want me for Neill.*

'Stay there.'

He walked softly along the hallway to his room and peeked around the edge of the curtain. A police car and an unmarked, double-parked outside the house. Two bored uniforms on the footpath. Two suits waiting for someone to answer the knock.

He rejoined Claire, who asked, 'They looking for Neve?'

Of course. That was the logical explanation. The pounding started again. 'Wish me luck.'

He trotted down the hallway again, opened the front door. 'Sorry, I was in the kitchen. Can I help you?'

A heavyset detective, the other the size of a jockey, and they looked Auhl up and down: Auhl in shorts and a sweaty T-shirt, yet to shower and shave. The little one said: 'You are?'

'I know who I am. Who are you and what do you want?'

'Are you Alan Auhl?' the stocky one said.

'Yes.'

'Does a Mrs Neve Fanning live here?'

'Yes, but she's not—'

The jockey waved a paper in Auhl's face. 'We have a warrant to search these premises, so if you'll—'

Auhl blocked him. 'Don't get in my face, okay? If you've done your homework you'll know I'm also a police member. A bit of fucking respect.'

'Yeah, yeah, keep your shirt on,' the stocky one said.

'Let's start again. Tell me why you wish to search my house.'

'We have reason to believe that Mrs Neve Fanning and her daughter Pia are hiding on these premises. All right? That respectful enough for you?'

The little one was Fenwick, the stocky one Logan, and they were tired, about to come off nightshift and disinclined to give favours. But Logan, seeing Auhl's bewilderment, unbent sufficiently to explain.

'We know about the court case. We know she pinched your car. But we do have to cover all bases.'

'In case I'm hiding mother and daughter under the bed.'

'Exactly.'

'Any sign of my car? Numberplate recognition?'

'It went out on the Tullamarine Freeway yesterday afternoon. Heading for Sydney? Who knows. The thing is, last night it came back, then disappeared.'

'Huh.'

'So we do need to search these premises. Let us have a quick squiz and we'll be out of your hair.'

'I want to examine the warrant.'

Logan handed it to Auhl. 'Knock yourself out.'

Auhl looked and said, 'I'm challenging this. Tenants live here. They have their own rooms or suites of rooms and lead lives independent of me and the other tenants. You are not searching their rooms. If you're smart, you won't even wake them. If you give me a hard time on this, I'm getting in a lawyer and I'll tie you up in front of a bad-tempered magistrate until way past your knock-off time.'

'Fucksake,' breathed Fenwick.

But Logan said, 'Have it your way, hot shot. So where can we look?'

'The public areas, like the kitchen, laundry, sitting room. My room if you like. Mrs Fanning's room. The yard, the garage.'

'Jesus Christ.'

They bustled in and halted when they saw Claire. 'And you are?'

'A work colleague who happens to rent a room here,' Claire said.

'I bet.'

Claire curled her lip but let it go. She stood at the door of the spare room and gestured. 'Why don't you two sweethearts start here, so I can get ready for work?'

Auhl and Claire watched from the doorway. Logan peered under Claire's bed, Fenwick into the wardrobe. Auhl said: 'You do know you look ridiculous.'

'Part and parcel, mate.' Logan was unabashed.

He re-entered the hallway with Fenwick. Leaned down and reached a hand to Cynthia, who arched her back instantly, all claws and bared teeth. *Fuck.*

'Good girl,' Claire said, giving both men a winning smile.

Then out into the garden and the morning dew and shadows. Auhl watched them enter the car shed, return to the yard. 'See? No car. They're not here. Mrs Fanning called me yesterday to apologise, but wouldn't say where she was.'

'If you say so.'

'Do you have an arrest warrant for Mrs Fanning?'

Logan, about to re-enter the house, said, 'Are you her lawyer now?'

Auhl didn't answer that. 'Claire and I need to get to work.'

'Mate, I need to get to bed, but we don't always get what we want.'

'Wouldn't have picked you for a Stones fan.'

'Showing your age, mate,' Logan said, pushing through to the kitchen again.

199

31

AUHL POKED HIS head into Helen Colfax's office. 'Am I still gainfully employed?'

The boss patted her pockets absently, poked around in her bag, opened and closed her top drawer. She looked at Auhl in defeat. 'Why wouldn't you be?'

'Just checking.'

She waved him off. 'Carmen Shirlow's coming in mid-morning. Until then, go and solve crimes.'

AT TEN-THIRTY CARMEN Shirlow was shown into one of the victim suites.

She was late twenties, a gaunt woman with black hair, torn jeans and a flight of tiny blue tattooed birds climbing her neck from within her T-shirt. Chewed nails—everything about her looked chewed. Jittery. Uncomfortable about being in a police station. But her eyes were clear, her teeth healthy. She was careful and precise with her words.

'I found some more photos.'

Digging around in a grubby daypack, she produced several, including the ones she'd emailed.

'See? It's him.' She flashed a look at each of them. 'You can check my DNA if you like, I don't mind.'

'We will,' smiled Helen. 'Now, you said the other day your brother wasn't perfect. What did you mean?'

Carmen wriggled around as if that would help her gild the lily. 'He wasn't a junkie. But he did do a bit of dealing.'

'You two were close?'

'Our dad ran off and Mum, well, she didn't cope all that well, so it was me and Rob looking out for each other.'

'Were you living with him at the time he disappeared?'

'No. I was living with Mum. Someone had to.'

'Where was that?'

'Cranbourne.'

'So not all that far from where your brother was living.'

She looked at them defiantly. 'Where he was *living with Mary*, don't you mean? Elephant in the room?'

Auhl gave her a small wry smile. 'Mary Peart.'

'Yes.'

'How well did you know her?'

'A bit. I used to visit.'

She was still defiant, waiting for them to get to it. Colfax obliged. 'Is there anything you can tell us about Mary's murder, or Robert's involvement in it?'

The defiance evaporated. 'Look, I was still in Year 11. I only visited them two or three times.'

'To be clear: they were living together?'

'Yes.'

'In an old house on a rural block in Pearcedale?'

'Yes.'

'The theory back then was Robert killed Mary on September the ninth and did a runner, maybe somewhere overseas.'

Carmen Shirlow shrugged. 'I don't believe that.'

'If as you say the man under the slab is your brother, we need to ascertain if he was murdered by the same person who murdered Mary, and at the same time.'

Another shrug. 'Okay, that seems reasonable.'

Seemed reasonable to Auhl, too. 'Can you think who might have wanted them both dead?'

'Maybe Mary had an ex-boyfriend? Like I said, I was just a kid, still at home, not part of Rob's life. He did a bit of dealing and a bit of nicking stuff, so maybe he rubbed someone up the wrong way.'

'*Did* Mary have an ex-boyfriend?'

'I don't know, do I?' Carmen wrapped her thin arms across her chest, clutched her shoulders. 'Far as I was concerned, Rob would never, ever have hurt Mary. They were mad about each other. I knew something bad had happened to him. I tried telling the police that but no one listened.'

Claire said, 'You didn't, in the corner of your mind, wonder if Robert had maybe shot Mary and gone into hiding?'

She squirmed. 'Maybe a tiny bit. I mean, the cops wouldn't leave me and Mum alone. Where's Rob? Did you help Rob? Did you deal drugs for him? Go easy on yourself and tell us where Rob is. That kind of thing. So yeah, I had a couple of doubts. Then I'd just think: no, not possible.'

Helen said, 'Did you ever see Robert or Mary with other people?'

'At their house? No.'

'Did they ever talk about the other people in their lives?'

'Mary talked about her sister a couple of times. Can't remember her name…Maybe Rachel? Or Ruth. Anyway they were brought up strict and Mary ran off when she met Rob.'

'And Rob? Did he mention anybody, friends, people he worked with?'

'No. Him and Mary were really happy and he wasn't doing

anything dodgy with her around. All he did was fix up the house in between odd jobs for people.'

Auhl leaned forward, frowning. 'The old house in Pearcedale?'

Carmen gave him a haven't-you-been-listening look. 'Yes. It was a bit of a wreck.'

'What kind of doing up?'

'Plastering over holes in the walls, new guttering, replacing floorboards, painting, that kind of thing. He was good with his hands. Do anything. Odd jobs, maintenance, gardening, house-painting, a bit of carpentry.'

'That was his job at the time? Was he employed by a firm, or self-employed?'

'Self-employed.'

Auhl thought he'd taken that line of questioning as far as it would go. 'Is there anything else you can tell us about Mary Peart?'

'Nope. Strict background, worried about her sister.'

The police reports were also sketchy. Mary Peart's place and date of birth, the name of the family who'd taken in the sisters when their parents died, a brief employment history. At the time of her death, Mary Peart had been working as a veterinary assistant in Cranbourne.

'What if I'm next?' Carmen said.

They all blinked. 'Next?' asked Josh.

'Yeah, like, I kind of went underground after it happened. It was too much, you know? Mary. Rob. The police on my back. This guy hassling me. I got scared. Me and Mum cleared out.'

Auhl said, 'What guy? Police?'

'Not police. An older guy. Sort of like a businessman but not, you know? Like well dressed and that, but…scary, wore these dark glasses and demanded to know was I part of it? Where was the rest? Questions like that.'

'The rest of what?'

'I don't know, do I? Whatever Rob and Mary were up to, I

203

suppose. Drugs. Nothing to do with me and I told him that.'

'Did he actually mention drugs?'

A shrug. 'No.'

'Did he give you his name?'

'Nope.'

'And you're sure he wasn't police.'

'I just don't know, all right? I wasn't part of anything, I was trying to get through Year 11, trying to keep Mum from fucking up her life.' She shot them a look. 'She was an alcoholic. Anyway, we cleared out to Queensland. Grandma and Grandpa helped us.' She paused. 'They're all dead now, there's only me. But no way am I coming back here to live. I feel safe up north. I can keep my head down.'

'Have there been any recent attempts to contact you? This so-called businessman, for example?'

'No. Anyway, I made it quite clear to him I didn't know what he was talking about, but I didn't want to take any chances, so we went up to Cairns.'

'Wise move,' Helen said, reaching out to touch a jittery forearm. 'Let's wrap this up, shall we? Josh, could you arrange a hotel for Ms Shirlow? Carmen, we need you to stay in town for a few days, is that all right? The police will pay.'

'A hotel? Cool.'

AUHL, RETURNING TO the Cold Case office with Claire Pascal, found the man named Logan waiting in the corridor. 'Things are just getting better and better for you, mate.'

The tone was cocky but the face oddly sympathetic, and Claire hesitated. 'Alan?'

He waved her on. 'You go, don't wait for me.'

She opened the door, glancing back once over her shoulder at the two men, then disappeared inside. Auhl turned to Logan. 'I thought you were finished for the day.'

'No rest for the wicked,' Logan said. 'Your car's been found.'

Auhl waited. When Logan didn't elaborate, he said, 'My car's been found, but neither Mrs Fanning nor her daughter was in it, is that what you're saying?'

'Correct. They'd have been burnt to a crisp if they *had* been in it, mind you.'

Auhl closed and opened his eyes. 'She torched it?'

'Can we go somewhere more comfortable?'

Auhl took Logan upstairs to the tearoom along the corridor from the Arson Squad. Sat at the stained Laminex table and pushed out a chair with his foot. 'Sit.'

When Logan was sitting, Auhl said flatly, 'Just get it over with.'

'As you know, we tracked your car north on the Hume, then back to the city several hours later. Anyway, we took a closer look at the freeway camera images. A couple of young guys in the front, no one in the back.' Logan shook his head commiseratively. 'Then about an hour ago we found it torched in Footscray.'

'It wasn't a car you'd bother taking to a chop shop,' Auhl said, trying for humour to stave off what was still to come.

Logan acknowledged it with a brief, fatigued grimace. 'Anyway, we were monitoring Mrs Fanning's Visa card, and she rented a Hyundai from Budget in Albury–Wodonga. We're presuming that's where she left your car, maybe with the keys in the ignition.'

'She kept going?'

Logan shook his head. 'The opposite. She drove all the way back here, through the city and down to Geelong.'

Auhl was hopeful. 'To her parents'?'

'To her husband's.'

'Mate, don't string it out.'

Logan said, 'It seems mother and daughter trashed the place. Threw paint over the carpets, left taps running into plugged sinks and the bathtub, smashed windows.'

Auhl was holding himself tightly.

Logan took a breath. 'And that's all I know so far.' He gave Auhl a sharp look. 'You need to tell her to give herself up.'

Auhl got to his feet and stood, irresolute. A civilian clerk hurried in with an armful of folders, looking for someone. Glanced at the two men oddly but said nothing and went out again. Auhl said, 'I'm not in contact with her.'

'You need to tell us where she is.'

Auhl strode away. 'I'm not in contact with her.'

CLAIRE PASCAL WAS pretending to read files when he returned. She took one look at him and got to her feet.

'Are you all right?'

Auhl explained. She wrapped him in a brief hug. 'What a shitty situation.'

'Out of my hands now,' Auhl said, wondering if that were true.

He buried himself in work, phone calls, internet searches.

And eventually learned that the family who'd taken in Mary Peart and her sister was not just any old family.

32

'MASCOT AND HIS team—bad case of tunnel vision,' said Auhl.

Friday morning, and he was in the passenger seat, his lap piled with Google printouts and Rhys Mascot's files, Helen Colfax behind the wheel, the traffic slow-moving now that they'd left the M1 and were heading along Wellington Road. Destination, the hill town of Emerald.

'Tunnel vision…' Helen Colfax said encouragingly.

Auhl lifted a thin file. 'With Robert Shirlow in the frame, there was barely any follow-up on the sister or the family that took the girls in. Nothing about them being fundamentalist crackpots.'

When Colfax stopped for a red light, he slid a photo under her nose. 'Warren Hince, leader of the Assemblies of Jehovah International.'

Printed from a news website, the photograph showed a portly man in a dark suit, his beaming, well-fed face crowned with a proud mane of swept-back white hair. He was shaking hands with a former Liberal prime minister, also beaming.

'Look who he's with,' Colfax said.

'Must have been an election on,' Auhl said.

'Anything for a vote,' Colfax agreed. The light changed, she accelerated smoothly away. 'What else?'

Auhl continued. The AJI was small, secretive, homophobic, misogynistic and well heeled. First established in Scotland—by Hince—in 1974, offshoots following in Germany, the USA, New Zealand and Australia. 'Hervey Bay in the mid-nineteen eighties,' Auhl said, 'then the Gold Coast, Byron Bay, Darwin, the Adelaide Hills, the Blue Mountains and finally Emerald.'

Where Hince now lived with his wife and their son. Auhl had checked out the estate on Google Earth: several hectares in size, with a sizeable main residence and several smaller buildings set amid pines and gum trees on a slope leading to a pond fed by a small creek. Other images confirmed Warren Hince's status: presiding over a baptism in that same pond; stepping out of a black Mercedes; boarding a small plane emblazoned *Assemblies*.

'Not short of a dollar,' Auhl said. 'Donations, plus many of the flock run successful businesses. Hince and his family have built a few small-scale housing developments and shopping centres.'

He went on. The church had flown under the radar for many years, enjoying its tax-exempt status, before cracks began to appear. Some members left the fold and began to speak out. A few returned, having found the outside world hard and bewildering. Those who did not were excommunicated. The few who agreed to be interviewed told reporters that their 'sins' had ranged from buying a computer, or some other trapping of a worldly society, to being 'immoral', encouraging their children to get an education, and questioning the elders.

'You could say there was quite a bit to question,' Auhl said.

Such as church elders arranging marriages. Urging husbands to beat disobedient wives. Exploiting the authority of their position to sexually abuse the children of parishioners. Their website opposed gay marriage, listed 'Crimes by Muslims' and claimed the

Black Sunday bushfires were God's punishment for the country's lax abortion laws.

Helen snorted, shook her head.

'Things really came unstuck for Hince when he urged his congregation to donate money to an anti-Islamic political party—which he happened to head,' Auhl said. 'Labor politicians finally got off their arses and argued the church was not a charity, and therefore its tax-exempt status should be revoked. Hince denied it, of course, and for a while no one did anything.'

'Friends in high places.'

'Friends like prime ministers,' Auhl said. 'And meanwhile there was the child sex abuse Royal Commission. As soon as that started to build up steam, Warren stepped down and handed the reins to his son.'

'Because he was named?'

'Not named but…implicated.'

They'd reached another red light. This time Auhl handed Helen a Hince family photograph. Warren, his son Adam, his wife Judith. Adam was a tall, stocky, bull-headed young man, not yet portly like his father but heading that way. Soft-looking; not commanding. And he stood glued to his mother's flank, as though cringing from his father.

'How old was the son in 2009?'

'Twenty-one.'

Colfax nodded and Auhl knew what she was thinking: Adam Hince was in the frame. He'd been a young man, not a child, when Mary Peart died.

'And the Royal Commission?'

'Father and son were asked to appear in late 2016,' Auhl said. 'They didn't, in the end. No witnesses, only vague allegations. Adam claimed he knew nothing about the actions of the elders and Warren was excused on the grounds he has dementia.'

Auhl found another printout, a report from the *Herald Sun*.

'Meanwhile the church could be struggling financially. Last year their charity status was revoked, meaning they've been hit with hefty tax-concession repayments.'

'That's the big picture. What about the smaller picture? Would these people murder someone who left the fold?'

Auhl thought about it. 'Mary Peart wasn't the only one who left. And are we asking if they murdered Robert because he lured her away? That seems…extravagant.'

'Carmen Shirlow said an older man hassled her and demanded to know where something was. Are we thinking it was Warren Hince?'

Auhl nodded. 'Good question. We need to show her his photograph.'

THE ROAD WOUND INTO the hills. Helen Colfax said, 'Dementia. Real or pretence?'

'Apparently real,' Auhl said, but thought back to a news clip he'd found yesterday, Warren Hince in a wheelchair outside the Royal Commission, his son pushing it. The old man's face vacant, almost drooling; then a nasty couple of seconds when a reporter shoved a microphone in his face and his expression sharpened to a fleeting, hard malice.

'If the old man's senile, we may not get much out of anyone,' Colfax said.

'There's Mary Peart's sister.'

'If she's still there.'

'The wife, the son.'

'Who will be heavily invested in protecting the old patriarch,' Helen said.

'A patriarch who runs a building firm,' Auhl said.

'Digging a grave, pouring a slab, patching and painting over bullet holes and bloodstains?' She shrugged. 'Anyone with DIY skills can do those sorts of things.'

They rode in silence until Helen said, 'Any word from Mrs Fanning or her daughter?'

How much did she know? Auhl said, 'I'm not in contact,' and told her what Logan had told him.

'And the situation with Claire?'

Startled, Auhl waited a beat. 'She's fine.' He paused, wound his window down a crack. 'She's been staying at my place.'

'I know,' Colfax said with a hard edge. 'That's why I asked.'

'She's going back to her husband sometime on the weekend,' said Auhl, also with an edge to his voice. 'And not that it's anyone's business, but I am not involved with Claire or Neve. I'm a *friend*.'

'Don't be naive. Sooner or later some tabloid hack is going to start sniffing around.'

Auhl knew she was right. 'Boss.'

'You need to do what I do, keep the public and the private at arm's length.'

Don't get involved, in other words. Auhl, realising he knew little about his boss's life outside the job, said, 'What does your...your partner do?'

Colfax laughed. 'My *husband* is a photographer for the local newspaper. No crime scenes, just garden fetes and netball finals and shopkeepers. My son plays football, my daughter thumps around in a pink tutu on Saturday mornings. A few hundred dollars to the Royal Children's each year and my conscience is clear.'

Auhl wondered if he quite liked his boss. 'Uh huh.'

'All I'm saying is keep your nose clean.'

'Don't bring the force into disrepute.'

'Something like that.'

Google Maps announced they'd arrived at their destination.

EXPECTING A WALLED compound shut away from the world in miserable secrecy, Auhl and Colfax found a generic outer-suburban McMansion with a small builders truck and a glossy black Ford

Territory parked in the driveway. The former was loaded with ladders, toolboxes and polythene pipes and had *W. and A. Hince Builders* painted on the doors; the latter had a bumper sticker: *What would Jesus do?* To one side was a low hedge and a wooden gate signposted *Assemblies of Jehovah International*, leading to a track that wound downslope through a cluster of small buildings— chapels? meeting rooms?—to the baptism pond Auhl had seen on Google.

They were expected—Colfax hadn't wanted to cold call on a church—and Adam Hince answered their knock. Barely thirty but wearing his years badly: tall and running to fat. Behind the eager greetings and handshakes, Auhl sensed a small, shy boy trapped inside a bewilderingly large and somewhat alien body.

'Come in, come in,' Hince said.

He filled out grey suit pants, a white shirt and black shoes; the leather soles slapped as he led them along a hallway to a plain sitting room with a dining alcove at the far end. No TV, no flowers, no books or magazines apart from a bible on a wooden stand. Off-white walls, unfussy leather sofa and armchairs, a handful of photographs on a mantel: Warren Hince with the prime minister, Warren Hince with his wife and son, Warren Hince with eyes closed and hand raised in an unadorned chapel.

Warren himself was in the room, slumped at one end of the sofa beside his wife, a walking stick resting against his knee. He gave the detectives a dazed, open-mouthed, wondering look. Some of his old weight had been stripped away by time and illness.

Judith Hince rose to greet them, a slender, harried woman wearing a long navy skirt with a lighter blue cardigan over a white top. An unremarkable face, a hint of worry, the fingers of one hand twisting a large ring on her other hand. Were the women of this church allowed to wear jewellery? Auhl wondered. This one was a chunk of milky opal set among small diamonds—probably valuable, but unexpectedly garish.

Behind the sofa, in a patch of shadows, hovered a third person. She was mid-twenties but as full of elbows, knees, ankles and wrist bones as a teenager in full growth-spurt. Tall, with a long, thin neck, and dressed, like Judith, in a plain skirt and top. No rings, earrings or bracelets. Thick black shoulder-length hair, pale skin, eyes bruised by fatigue or anxiety. The hair, the skin, the eyes—a natural goth but without the clothing and makeup.

Auhl snorted to himself. She probably didn't know what a goth was.

She looked tense, jaw clenching, nails bitten to the quick. He could see from the vibration of her torso that one leg was jiggling.

'Tea? Coffee?' asked Adam Hince. 'Ruth, please put the kettle on.'

The younger woman slipped silently from the room. Helen Colfax said, 'Ruth, as in Mary's sister?'

'Mary's sister, yes.'

'We'll wait till she comes back.'

'She doesn't really know anything,' Judith Hince said, her voice an odd, sultry rasp.

'Even so,' Auhl said.

Colfax crossed the dark grey carpet and stuck her hand out to Warren Hince. Auhl knew what she was doing—she was taking charge of the room. 'Mr Hince? My colleague and I are here to talk about Mary.'

His voice came in a weak croak. 'Who?'

'He doesn't remember her,' Judith said, with an apologetic wince. 'Or rather, his memory comes and goes.'

'It's up to me now,' Adam said. 'I keep the flame burning.'

Auhl said, 'With your mother's help?'

Judith placed her hand at her throat in dismay. 'Goodness, no. I'm directed in God's purpose through Adam.'

Nice for Adam, Auhl thought. Or not.

Presently Ruth re-entered the room carrying a large tray with

213

tea things and a jar of instant coffee. She placed it on a glass-topped coffee table and stood back.

'Join us, please, Ruth,' Helen said. 'We're here to talk about your sister.'

Ruth ducked her head shyly. With an asking-permission glance at Adam she pulled a straight-backed chair from the dining table and placed it behind the sofa. Auhl was about to ask her to join the rough circle of chairs, but then decided this was a girl who knew her place. She'd be less useful to them if she felt uncomfortable.

Colfax began. Addressing Judith, she said, 'Your family kindly took in Mary and Ruth on the death of their parents?'

'They were dead to us, yes. We did our Christian duty by the girls.'

With a frown at the syntax, Colfax said, 'And a few years later Mary formed an attachment with a young man named Robert Shirlow?'

It was Adam who answered. 'Robert did some odd jobs for us on various building sites and in the grounds of our church.' He gestured to the buildings and parkland slope outside. 'The devil was strong in him, I fear, and soon strong in Mary.'

Auhl watched Ruth for a reaction. Nothing. She stared at her lap. He swung his gaze onto Adam. 'Would you care to elaborate? The devil was in her?'

'She began to question our faith, our beliefs. She wore indecent clothes. She became disruptive.'

Colfax said, 'The girls lived here in the house? I saw what looked to be cabin accommodation in among your other buildings.'

'They lived here with us, yes.'

'Was Robert allowed into the house?'

Judith said, 'Absolutely not.'

Ruth was sinking deeper into her chair. Auhl said, 'Did everyone feel that way about Mary? You all argued with her?'

'We told her our position,' Adam said, 'but ultimately she was not able to overcome her earthly concerns, and she ran away with Mr Shirlow.'

'Were you friends with him, Mr Hince?'

Adam said stiffly, 'We were the same age but certainly not friends. He was a casual employee.'

'You are aware that Robert and Mary shacked up together?' Auhl said harshly. 'In an old farmhouse near Pearcedale?'

'We may not be entirely *of* the modern world and its madness,' Adam Hince said, 'but nor are we ignorant. I for one was well aware of the nature of Mary and Robert's cohabitation.'

Did any thirty-year-old anywhere speak like this weirdo? wondered Auhl. 'Yes, but did you visit them? Try to get Mary to return? Try to bring Robert into the fold?'

'We did not. To have done so would have been to battle hard with the devil. Mary and Robert were not inclined to share in God's grace with us, nor ready to hear God's call.'

Colfax said, 'Ruth, did you visit your sister?'

Ruth gave Adam a frightened glance and received a pinched nod. She said in a hesitant whisper, 'No.'

'May I ask why not?'

Judith said, 'Mary was quite wilful and disruptive. It was difficult for Ruth to withstand her, so we thought it best if she did not visit.'

Colfax cocked her head. 'Ruth?'

As if spotlights were trained on her, Ruth shrank and gave a tiny nod. 'I thought going to see Mary wasn't the right thing to do.'

Adam and Judith beamed at her. Auhl realised they'd been worried what she might say. Glancing from one to the other he said, 'Did Robert and Mary live alone?'

'As I understand it,' Adam said.

'And when Robert worked here prior to that, did he ever have friends with him? Was he ever visited by friends?'

'Certainly not.'

'And Mary, what about her friends?'

'Mary's friends were here,' Judith said, 'among our congregants.'

Her son added, 'But Robert was somewhat wild. He might well have associated with the wrong people.'

'You didn't see anyone else at the old house?'

'As I think I told you, Acting Sergeant Auhl, we did not visit.'

Helen Colfax cut in, almost tauntingly: 'Robert making a cosy little love nest for himself and Mary, it must have been a slap in the face for you all.'

'It's not fair to talk about them like that,' said Ruth suddenly, her voice soft but with some steel in it. 'They were renovating the house for the owner.'

'So you *did* visit them, Ruth?'

But the room's atmosphere had shifted. Ruth shook her head, sank in her chair.

'What about Mr Hince?' Colfax said. 'Surely he dropped in on Mary to see that she was all right? Or you did, Judith? Or Adam?'

Judith said, 'What Mary and Robert did together was no longer any of our concern. I wish you would listen.'

WHEN ALL THEIR questions were exhausted and nothing new had been learnt, Auhl and Colfax stood ready to leave. The old man had said nothing, and remained seated as they all moved to the hallway door.

Auhl held back a little and let his hand brush Ruth Peart's. She jumped to feel the stiff edge of his business card, and for a moment he thought she'd baulk, but then her fingers closed on the card and it was whisked into a pocket.

At the front door Adam said, as though to be polite, 'Would you care to worship with us for half an hour?'

Colfax said briskly, 'Sorry, we'll be battling Friday traffic as it is.'

Hince turned to Auhl. 'And you, Mr Auhl? Are you ready to hear God's call?'

'I'm always hearing calls, but they're not the kind anyone else wants to hear. Besides, I do my best work on my feet, not my knees.'

Hince gave him a huge satisfied smile and wagged a finger. 'Ah, but it's hard to stumble when you're on your knees.'

Auhl said, 'If I pull that finger, will you toot?'

33

'BLACK MARK FOR antagonising the public, Acting Sergeant Auhl,' said Colfax in the car.

But there was humour in her voice. Late Friday morning, the traffic building up, as if everyone was headed somewhere for lunch.

'So,' she went on, 'was it the father or the son?'

Auhl shrugged. 'Or both. The thing is, why the delay? Those kids ran off in May. They weren't shot till September.'

'Maybe the need for punishment built up over time.'

'You think that's what it was, punishment?'

'Punish Mary for leaving the church and the boyfriend for luring her away,' Colfax said. 'Unless something else set off the killings, like sexual jealousy.'

Auhl mused on it. 'We have the gun, we have the prints. At the very least we should see if they match anyone.'

'Have to arrest them first—unless you smuggled out a teacup just now? They'll surround themselves with lawyers, who'll argue Warren is gaga and the son was just a kid at the time.'

Auhl muttered his disappointment. 'Pity we weren't able

to speak to each of them alone. I'd like to pin down times and movements. Did they know the actual address where Mary was living? Did Ruth visit? Was someone from the church watching the house, told them when to strike?'

'Or, you know, the Hinces are blameless.'

They fell into silence until Helen Colfax said, 'We need to know if Carmen Shirlow can ID Hince.'

'I can do that now,' Auhl said. He snapped the clearest file shot of Warren Hince with his phone and texted it to Shirlow. The reply came within a couple of minutes. *Nothing like him.*

'Worth a shot,' Colfax sighed.

THEY'D RETURNED THE unmarked car and were riding the elevator when Auhl's phone rang. A landline number he didn't recognise.

He picked up, and a whispery voice said, 'You gave me your card.'

The doors opening, Auhl signalled to Colfax to follow him to a quiet corner of the corridor, mouthing: *Ruth Peart.* Leaning against the wall he said, 'Ruth, I understand if you can't talk now, or not for long, but is there a chance you can get away later?'

She said in a rush, 'Not today. Tomorrow morning.'

'Is there any chance you can come to us? We can send a car for you, if you like.'

'No! No time. I can get away for half an hour when I do the shopping.'

'Okay, maybe we can meet in your bakery or the—'

'No! The baker's an elder in our church. Ten-thirty in the Catholic op shop behind the Coles car park.' With a derisive snort she added, 'None of our congregants would dream of going in there.'

AUHL SPENT THE REMAINDER of the day digging deeper into the Assemblies of Jehovah. He tried calling Neve and Pia, but their phones were apparently off. Then at knock-off time, as he was leaving with Claire Pascal, Logan bailed him up in the foyer.

'A word?'

Logan looked deeply fatigued. Still barrelly and stolid, but now a flicker of sadness showed on his heavy features.

'Bad news,' said Auhl flatly.

'You could say that.'

Logan glanced at Claire, who said mulishly, 'I'm staying.'

Logan shrugged. 'Suit yourself.'

Auhl said, 'Let's do this in the tearoom.'

'I won't, I need to crash, been racing around all day.'

Auhl folded his arms. 'Okay, what happened?'

'Long story short, Mrs Fanning ran her rental car into a tree on a back road near Mount Gambier and she's in a coma.'

Auhl realised he was gaping. He felt Claire Pascal grab the crook of his arm. 'What about Pia? Was she in the car?'

'She was. A bit knocked about, broken leg, broken ribs; otherwise okay. They were both airlifted to Adelaide, different hospitals.'

Claire's fingers were a clamp on Auhl's arm. 'Is anyone with them?'

'Mrs Fanning's parents are on their way over,' Logan said. Then he shook his head. 'Meanwhile I've got the husband's lawyer hassling me.'

Auhl took out his wallet, fished around for Georgina Towne's business card. 'Neve's lawyer,' he said. 'Might be able to run interference for you.'

Pocketing the card, Logan looked pityingly at Auhl. 'I spoke to people who knew Mrs Fanning in Geelong. Seems the husband's a shithead and she's a nice lady, had a rough trot.'

'She is,' Auhl said.

'Anyway, nothing's going to come back on you.'

Auhl flexed his jaw, his fists. He wished Logan hadn't said that. 'Last thing on my mind, all right?'

Logan raised his hands, placating, nodded goodbye and left the building.

Auhl tried calling Pia's phone. A man's voice said, 'Who is this?'

Auhl broke the connection.

34

FIRST THING ON Saturday morning, Auhl made contact with Neve's parents. They'd rented a flat in Adelaide and would stay until their daughter and granddaughter had recovered. No real change, but Pia was doing pretty well. They were beside her bed, in fact. Would Auhl like to talk to her?

'A. A.!' A screech of pleasure, before the child remembered herself.

'Hello, Bub. I'll come and see you as soon as I can, all right?'

Her voice hollower now, she said, 'All right.'

'Claire sends her love.'

But all Pia said to that was, 'Will I have to live with Dad now?'

THEN TO WORK.

By ten-fifteen Auhl and Pascal had found the Catholic op shop in Emerald. Musty air, a couple of women flicking expertly through racks of T-shirts, three small children on the floor with picture books. And Ruth Peart, tense and pale, emerging from the shadows. 'Can we do this in your car?'

She was edgy as they walked, holding herself stiffly, wanting to hurry but unable to. 'Please, I might not have much time.'

'Are you hurt?'

'Please, someone might see.'

And she took an age to relax her spine against the seat back as they settled in the car, Claire beside her, Auhl in the front. Again Auhl said, 'Ruth, are you hurt?'

'Fine,' she gasped.

'I think someone hurt you, Ruth.'

Claire reached out, took her arm and pushed the sleeve to the elbow. Finger bruises. 'Who did this to you, Ruth?'

'It doesn't matter.'

'We can help you. Come with us, right now, no looking back.'

'No.' Doubt and wretchedness and a vigorous headshake. 'Not just yet.'

Claire nodded. 'That's fine, we understand. What's happening at the house? Are they all there?'

She nodded. But holding back, Auhl thought. 'Ruth, what happened?'

'Your visit yesterday set them off.'

'Set them off in what way?'

'They're worried. They're angry.'

'They hit you.'

She hung her head, moved futilely to get comfortable.

'What was it about our visit that upset them?'

She looked anguished. 'It's partly they're tired of all the attention, they hate people snooping around. And then knowing Robert and Mary were both killed. But mainly it's what I said.'

Claire said, 'I don't recall you saying anything.'

'Remember? I said about Robert and Mary doing up the old house?'

Auhl was baffled; he could see Claire was baffled. 'Let's start with why you wanted to meet with us.'

With another little gasp of pain, Ruth Peart said, 'Until you came yesterday I had no idea about Robert.'

'That his body had been found?'

She nodded.

'The others didn't tell you? You didn't see it on the news?'

'No. We don't watch the news.'

'It's against your religion,' Auhl said sourly.

Ruth didn't register the tone, simply nodded ingenuously. 'That's right.'

Claire gave Auhl a look. 'But you've always known about Mary's death. That wasn't hidden from you.'

'It was awful,' Peart said. She paused, looking into the distance, concentrating. 'Half of me believed Robert killed her but the other half didn't. Does that make sense?'

Auhl smiled. 'I'm forever holding contradictory positions in my head, convinced they're equally valid.'

The smile didn't work. Ruth Peart said, 'Everyone said he did it. Adam and Judith and the Father and the elders, *everyone*.'

'When you say the Father: is that Warren?'

A middle-aged man was approaching the car, carrying supermarket bags. Ruth Peart froze, sank in her seat, not relaxing until he was past. 'Yes.'

Claire said gently, 'When you say a part of you *didn't* think Robert killed your sister, what do you mean?'

'Because he was so in love with her. And Mary was in love with him.' She looked away. 'I…'

They waited. Presently Claire prompted: 'What was it you wanted to say?'

It came out in a rush. 'Back then everything was upside down for me. I know it's wrong but I was confused and hurt by what Mary did.'

Again, they waited. Auhl said, 'What did she do?'

'Turned her back on us. *Me*. Left me behind to suffer.'

Auhl chose his words. 'I understand that when your parents died, you and Mary were taken in by Mr Hince and his family?'

She gave him a complicated look. 'My parents didn't die.'

He waited. Eventually she said, 'They were excommunicated.'

Claire said, 'Can I ask why?'

'Falling out with the elders.'

The elders again. Auhl said, 'What kind of falling-out? Was it over doctrine?'

'Over a computer. Mum and Dad bought us a computer.'

Seeing their bafflement, she went on, faintly exasperated: 'The Assemblies doesn't allow computers or TV. No immoral behaviour, no going against the elders' decisions, no going to university.'

'I see,' said Auhl, who didn't yet.

'So Mum and Dad were excommunicated.'

'What exactly did that entail?'

Ruth looked at Auhl, astounded. 'They were *excommunicated*. They were banned.'

'In effect, they were dead to the church?'

'Yes. I'm in touch with them now, though. They still kind of believe in the faith.' She clutched Claire's sleeve. 'Please don't tell Adam or Judith.'

'We won't.'

Auhl said, 'Ruth, if you're being mistreated, leave. Surely your parents would have you back?'

'I can't go against my husband,' she said wretchedly.

Ah. 'You're married to Adam,' Auhl said.

'Yes.'

'Are your parents nearby?'

Ruth gestured languidly at the hills around them. 'Not far.' She winced again, the pain physical and emotional. 'Why didn't they try harder?'

Claire touched her wrist. 'How old were you when the Hinces took you in?'

225

'Nine. Mary was twelve and about to start high school and that's why Mum and Dad thought we needed a computer.'

'Were you ever allowed to see your parents?'

'No. But last year Mum saw me in the street and I've seen her a couple of times.' Again she beseeched them, 'Don't tell Adam.'

Auhl wondered what might have happened if police had followed up on the Peart family back in 2009. Would Ruth have stayed with the Hinces? But even if Rhys Mascot had found and interviewed the parents, they still 'kind of' believed. He might not have got anything from them anyway.

'Have you been married long?'

'A year.' Looking away awkwardly she said, 'He used to be in love with Mary.'

Auhl exchanged a glance with Claire. 'It must have made him mad when she ran off with Robert.'

She glanced at each of them as if regretting that she'd spoken. 'He'd never kill anyone.'

Famous last words. Before Auhl could follow up, Claire leaned close to Ruth Peart, placing a hand over the young woman's forearm. 'Ruth, you said Mary turned her back on you, left you behind to suffer.'

Peart looked away. 'Father could be strict.'

Auhl exchanged another glance with Claire. He said, 'Mary ran away because he was strict, leaving you behind. You felt betrayed.'

Ruth Peart's knuckles as she clenched her fists were white pebbles. She ground out the words: 'She ran away because she was in love.' A pause. 'They took me with them.'

Sensing anguish and guilt, Auhl trod carefully, 'You went to their house with them?'

'Yes.'

'Did you stay long?'

'Only a day,' she whispered.

'How did you get back?'

'Rob drove me.'

'Why didn't you stay?'

'I hated the house, for a start.'

'Describe it.'

'It was horrible. I mean, Rob was doing it up but still, there were floorboards missing everywhere and holes in the walls and it was freezing cold and there were rats. I hated it. Plus...'

They waited.

In a burst she said, 'Plus it felt so *wrong*. I thought Mary should come back with me. I thought God would punish us.'

Ruth Peart stared at her lap. Auhl wondered what she was hiding. He said, 'If Mr Hince was strict, why not live with a different family? Or ask Mr Hince to mend bridges with your parents?'

Ruth looked at him in wonderment. 'In the Assemblies, children belong to the church, not their parents.'

'Oh,' said Auhl, as though he should have known.

Claire said, 'Are you in love with Adam?'

'He's my husband.'

Then Claire said, 'Did he abuse you, too?'

It was a clever question, well placed in the flow, and got a result. Ruth Peart slumped. When she lifted her face to them it was filled with pain. 'Can we please not talk about that?'

Auhl said, 'Ruth, we're police officers, we've heard everything. We don't judge. We don't need details. We simply need to know: were you and Mary abused by Mr Hince?'

'Yes.'

Claire said, 'Sexual abuse, Ruth? More than a sharp word or a slap on the legs?'

A nod that was barely there.

'But Adam wasn't part of it?'

A tiny headshake.

Auhl tried to provide a summing-up that would help her. 'You were still young when Mary asked you to run away with her.

227

You were, are, a good person, an obedient person. You still believed in the church. A part of you thought it was wrong of Mary to run. And she took you to live in a horrible old shack and it was all too much so you went back to live with Mr Hince.'

'Yes,' a mutter, almost inaudible.

'You went back to being abused,' Claire murmured.

Ruth Peart shrugged. 'Only for a while.'

Got too old? wondered Auhl. 'You did nothing wrong, Ruth.'

Those clenched fists again. 'That's just it: I *did* do something wrong.'

Claire touched her forearm.

Ruth Peart's eyes spurted. 'I told Father where they were living.'

There's our killer, Auhl thought. But the timing puzzled him. Mary had run away with her boyfriend in May. Murdered in September. A slow-burning fuse?

'When exactly did you tell him that?'

'As soon as Rob dropped me back.' She shifted in her seat. 'I sneaked in, which was stupid because of course Father knew I'd been gone.'

'That was a few months before the murders. Do you know if anyone, Mr Hince or Adam or Judith or the elders, tried to visit Mary and persuade her to come back?'

Ruth Peart shifted uncomfortably. 'I don't know. I've kept my head down ever since.'

Claire said, 'Was Robert also a member of the church?'

'No.'

'What did Mr Hince say when you got back?'

'He hit me. He said it was my fault.'

Auhl said gently, 'I hope you don't feel any blame now, Ruth.'

More tears. 'But I do! I was so confused about everything. I couldn't just walk away from what had been my whole life. It was like I couldn't think.'

'If Father was angry with you then he would have been furious with Mary.'

She shook her head. 'He was, like, good riddance to bad rubbish.'

Auhl tried not to seem dubious.

Ruth looked at each of them, distressed. 'I don't know if he killed Mary and Rob or not.'

'Let's pretend he did. Was his anger mounting, festering, by any chance? Or maybe something else happened to set him off?'

'He was always great at festering,' Ruth muttered with a harsh laugh.

Starting to show some backbone, Auhl thought. 'Who hit you, Ruth? Yesterday or this morning?'

She looked at her lap. 'I had to be punished.'

'Who?'

'Judith. And Adam.'

'Come with us, Ruth, right now.'

'Not yet. The time's not right.'

Claire said, 'Just let us know when and we'll help, won't we, Alan?'

Auhl nodded. 'We now think Robert was murdered at the same time as Mary, probably by the same person, who staged things to look like Robert was to blame. Keeping all that in mind, is there anything that puzzled you at the time that makes sense now?'

Ruth shifted again, uttered tiny huffs of pain. 'One day Judith gave me a big slap and said, "Were you in on it?"'

'When was this?'

'One minute she was telling me Mary had been found dead and the next she was hitting me.'

'What did she think you'd been involved in?'

'I have no idea.'

Auhl had been thinking about the house. 'When you say Robert was renovating—'

She cut in. 'He'd finished. Mary said he did a terrific job.'

Some witnesses told you everything, others nothing, and there were those who dribbled information and misunderstood the importance of crucial facts. Auhl said patiently, 'When did she tell you that?'

'When she tried to get me to go with them the second time.'

Auhl said patiently, 'Ruth, you'll have to be a bit clearer.'

Ruth Peart took a deep breath and said, 'I always go to the chapel when I get up in the mornings and one day they were there waiting for me.'

'When?'

She hunched her shoulders as if it pained her to say the words. 'The day before Mary was killed.'

'Did anyone see them?'

The replies were increasingly monosyllabic. 'Don't know.'

'But you still thought it was wrong to leave the church?'

She was impatient with Auhl's dimness. 'Well, yes, but they wanted to take me across to Perth, make a fresh start there.'

Then she hunched again, wouldn't look at him. Survivor guilt, thought Auhl. If she'd gone with them, she'd be dead now.

'Why leave,' said Claire, 'if the house was fixed?'

Peart frowned. 'Because it had been sold.'

The answer came to Auhl, a cold sensation, and it explained the panic in the Hince household. 'The house wasn't pulled down, was it?'

Ruth seemed to think that was self-evident. 'Rob said it would be cut into three sections and then put on trucks to take it to a new location.' She began to weep. 'You think the Father killed Mary and Rob, don't you?'

'Ninety-nine per cent sure,' Auhl said.

'I don't want to go back.'

35

'THE MONASH MEDICAL Centre,' said Auhl, speaking to Colfax on his mobile. He was in the passenger seat, Claire driving, out along Eastlink again. 'They're keeping her in for observation.'

'Blood in the urine? Must have been quite a beating.'

'I'm glad we had her checked,' Auhl said.

'She'll make a statement?'

'Possibly. Probably.'

Colfax was silent. But she was on a golf course and Auhl could hear voices, birdsong. Then she was saying, 'Doesn't matter, we can press charges. Meanwhile see what Angela Sullivan has to say for herself, find the house and have it forensically examined—that's if it's still standing.'

Arrests would mean fingerprints, thought Auhl. Then they could run those prints against the prints on the gun. 'Boss.'

OUTSIDE SULLIVAN'S HOUSE Auhl stretched the kinks in his spine. Too much charging around the countryside in a car. He followed Claire to the front door, pressed the bell. Nothing.

Pounded his fist. Nothing. 'Let's try around the back.'

The side path took them to a typical suburban yard: small garden beds, flowers, shrubs and a vegetable plot, all showing some semblance of design—rock borders painted white, a wooden garden seat artfully angled beneath a small gum tree, a wheelbarrow doubling as a flowerpot. Neat, but in an ongoing war with nature— Sullivan apparently happy for that to happen, thought Auhl, noting the weeds, the moss on the rocks, the dead stalks and bird shit.

Mostly he was interested in the sliding glass door beyond a stretch of sun-faded patio boards. It stood open.

Auhl shouted, 'Police,' as he followed Claire up onto the patio and now he heard a muffled voice and thumping sounds.

Angela Sullivan was in her kitchen, duct-taped to a chair.

'Do you need a doctor?'

Sullivan, ashen, trembling, said, 'I'm all right.'

A bruise coming up on her cheek, finger bruises on her upper arms. No blood or broken bones. Smudged and reddened skin where she'd been taped. 'He punched me in the stomach and had me on the chair before I knew what happened.'

'Describe him.'

She cocked her head at Auhl. 'About your age.'

'Did he tell you his name?'

She shook her head. Auhl took out his phone and showed her the picture of Warren Hince. 'Is this him?'

'No.'

A photo of Adam Hince.

'No, too young.'

Claire handed her a glass of water. Sullivan clasped it in both hands as though fearful it might abandon her. It was the body language of a child.

'Just one man. No woman.'

'No.'

'Okay, moving on,' Auhl said, pocketing his phone. 'My colleague and I think you've been giving us a lot of bullshit, Angela. What did your visitor want?'

'What else? Money for drugs.'

'You can do better than that.'

He moved behind her, rested his rump against the bench. She would need to turn her head to see him and he could see she hated that.

Claire took over. 'Angela? Look at me. What did he want?'

A shrug.

'This involves two murders, Angela. You don't get to play dumb.'

Sullivan finally looked at Pascal, then around at Auhl, less sulky now, a little conniving hardness in her face. 'If you must know, he asked about the old house.'

'Now we're getting to it. The house you'd demolished.'

She looked away. 'Yes.'

'Angela, look at me. You lied to the police in a murder investigation. The house was not demolished. Robert Shirlow fixed it up, then you sold it and it was moved to a new location.'

'So what? No law against it.'

'There is against lying to the police,' Auhl said.

'The house was—is—a crime scene,' Pascal said. 'It might still contain evidence.'

Sullivan gave a little scoffing grimace. 'After all this time? Don't be stupid.'

Auhl said, 'Why did you lie?'

Craning her neck, she shot him a quick, hunted look.

'Angela,' Auhl said, a touch of the whip in his voice, 'why did you lie about the house?'

She shouted, 'Because of the asbestos.'

The air went out of Auhl. 'Oh, for Christ's sake.'

Still heated, Sullivan said, 'It was a fibro house, meaning asbestos, and I would've needed a permit to demolish it, which

233

would've cost *ten thousand dollars* because of the biohazard regulations and whatever. So I sold it.'

Auhl understood. 'You didn't tell the new owner.'

She stared at the floor.

'Who bought it, Angela? Where is it?'

It was as if she hadn't heard him. 'You can't blame me. I was scared back then. All those police questions, did I know what was going on in my place, did I have anything to do with the killing, did I know where Robert was.' She hugged herself. 'Now I'm scared all over again.'

'*Angela.*'

She jumped.

'*Who bought the house and where did they put it?*'

She gave them a name and an address in Skye. And, as if they were merely chatting, said, 'Not that far from here, really. I drive past it now and then. It's amazing what Mr Lang's done with the old place. It actually looks quite pretty,' she added wistfully.

36

AUHL DROVE. PASCAL worked the radio, calling for backup, a standby ambulance and a firetruck.

Skye turned out to be a region of small acreage hobby farms and rural businesses set back from the road on slightly undulating country. They passed an alpaca farm, an alternative healing clinic, a haulage contractor. Neat, modest properties alongside a sprinkling of hideous starter castles and hovels landscaped with rusted washing machines.

Suddenly Claire pulled out her phone; gave Auhl a half-smile. 'Just calling the hospital, okay?'

Auhl drove, listening. It took some time, but then she was talking.

'Ruth, it's Claire. Quick question: do you know a man named Rex Osprey?'

'Of course,' muttered Auhl. Getting old, losing his touch.

Claire concluded the call, grinned at him. 'An elder of the church.'

Auhl thought it through. 'The Hinces stay in Emerald in case the police are watching and send their errand boy to… To what? Burn the place down in case there's forensic evidence tying Warren or Adam to the murders? They must be mad.'

'Well, der. They *are* mad.'

THEY FOUND ANGELA Sullivan's old farmhouse along a dirt road choked with spring grasses. As she'd said, it was a pretty house, cream with a green roof and a new veranda. But not peaceful right now.

Auhl shot the car into the driveway and braked hard. They piled out, Auhl trying to read the situation in a glance. A Holden station wagon parked at the side, a black SUV in the driveway. A man he didn't know backing up, swinging a garden rake while Rex Osprey menaced him with a small pry bar. The two of them enacting a tense, jerky dance of fear and threat.

Osprey hadn't registered their arrival. Auhl darted in, shooting a glance at the veranda. Two crowbars and a hammer lay on the decking. A petrol can on its side, fuel darkening the wood, a rainbow film blooming as the sun caught the spill. No flames, but Auhl could picture them starting, blooming, feeding on the wood-preserving oils, leaves and debris…

Was anyone still inside the house?

Save the stranger first. If it was the owner, Lang, he was blood drenched, uttering awful cries, his jaw at a cruel angle. A moment later, Osprey's pry bar swiped the rake aside, swiped the other way, hitting the injured man on the shoulder. He fell, scrabbling away on his back as Osprey advanced.

Coming in hard and fast, Auhl kidney-punched the church elder. '*Enough.*'

With slow articulations of his knees, hips and hands, Osprey lowered himself to the ground. Otherwise he seemed indignant. 'We have a right.'

'You're under arrest for assault, with other charges to follow,'

Auhl said, snapping handcuffs on Osprey's wrists.

'*We have a right.*'

Auhl told him to shut up and joined Claire in helping the other man get to his feet. 'Are you Mr Lang?'

A nod, Lang trying to get his words out but whimpering with the pain, a hand to his jaw. He was about fifty, and seemed as angry as Osprey, pointing incredulously, whimpering again.

'An ambulance is coming, Mr Lang. Don't try to speak, just nod. Did this man hit you?'

Lang nodded, pointed. The pry bar. Evidence, and apt to be overlooked once emergency vehicles and other police arrived. 'I'll be back in a tick,' Auhl said, drawing out his phone. He photographed the bar, used his handkerchief to pick it up, and ran with it to the car. Securing it on the back seat, he returned to Lang in time to stop him from stepping onto the veranda.

'Stay here, Mr Lang. Is anyone inside?'

The man shook his head but he was agitated. 'My house,' he slurred, then placed his palm over his jaw and whimpered again.

Auhl turned as a leisurely police car rolled up. Two uniforms got out and approached curiously. Ascertaining they were from Frankston, Claire gestured at Osprey. 'This man is under arrest, assault and deprivation of liberty, for starters. Get him checked by a doctor, we'll be along to interview him shortly.'

As the car bumped away, an ambulance turned in. Auhl watched it, trying to figure out his next move, events passing too quickly. Speaking a little too loudly, too slowly, he said to the man with the broken jaw, 'Mr Lang, is there someone we can call? Partner, friend, neighbour? Son or daughter?'

Lang nodded and began digging into his hip pocket. He fished out an iPhone in a leather flip case and, as Auhl watched, activated the screen and scrolled through his contacts list. He stopped at *Bonnie* and a mobile number, proffered the phone to Auhl.

'Is Bonnie your daughter?'

Lang nodded.

Auhl pressed the call symbol and a woman answered. He explained, explained a second time, the daughter increasingly querulous. He was a policeman. Her father had been assaulted. He was okay but an ambulance would be taking him to Frankston Hospital with a suspected broken jaw. His house was a crime scene and would be forensically examined, meaning it might be some days before he could return to it.

When the ambulance had left, he said, 'What do you think Osprey was talking about? Right to what?'

Claire shrugged. 'No idea.'

They stepped onto the veranda, Auhl photographing the petrol can, the crowbar and hammer. They stepped inside. The hall and rooms were neat, a mix of Ikea and furniture-store chairs, tables, bookshelves and beds. It wouldn't stay that way. He called for a forensic team.

37

FRANKSTON POLICE would prosecute Osprey for the attack on Lang, but were happy for Auhl and Pascal to interview him in regard to the Slab Man investigation.

They were escorted to a room halfway down an airless corridor, where Osprey was seated at a scuffed plastic table with a young Legal Aid solicitor called Rundle. Auhl pulled out a chair. 'Mr Osprey, I understand you've been cleared by the doctor for interview?'

A soft voice emerged from fleshless lips. 'Yes.'

'But my client suffers from asthma and I may need to ask you to stop the questioning if he becomes distressed,' Rundle said.

'If he has asthma he shouldn't go around exerting himself,' Auhl said.

The lawyer was about to object, but Osprey touched his arm. 'It's all right.'

Claire Pascal started the recordings, audio and visual. The usual disclaimers and notifications and the names of all present. The fifth player was the room: cramped, airless, cheerless.

Auhl, certain that his chair suffered from plastic fatigue, hardly dared shift in it. He said, 'Mr Osprey, have you been advised that you face charges in relation to certain matters that occurred today?'

'My client,' Rundle said, 'is aware of his rights and obligations and is willing to cooperate in any way possible, but we would question the severity of those charges. And I understand that this interview is *not* in relation to those charges but certain historical matters?'

'That is correct,' Auhl said.

He wondered briefly why Osprey had not requested a pricey Assemblies of Jehovah hack. Rundle was young, bright, up for a stoush, but he didn't seem to have much at stake in the proceedings. Not bored—looking to have fun, if anything—his engagement more intellectual than emotional, in Auhl's judgment. Maybe it was the look. An earring. Designer spectacles. Unshaven in the regrettable style made ubiquitous by the makers of TV commercials.

Rundle seemed to read Auhl's thoughts and gave a whisper of the shadow of a smile.

'Mr Osprey, why don't we begin with why you were at Mr Lang's house,' Claire said.

Osprey mulled on that, a grey-faced spectre on the other side of the table. 'Will I go to jail?'

'Quite possibly,' Auhl said. 'You committed serious assaults on Mr Lang and Ms Sullivan, and hindered a murder investigation.'

'May I remind you why we're here?' Rundle said.

'All right, we'll start at the beginning,' Claire said. 'Mr Osprey, you are an elder of the Assemblies of Whatever church.'

Osprey said stiffly, 'I'd rather you didn't mock my beliefs.'

Claire went on blithely, 'A vehicle apparently stolen from your car yard was used in the commission of two murders. One of the victims, Mary Peart, being *a young Assemblies church member*. Isn't that rather a coincidence?'

'Ex-member.'

'I said, that's quite a coincidence.'

'The vehicle in question was *stolen*,' Osprey said.

'You're really going with that story?' Auhl said.

Osprey flushed. 'If you are trying to say *I* stole the car and then went and shot someone then I'm refusing to say anything more.'

'Can you account for your movements back then?'

He was triumphant. 'I can indeed.'

He glanced at Rundle, who opened a folder and retrieved an envelope. 'My client had this in his pocket when he was processed earlier today.'

Auhl was curious. Well prepared? Expecting arrest? 'Why don't you give us the gist, Mr Osprey?'

'Receipts, hospital paperwork. I had a cataract operation at the time the Suzuki was stolen. I couldn't drive anywhere. I was half-blind for a few days. I didn't kill anyone. I would never do such a thing.'

The man was talking freely, so Auhl pushed a little. 'Mr Osprey, were you coerced to do what you did today?'

No answer, but the man shifted in his chair.

'Did you fear it might all go pear-shaped?'

No answer.

'Mr Osprey,' Claire said, 'I understand that you're a devoted member of the Assemblies of Jehovah congregation. Loyal, faithful, eager to do the right thing. But matters are coming to a head. I put it to you that you were asked to provide the leader of your church, Warren Hince, with a vehicle that was subsequently used in a double homicide.'

Osprey sagged a little. He gave his lawyer an anguished look. Rundle's shrug was almost imperceptible.

'Were there other crimes you were a party to on behalf of Mr Hince? The sexual abuse of the children of your congregants, for example.'

'What?' That straightened him up. 'Not me. Never.'

'Then how do you explain today's actions?' Auhl said. At a look

241

from Rundle, he held up his hand. 'My question refers to the hold these people seem to have over your client.'

'You can answer, Mr Osprey,' Rundle said with a hint of enjoyment. He was curious, too. 'Were you asked or ordered or blackmailed in any way?'

'We don't believe for a moment that you killed anyone or knowingly provided the means,' Auhl said. 'You didn't drive the vehicle, shoot the gun, hide the gun. But we do believe you know more than you're telling us.'

'Gun? What gun?'

Auhl was flat and hard. 'The gun used to kill Mary Peart and probably her boyfriend was found hidden in the Suzuki stolen from your yard.'

Osprey blanched. He swallowed. Rundle looked at him with interest. Time passed. Auhl, looking at the way Osprey chewed his bottom lip, thought they'd lost him.

Then: 'Warren Hince came to me and said he needed to borrow a vehicle for a couple of days. I wasn't to ask why, it was church business. When he didn't return it I asked for it back and he said it had been stolen from him. He paid me the value of the vehicle and I thought nothing of it.'

'But you reported it stolen, to make it official.'

'Well, it *was* stolen. Warren borrowed it from me, then it was stolen from him before he could return it, the idiot.' He gave a twist of his mouth. 'I hate to speak ill of the fellow and I'm not saying he can't whip up a congregation, but really he isn't, wasn't, all that bright.'

They watched him. Auhl said, 'Mr Osprey, were you asked to intimidate Carmen Shirlow? She said an older man, a business type, hassled her afterwards.'

A slight, conceding shrug as Osprey looked down at his pale fingers. 'Not proud of it. Warren asked me to. Said if I wanted the money for the Suzuki I had to do it.'

'We need a statement, Mr Osprey. And we must caution you in relation to this matter.'

Osprey was resigned now, almost relieved. 'Whatever it takes. I've had enough. The church is more or less bankrupt anyway, and why should I take all the blame?'

Claire looked at him and said, very gently, 'Mr Osprey, you have a daughter.'

Osprey's face changed, transformed by an expression of pure misery. 'You will not talk to me about that. Please don't talk to me about that. I'll help you with anything else you like, but I don't want her dragged into anything.'

Warren Hince, thought Auhl. And he's lived with it, unable to see or, if he saw, to do anything about it, and it's pulled him apart.

'All right. Now, did Mr Hince say anything at all about why he needed the Suzuki?'

'No. I just did as I was told.'

'Did you later connect it to the murder of Mary Peart?'

'I had no reason to—not until you spoke to me the other day.'

'And today? What was that all about? You were doing the Hinces' bidding again, destroying evidence for them?'

Osprey shook his head. 'It was all about the money, it was only ever about the money.'

Auhl looked at Pascal; she looked back at him. Sighed: a tiny noise of fulfilment. 'All right, Mr Osprey. Tell us about the money.'

38

THAT WAS SATURDAY.

As soon as they were back at Chateau Auhl, Claire packed, kissed Auhl on the cheek, gave him a bottle of good wine and called for a taxi to take her home. The house seemed empty around him that night.

Waking at 6.00 a.m. Sunday, Auhl walked, bought croissants. Coffee, croissants and the *Sunday Age* at the mossy wrought iron table in the backyard, dimly bathed in sunlight. Cynthia stretched on the sun-warmed crazy path. At eight Liz appeared, freshly showered, overnight bag in her hand. 'Sorry, I'm meeting people for lunch in Queenscliff, I'd better rush.' And she was gone.

Auhl blinked: he hadn't even known she'd stayed the night. Meeting people for lunch... Or meeting a special person. He realised it didn't matter so much anymore. Tried to tell himself that, anyway.

Then Bec, half-awake, grabbed a croissant and waved goodbye. 'I have to open the shop, Tanya lost her keys.'

She was always floating names at him. Friends, co-workers,

people he'd forgotten meeting or would never meet or who too closely resembled one of the others, so he just smiled benignly. She kissed him and clattered along the hallway and out the door.

It was time for Auhl to move his weary bones.

A NURSE WAS ARRANGED for Warren Hince, while the wife and son were arrested and brought to the city for questioning.

Separate cars, separate interview rooms.

The first thing Judith Hince said was, 'You do realise it's the Sabbath?'

'Means nothing to us, Mrs Hince,' Claire said. She looked subdued.

'The law never rests,' Auhl said. 'Speaking of which: you're entitled to a lawyer.'

'I don't need a lawyer,' Judith Hince said, 'and my son doesn't need a lawyer. We've done nothing wrong.'

Auhl and Pascal smiled noncommittally, settled her in one of the interview rooms with a uniform at the door, then conferred in the corridor. 'How do you want to play this?' Claire asked.

'Adam first.'

'Agreed. He might be the dear leader but his mother holds the reins.'

They walked up to the next level. 'So, how are things at home?'

They walked, Claire silent. Then: 'If you must know, Michael lost it when I said I had to work today.'

'The case does have momentum,' Auhl said.

'Except that the weekend is shot to hell.'

'Well, you know there's a room at my place.'

'Alan, I've barely started phase two of my marriage.'

THEY FOUND ADAM fidgeting at an interview-room table. 'Why am I here? It's the Sabbath.'

'You know why you're here. You assaulted your wife. Also, you either committed or helped cover up two murders.'

'That's ridiculous.'

'Was it you or your mother who asked Mr Osprey to find and destroy the house?'

'I don't know anything about that.'

'He said it was your mother.'

Adam shot each of them a blunt, frightened look. Seemed to see conviction on their faces. 'All right,' he said quickly, 'if you must know, it was me, I asked him, Mum had nothing to do with it.'

'What a loyal son you are,' Claire said, with her sweet smile.

How much did the guy know? Auhl sharpened his voice. 'You asked him to destroy a house, yes? Why?'

'Umm.' Hince hesitated. 'To destroy evidence.'

'What evidence?'

Hince frowned, concentrating. 'Well, bloodstains. DNA. Fingerprints. Bullet holes in the...the...the floor. The walls.'

'And why might those things have been present?'

Adam Hince drew himself up onto surer ground. 'A few years ago, when my father's mind was starting to go, he let slip that he'd done a terrible thing, murdered Mary and Robert. It tormented his conscience. Then those Royal Commission allegations, it was the ruin of him. You saw him—he has dementia. He was a proud man and to see him brought down...well. Too late now, of course, you've found the house, but I didn't want to see him diminished further in the eyes of the world and that's why I asked Mr Osprey to destroy the evidence.'

Claire snorted. 'You didn't even know about the house until two days ago. The truth was under your nose the whole time but you and your mother and your father treated Ruth like she barely existed.'

'I love my wife.'

Claire brushed that aside. 'To be clear for the tape, Mr Hince: you are admitting you've known for some years that your father was

246

responsible for the murders of Mary Peart and Robert Shirlow in September 2009?'

'Yes.'

'You shot them both?'

'What? No. My father did.'

'Inside the house they were living in at the time?'

'Yes.'

'And the three of you staged matters so that it appeared Robert was the killer?'

'Yes. I mean, no, my father did.'

'Drove Mary's body to a nature reserve and buried Robert under a slab?'

'Yes.'

'He told you all this?'

'Like I said, he confessed to my mother and me many years later. His mind was going and everyone was hounding us, and he had a bit of a breakdown and told us what he'd done.' With an expression of the profoundest indignation and regret, he added, 'I think the way he was treated tipped the balance into senility.'

'You didn't think to tell the police?'

'He's my father!'

'It's a hell of a big job,' Auhl said, 'killing two people and staging a false scene. Driving a body all round the countryside. Are you sure he didn't have help?'

Claire Pascal leaned forward. 'Adam, I put it to you that you helped your father carry out the killings and cover them up. What do you have to say in regard to that matter?'

'An absolute lie.'

'Big strapping bloke like you—surely you didn't let your father dig the hole,' Claire persisted.

'I wasn't there.' Adam tried to fold his arms over his chest but his bulk defeated him. 'It was all my father, I'm sorry to say. It devastated me. And my mother.'

'I expect it did,' Auhl said. He cocked his head. 'According to the autopsies, two bullets hit Mary in the head, and one in the chest, and Robert was shot once in the head and twice in the torso with bullets from a Smith and Wesson point three-two revolver.'

Adam nodded briskly. 'That's right. My father showed us the gun. My mother said she didn't want it in the house and made me get rid of it.'

'Where?'

'Where no one can ever find or use it, mixed into a concrete pour under a strip of shops we put up.' Hince paused. 'I think my mother was scared Dad would shoot himself.'

'When police searched the house after Mary was found, they saw no evidence of blood or bullet holes. Your father must have done a good job cleaning up after himself.'

Hince shrugged. 'He's a builder. But then when Robert was found we got worried that the police would use...ah, new techniques. To find blood and so on.'

'So let's get the story sorted,' Auhl said. 'You were in love with Mary, hated it that she ran off with Robert, and shot them both.'

'What? No,' Hince snarled. 'Aren't you even listening?'

'We have it on good authority that you were in love with her.'

'She was my friend. We kind of grew up together after she came to live with us.'

'But she wanted someone else, right? So you got rid of her, then married her sister.'

'Stop it.'

'Did your father love your wife in the way he loved Mary?'

'What do you mean? I don't...'

'Adam,' said Claire Pascal, 'why did your father kill Mary?'

He'd glimpsed the angry scarring on her forearm and didn't take his eyes from it. 'Punishment.'

'For what?'

Hince looked up. 'Leaving the family of our church and living in sin,' he said, as if this was the only conceivable reason.

'Mary was the main target, and Robert was unlucky enough to be there when you shot her?'

'When my *father* shot her, yes.'

'But Mary had left the church *several months earlier*,' Claire said. 'Why wait so long?'

'Dad wasn't certain where she was.'

Auhl watched Hince expressionlessly. 'We have reason to believe that Mary left the church because she'd been sexually abused by your father. It's possible she was also abused by the elders. It's possible she was also abused by you. If not for that, she might never have left.'

'That's a filthy lie.' Hince spat the words. 'I would never do such a terrible thing. And my father loved his flock. He wouldn't harm a soul.'

'Except for the small matter of a double murder, right? Anyway, he's gaga now, your father,' Claire said lightly. 'Conveniently unable to account for his actions.'

Hince composed himself. 'My father is suffering some memory loss, owing to his age. He's forgetful. He's not well. But he's a good, decent man and the hounding he's received is unforgivable.'

'Unforgivable,' Claire said. 'Adam, let's try this question for size: where would a young guy like you, a devout churchgoer, get hold of a Smith and Wesson revolver?'

Hince shook his head sadly. 'There you go again. I played no part in my father's crimes. Where he got the revolver from, I have no idea. We do employ some quite rough men on our building sites from time to time.'

'Did you visit Mary?'

'I didn't know where she was living.'

'Didn't try to get her to come back to you? Or to the church?'

'No.'

Auhl said, 'Did you own a car back then, Adam?'

'No.'

249

'So how did you get to the house to kill those poor young people?'

'My father. He drove there, by himself, in an Assembly car. We have a lot of cars at our disposal.'

'Why didn't he simply burn down the house when he'd finished killing Mary and Robert?'

'He told me later that he wanted blame to fall on Robert. He was worried a fire would attract too much attention.'

'Ruth has made a statement, Adam, you know that, don't you? About the events of ten years ago, and last Friday?'

Hince flushed. 'She shouldn't be dwelling on the past. Poor Ruth—obviously the discovery of Robert's body dredged up old memories. But she doesn't know anything.'

'No one bothered to involve her, did they?' Claire said. 'No one bothered to talk to her at all, really. I guess she was just your servant, wasn't she? And sex toy.'

'Can she talk to me like that?' Hince asked Auhl. He swung back to Claire. 'You can't talk to me about private family matters like that.'

Christ, Auhl thought, this patsy. This soft young man in thrall to his bullying father and his crackpot faith. 'All the disasters that have befallen the Assemblies, you must really be struggling financially.'

Faintly perplexed, Adam Hince said, 'With God's grace, we'll survive.'

'Still,' Auhl persisted, 'if a big bundle of cash had gone missing, you'd want to get it back. All those legal costs…'

Adam Hince looked puzzled. It wasn't an act: he didn't know what Osprey knew. About the money.

'We'll take a short break,' Auhl said.

39

A LONG BREAK, SO they could question Judith Hince.

As they headed down the corridor to the second interview room, Auhl said, 'He doesn't know the real reason why his father killed those kids.'

'I agree.'

'He didn't know about the money in 2009, and doesn't know about it now. After our visit on Friday, I'm betting Judith coached him in a story that made some kind of sense: yes, Warren was to blame for everything but they did have a duty to protect his name as much as possible. As to who exactly was—'

Claire's mobile chirped. She glanced at the screen, stopped dead in her tracks and gave Auhl a broad grin. 'Judith.'

'Judith what?'

'Fingerprint match: Judith handled the gun. She was there—or she shoved it behind the dashboard of the Suzuki, at the very least.'

'*Yes*,' Auhl barked. He clapped his hands, strode on again. 'Excellent.'

*

Judith Hince was tidy, composed, but there was a tired sag beneath her eyes. Auhl said, 'You still don't want a lawyer, Mrs Hince? Surely the church can afford a good one?'

She laughed and it was derisive. 'We're broke. It's all gone on legal fees.'

'Good,' said Auhl. 'Straight to the main issue: the money.'

Judith Hince went blank and tried to hold it. 'I have no idea what you're talking about. All I know is I've done nothing wrong.'

'Put Ruth in hospital.'

'How *is* the dear girl? When may I see her?'

'Probably fifteen to twenty,' Claire said. 'Meanwhile, in addition to hurting your son's wife, you are accessory to certain acts carried out by Mr Rex Osprey yesterday.'

She shrugged. 'Mr Osprey is quite capable of making his own decisions.'

'And you also,' Auhl said, 'murdered, or helped cover up the murders of, Robert Shirlow and Mary Peart.'

Her demeanour didn't alter. 'Don't be ridiculous. That was a long time ago and has nothing to do with me.'

'You took Mary Peart and her younger sister into your home when their parents were excommunicated, is that correct?'

'Yes.'

Claire said, 'Did your husband sexually abuse Mary?'

'Yes.' No flicker in the blank face.

'Ruth?'

'Yes.'

'Did your son abuse them?'

'*No.*' Angry now. 'And don't you try pinning it on him.'

They were silent. Auhl contemplated her, the hint of pink rising in her cheeks. Wondered if she'd had enough of the Assembly and its menfolk.

But the prints on the gun.

'Mary met Robert Shirlow when he was hired to do gardening

work and yard maintenance at your property in Emerald?'

'Yes.'

'A relationship developed?'

'Yes. A friendship really, at first.'

'Did you disapprove?'

'Back then, yes. My husband disapproved, therefore I disapproved. Now I think: good luck to young lovers. Except the luck didn't last for those two.'

'Are you fed up with the men who run your church, Mrs Hince? Is that it? Fed up with your husband's actions? The betrayal?'

'He's…he was a weak man.'

'So, Robert and Mary. They became lovers and Mary ran away.'

The woman shrugged. 'Ran away from Warren or ran towards love? One or both.'

'She took Ruth with her.'

'Poor girl, she came back the next day. But Mary always had more spunk.'

'On Friday you said Ruth *didn't* go to the house where Mary was living.'

'I forgot. It wasn't important.'

'Back when Mary was murdered, the media ran with the story that Robert was dealing drugs and things got out of hand and he murdered Mary and disappeared.'

'Well, I think you know the real story,' Judith Hince said, in her abrupt, get-on-with-it manner. 'It was Warren.'

'With the help, willing or otherwise, of your son,' Claire Pascal said. 'Were you there? Did you help?'

The woman snarled, 'Adam had nothing to do with any of it. Nor did I. Not then, and only to a limited extent now. My husband shot both those youngsters. He was away for two days.'

'Your son had nothing to do with it?'

'Correct.'

'You had nothing to do with it?'

'Correct.'

'Everything was carefully staged. Mary's body was moved, Robert's was buried under a slab, the scene was cleaned up, there was misdirection. Is your husband capable of that kind of meticulousness?'

'He set up a successful church, didn't he? Ran a successful business? He's bright. And he's good with his hands.'

'Is he mentally competent?'

'No. The dementia is real. Talk to the doctors.'

'We will. When your husband returned from his two days away, he told you what he'd done?'

'Yes.'

'You didn't think to report it to the police at the time?'

'Of course not.'

'He just went off to kill Mary Peart for leaving the church,' Auhl said, 'and while he was about it he also shot Robert Shirlow, and then he came back again and life went on as normal.'

'Correct.'

'But Adam just told us he knew nothing about any of it until some years later.'

'Correct. There are matters kept secret between husbands and wives. There was no need to trouble Adam. But then my husband's name was dragged through the mud and he kept wailing and gnashing his teeth and it all came out.'

'And, what, it triggered senility?'

She shrugged. 'Who knows?'

'Mrs Hince. Are you able to explain why your fingerprints were found on the gun that was used to shoot Mary Peart?'

40

LATE AFTERNOON NOW, Judith Hince sour and washed out in the interview room.

This time she had a lawyer with her, a woman in her fifties with sharp eyes and nervy fingers, who kept fidgeting as if she wanted to leap in with objections and warnings. 'My client has, since her earlier interview, decided to acknowledge that she helped her husband in the commission of the two murders. She did not fire the gun but merely handled it.'

Auhl said, 'Well, that saves time and paperwork. Where did you get the gun?'

Hince said, 'I don't know where my husband got it. However, he was a builder. He's employed many men over the years, from all kinds of backgrounds.'

An echo of the interview with Adam. 'Okay. Explain why you placed it behind the dashboard of the Suzuki you borrowed from Mr Osprey's yard.'

At the sound of Osprey's name, Judith Hince looked uneasy. She said, 'We were on our way back and saw a booze bus and in a panic I hid the gun. Then we had to stop for petrol and that's when someone stole the car. I couldn't believe it.'

'Very well. So you helped your husband commit two murders?'

'Yes. I'm not proud of it. In fact, I didn't even know he intended to do it.'

'He asked you to accompany him to the house where Mary was living with her boyfriend?'

'Yes.'

'Did he say why?'

'To ask Mary to reconsider.'

'And, what, she refused? Things got rough?'

'Yes.'

'Your husband thought he could persuade Mary with a gun?'

'The gun was for protection. Robert was young and he was tough and he was a nasty little shit, excuse the language.'

'Robert was mild-tempered and physically small, from all accounts. I put it to you that you went with your husband with the intention of punishing Mary for leaving the fold and punishing Robert for luring her away.'

Hince flared at him. 'So what? It wasn't my idea. It was Warren's. He was always banging on about the need to punish disobedience.'

Claire Pascal said, 'That's quite a ring you've got there.'

Judith Hince had been worrying the ring. Now she went very still. She turned to her lawyer. 'I do not intend to answer any more questions. If asked questions, I will simply answer no comment.'

'You're suddenly a bit touchy, Judith. I wonder if it's because you ripped that ring off Mary's finger?'

'No comment.'

Judith Hince's lawyer smiled. Her hands were quiet now.

BACK TO THE BEWILDERED wreck of Adam Hince, sitting two doors away from his mother.

Staring at the great lump of a boy opposite him, Auhl said, 'We've

256

been puzzled about a certain injury to one of Mary Peart's fingers.'

Adam Hince's gaze flicked about the room. He's trying to guess what his mother said, Auhl thought.

'It must have happened when Dad moved her.'

'We think her finger was broken when this was forcibly removed,' Claire Pascal said, placing Judith Hince's ring at the centre of the table.

Hince stared at it in confusion. 'Don't know what you mean.'

Auhl said, 'You maintain that your father went to the house where Mary and Robert were living and shot Mary for running away from the church.'

'Yes, for the hundredth time.'

It was time to haul out Rex Osprey's story. 'I put it to you that your parents went to the house to get back several hundred thousand dollars, plus quite a bit of your mother's jewellery.'

Adam Hince shook his head wildly. He was halfway capable of accepting that his father had killed in order to punish. There was a nice Old Testament ring to that. Nothing righteous about murder for money, though.

'Don't know what you mean.'

'We know that your father had amassed a huge sum from donations. Very little of it benefited the church. He was keeping it for himself, fearful the church would lose its tax-exempt status. For years there had been rumbling, people speaking out, calling the Assemblies of Jehovah a sham.'

'*Not* a sham.'

'He stowed that cash and your mother's jewellery in a safe in his study. Mary knew about the safe. She knew the combination. Your father had probably scribbled it on a slip of paper which he stuck under the desk. Perhaps she saw it when he was raping her on the floor one day. She told Robert about the abuse. She told Robert about the money. Sometime in September they sneaked back and robbed the safe. Call it revenge. Call it greed, if you like. They were also getting ready to leave the state and tried again to get Ruth to accompany them. She said no. It's possible she told your father, or he saw them on the property—it doesn't matter, he soon worked out who'd robbed him, and he went after them with the direct help of your mother and the indirect help of Rex Osprey.'

Hince was lost. 'My mother can't have told you these lies. It was Mr Osprey. He's a liar, trying to save his own skin.'

'They went to the house but all they got was that ring, which your charming mother tore off Mary's finger. It must have been a chaotic situation—a gun waved around, a struggle, with the result that Mary and Robert were shot before your darling parents got the money back.'

Pascal added, 'He was an impatient man, wasn't he, your father? Aggressive? The kind to go in swinging. But it all went badly wrong, and suddenly Mary and Robert were dead and he still didn't know where the money was hidden.'

Hince rolled his shoulders, but Auhl could see that the scenario made sense to him. He could visualise it.

Pascal went on: 'All your parents found was the ring on Mary's finger. Robert was restoring the house, remember. Perhaps there were a couple of floorboards still loose, so he stowed the money under them while he and Mary got ready to leave.'

'Of course an honest person would have gone to the police,' Auhl said, 'but your father wasn't honest. He didn't want reporters—or the tax office, or the elders—to know he was squirrelling money away.'

'Later on he thought it through, and went back to search the house,' Pascal said, 'but by then it was gone, and he had no luck finding anyone connected to Mary or Robert who might have the money.'

'You people really should have paid more attention to Ruth.' Auhl couldn't help himself.

Hince tried to rally. 'If what you're saying is correct, that money's rightfully ours.'

'Good luck with that,' Claire said. 'We'll find it long before you lot get your grubby little hands on it.'

'I expect it would come in handy about now,' Auhl said. 'Barristers' fees, victims demanding compensation. Not to mention ordinary greed.'

'My father has dementia. He's not liable.'

'Your father is a rapist,' said Claire.

Adam Hince drew himself up. 'Either way, it was my father who did those murders. Not me. Not my mother.'

'We have the gun, Adam,' Claire said.

Hince said warily, 'So what?'

'Your mother's prints are on it. She was there. Pulled the trigger for all we know.'

'Or all three of you were there.'

Judith had said not, though, and the mix of emotions on Adam Hince's face bore that out.

'Not really all that bright, your father,' Auhl said. 'Your mother knew she couldn't trust him to get it right.'

Hince looked like a man realising he was now truly alone. 'She would never hurt anyone.'

Then Auhl felt his phone vibrate in his pocket. Fished it out, saw the number for the crime-scene manager. Excused himself and took the call in the corridor.

'About the house in Skye?' queried the technician. 'We're wondering if we were properly briefed.'

Auhl said patiently, 'We're hoping you'll find evidence of a double homicide, plus cash and jewellery concealed under the floorboards or inside the walls.'

But just then Auhl felt a prickle of...what? Not alarm: *anticipation*. The feeling opening like a late flower as the forensics guy said, 'But someone's already searched the place.'

Floorboards prised up, he told Auhl. A wall panel removed.

41

THEY WERE FINISHED by mid-afternoon, charges laid.

Auhl dragged himself onto a Swanston Street tram, the week-end's adrenaline rush depleted. Thinking now only of Neve Fanning lying in hospital. Pia Fanning in fear of the prospect of living with her father. Lang with his broken jaw, his home a crime scene.

Not wanting to return to an empty house, he wandered down to the private gallery in Rathdowne Street. 'Just looking,' he said. But before he quite realised it he was buying a little Charles Blackman drawing of a schoolgirl. Was it a treat, a reward?

He left the gallery, faintly dazed, with a feeling that his Sunday was filling up strangely. And almost immediately experienced an odd echo of the case just closed. A poster on a side wall—rock concerts, experimental theatre, pub gigs and lost dogs—and a word catching his eye. *Assemble.* It was a flyer for a march on Parliament, but Auhl saw only Rex Osprey and the deluded neophytes of the Assemblies of Jehovah International.

He called Claire Pascal. 'Fancy a trip to Frankston tomorrow?'

'Sorry. Got some patching up to do.'

So Auhl made the trip alone on Monday, an Uber delivering him to the public hospital by 10.00 a.m. He asked for Lang's room and was directed to a small ward. Lang still looked dazed, but recognised him, and cast a reassuring look at the young woman with him, who proved to be the daughter. After the introductions Auhl said, 'Mr Lang, did anyone visit you in the past couple of days? A stranger?'

Lang nodded.

Scouting trip, thought Auhl. 'Did this person give a name?'

Lang gestured at his daughter, turning his wrist in a circle, and she reached for a notepad and pen on the bedside table. He wrote, printing the words neatly: *Can't remember.*

'Can you give me a description?'

Woman about 30, a bit alternative, tattoos of birds on neck.

Auhl smiled. 'Did she say what she wanted?'

Her brother used to live in my house. Dead now. She just wanted to see it.

I bet, thought Auhl. 'Did she say how she found you?'

Phoned house removalists.

As I should have done, Auhl thought—if it had occurred to me that the house was still intact.

Auhl didn't know how many tens of thousands of dollars Robert Shirlow had stashed in the old house, but he must have told his sister Carmen about it.

Auhl didn't think any of it was rightfully the property of the Hince family. And it shouldn't become the property of the state government, or languish in a police evidence safe. But nor should Carmen keep it all.

He climbed into the car and phoned her hotel: she'd checked out. He texted her: *Mary's sister Ruth should get half.*

He didn't expect a reply, but around the Ringwood off-ramp his phone pinged: *You think?*

Feeling a little buoyed, Auhl sat back and smiled. Carmen might have been having fun with him, of course; but he sensed he'd got her thinking.

He decided to give her the benefit of the doubt.

42

NOW IT WAS EARLY November.

Melbourne Cup Day came and went. The spring sun grew stronger, gearing up for summer, and all the world including retail knew Christmas was approaching fast. Helen Colfax's detectives took on new cold cases and wrapped up or put on hold current ones. The Hinces and Osprey were the responsibility of the OPP now.

Sometimes Auhl happened to encounter Jerry Debenham in the police building and receive the narrowed-gaze treatment that said, *I still don't trust you*—but Colfax said Debenham treated everyone that way, and meanwhile Janine Neill's toxicology results had come back: hypoglycaemic seizure, the theory being that Alec Neill had fed his non-diabetic wife a high dose of some glucose-lowering drug.

Pia Fanning still had her leg in a cast but was recovering quickly. Auhl phoned her regularly, and flew to Adelaide for a couple of days every fortnight or so. He'd sit quietly watching Neve or trying to talk her out of her coma, before heading to the Deanes' rented apartment where he'd read to Pia, chat, kid around. He didn't encounter Lloyd Fanning, but apparently he'd called in to see his daughter. Not his wife.

Pia said, 'If I'm better at Christmas he wants to take me to Bali for the whole of the holidays.'

Auhl cocked his head to read her. She was getting good at flat expressions. 'You don't want to go.'

'I want to be here in case Mum wakes up.'

'Tell him that.'

'He doesn't listen.' Pause. 'I have to go and live with him when I'm better, don't I?'

'I won't lie to you. Yes.'

'New school, new everything,' Pia said, her eyes filling.

'When your mum's better and her lawyer can swing into action, it's possible you won't have to live with him permanently.'

'That's not what he says. He says she's going to jail. He says I'm his forever.'

THEN ON A FRIDAY IN December Auhl let himself into Chateau Auhl, dumped his keys, wallet and jacket and dodged around Cynthia's sinuous greeting, and found Bec in the kitchen. She'd just got home from work, her GewGaws T-shirt wrinkled, damp with perspiration.

'A woman called a minute ago.'

Auhl stiffened whenever he heard these words. He'd think: *the hospital*. But usually it was a witness, a colleague.

'Who was she?'

A short wait while Bec gulped down a glass of water and gasped and swiped her hand across her mouth. 'She said she was from Pia's school. She wants a word with you.'

'Concerning?'

'She was a bit close-mouthed, Dad, but I said you'd be home about now, is that okay?' With a twirl of her fingers, Bec pounded up the stairs.

Auhl glanced at his watch: 5.30 p.m. He wanted a beer, but would that give the wrong impression? He sat in his favourite chair instead and coaxed Cynthia onto his lap.

ANSWERED THE KNOCK when it came, finding a young woman on his front step. Broad shoulders, short hair. Wary, yet apologetic and tentative, too. As if she wasn't sure of Auhl, wasn't sure of herself.

'Are you Mr Auhl?'

'I am.'

'Mrs Neve Fanning and her daughter Pia lived here until recently?'

'They did.'

She chewed at her bottom lip. 'Pia told me about you. She said you were a policeman.'

'Yes, I am.'

Further doubt and reluctance, the woman assessing him, a practical figure in a flowery skirt and plain T-shirt, a slim document wallet under her arm. Not ready to enter his house yet. Auhl said, 'You know my name but I don't know yours, or how you relate to Pia.'

She nodded abruptly, shot out her hand. 'Tina Acton, school counsellor.'

'Pia's school here in Carlton?'

'Yes, that's right.'

Auhl gestured. 'Let's continue this inside.'

But Acton was still not ready to move. 'Is Pia here?'

'She and her mother are still in Adelaide.'

Acton closed her eyes, took a breath and stepped past Auhl into the hallway. Then she stopped and he collided with her.

'Sorry, but I need to know, were you and Mrs Fanning, er—'

'Romantically involved? No,' said Auhl. 'Please. Come in.'

He took Acton through to the sitting room. 'Tea? Coffee? Something stronger?'

Acton shook her head. 'Water, please.'

Water was fetched and when they were seated and the cat had made itself comfortable in Acton's lap—Acton recoiling a little— Auhl said, 'Does this concern something Pia said or did? Something you noticed?'

'You're police, right?'

'Yes.'

A slow, troubled nod. Acton began to pat Cynthia. 'Well, the police might need to be involved.' She darted him a look.

Get on with it, he thought.

'A couple of days before Mrs Fanning came and, er, took Pia out of school and, er, didn't bring her back, I gave a talk to the Year 6 kids about appropriate adult behaviour.' She stopped, took a breath, carried on: 'Pia came up to me afterwards and said her dad sometimes touched her in ways that made her feel uncomfortable.'

She stopped as if afraid she'd said too much.

Auhl knew at once the reason for Acton's hesitancy. Mandated to report Pia's claim, she'd either failed to do it or she'd acted too late. He said harshly, 'Spit it out.'

Acton gave him a pained, twisted smile and said, 'He told Pia it was their special secret. She shouldn't tell anyone.'

'She told *you*.'

'Some kids find it easier to confide in someone less close, especially in the early stages.'

Auhl let his fury show. 'Cut to the chase, Tina. Did you or didn't you report it?'

'Look, I'm really sorry. I have now and I didn't mean to leave it so long, but I'm new in this job and I needed to be absolutely sure and then, you know, everything seemed to happen at once...'

'Did you tell Mrs Fanning?'

A whispered, 'Yes.'

'When?'

'The day before she ran off with Pia.'

'What exactly did you tell her?'

'I told her what Pia told me.'

'And what did she say? I need to know. Stop farting around.'

Acton hunched her shoulders and the words came in a flood. 'She said she had doubts. She was beating herself up over it. She said one night she saw her husband leaning over Pia in bed, touching himself, and she once heard Pia say, "You're my special pussy," in her sleep. And apparently last Christmas Pia tongue-kissed one of Neve's brothers when he gave her a present.'

Acton rocked in distress. 'I wish I'd done something sooner. This is all on me.'

Auhl wasn't going to absolve her. He idly wondered how the single expert, Kelso, would have responded if Neve had related the 'special pussy' incident. Asked if she liked cats?

'Will you attest to this in court? Will you make a statement?'

'Oh God yes,' Acton said, as though let off the hook. 'Absolutely.'

SHE LEFT. AUHL returned to the sitting room, too agitated to sit still. Stepped into the kitchen and poured himself a shaky glass of wine, and suddenly Bec was there, curious, sensitive to the moods of the house and her father.

'What did she want?'

Auhl told her, then they sat together at the table and finished the bottle, Bec spitting rage. He should do something, tell someone. Pia wouldn't be able to stay with her grandparents forever. Soon her father would have a clear shot at her.

Auhl was not heated. He felt icy cold as he traced the next steps in his mind. Report Lloyd Fanning to the sex crimes unit at St Kilda Road. They would refer him to the Sexual Offences and Child Abuse Investigation Team in Geelong. Their investigation would drag, given that two essential witnesses were presently in South Australia, one in a coma. And Lloyd Fanning would call in his lawyer, who would refer the SOCIT officers to Neve's behaviour.

'Abducting' his daughter from his house one weekend—with the help of a policeman, mind you. Abducting his daughter from school. Stealing a car. Trashing his house. A woman capable of all that would also be capable of putting ideas in her daughter's head. Talk to the eminent psychiatrist, Kelso—he knew exactly what Neve Fanning was like.

Auhl was cold, but that didn't stop the recriminations. He should have suspected earlier. Seen something. Pressed Neve. Her damned politeness and modest expectations and fear. Had she harboured suspicions but buried them? Hadn't let herself think the man she'd married would do that to their daughter?

Auhl flew to Adelaide on Boxing Day with a bike, which Pia accepted wanly. Her father's present: a card from Bali containing fifty dollars. Then Auhl took them all to visit Neve. Responding well to physical stimulation, according to the specialist: eyes fluttering, her arm jerking away if poked or squeezed. Could wake from the coma any day.

Pia hugged Auhl when he left. Asked after Bec and Cynthia, and nodded politely when he told her there'd always be a bed for her if she visited Melbourne.

Auhl liked Melbourne in January: less inner-city foot and car traffic, less noise, fewer toxins to starve the eucalypts and garden flowers, a sense that strangers might even smile if they encountered you walking at the end of a long, unrushed day.

'Meanwhile life goes on,' Helen Colfax said. She tapped a sheaf of papers together. 'Are you growing a beard?'

'Trying to,' Auhl said, fingering the wiry, itchy clumps of silvery growth.

The office was quiet, Josh Bugg on holidays until late January, Claire Pascal and her husband in Sydney. As for Colfax, she liked to leave work early and head for the beach. Brown arms, brown neck, showing beneath a plain T-shirt today. Red nose and frizzy hair. Rubbing cream into the backs of her hands when Auhl sauntered in to ask for time off.

Asking about his beard was a way for her to gather her thoughts. 'Time off, you say.'

'Just a few days.'

'You've only been here nine months.'

'True.'

'Then again, our cases are cold.'

'Almost frigid.'

She gave him a week.

43

BALI WAS HUMID AND overcrowded. The only decent accommodation Auhl could find was a rundown hotel near the airport, but it didn't matter. He was not holidaying. Early the next morning he hired a taxi, giving the driver an address he'd found in the handbag in the bedside table of Neve Fanning's hospital room.

The taxi took him north-west, hills in the distance, the towns giving way to roadside shanties, paddy fields behind them on either side. Whenever the taxi pulled up at stop signs, kids flocked to Auhl's window, offering cling-wrapped copies of *Newsweek*, the *Straits Times*, the *International Herald Tribune* and other newspapers and magazines. Taking pot luck, Auhl bought a November 2016 issue of the Melbourne *Age*. 'Huh,' he told the driver. 'Donald Trump's been elected President of the US.'

The driver grinned and accelerated past a brightly decorated three-wheeled taxi. Auhl placed the newspaper on the seat beside him and closed his eyes briefly.

Then the taxi was climbing into the hills. The road was narrow, busy with small Japanese and Korean cars heading down to the main road. Auhl wondered: what came first, narrow roads or narrow cars? They reached a handful of shanties and, realising he hadn't eaten, Auhl asked the driver to stop beside an old man pushing a cart. He bought dumplings, an unleavened bread parcel and a bottle of water. He offered the taxi driver a dumpling. The driver shook his head. A short distance away, downslope of the cart, a man was washing animal entrails in a ditch. Auhl asked the taxi driver about it. 'Is goat,' said the driver, 'be for to welcome new child.'

They drove on, past the shanties to more paddy fields, new rice shoots in still ponds, water rushing along the drainage ditches, a couple of large family compounds at the far end. Soon they reached the outskirts of a town in the folds of the coastal range, the driver slowing, saying, 'There house,' and pointing to a villa upslope of the coast road, at the highest edge of a village.

But as the driver began to accelerate, Auhl spotted a walled compound, a sign on the gate reading *Lotus Flower Yoga Retreat*. He asked the driver to stop, paid the man the fare and a hefty tip, and got out.

The retreat was an upmarket place, a huge house set deep inside a terraced garden. A security guard dressed in black with white armbands in a booth beside the front gate. The signs were in English, French and German. Auhl nodded to the guard, who seemed unsurprised to see a Westerner arrive so early, and he walked in as if he was known, expected, welcome.

It was not his destination; it was a short cut and useful cover. He walked around the side of the villa to where the rear wall looked onto the village and found a back gate. Another guard, equally unsurprised. Auhl left the grounds and continued to climb towards Lloyd Fanning's house. Paddy fields to his right, haphazard little streets on his right. Small houses, shuttered shops, walled villas with family temples shaded by coconut palms.

Auhl reached the road leading to Fanning's villa. More small houses, a school—and a small mosque. Not many of these in Bali,

Auhl thought. It was a modest building, white, with a tiled roof, two green domes and ornate mosaic work around doors and windows.

But mostly Auhl was interested in the villa. It overlooked the mosque from halfway up a slope. To reach it Auhl ran, doubled over, across the road to the surrounding wall. Concealed now, he skirted the building, making his way to the paddy system above. Finding a grove of trees on a bank, he sat where he couldn't be seen. Families were stirring in a couple of nearby houses, and from his vantage point Auhl saw hens pecking about, a goat straining its leash, TV sets flickering. Palm fronds whispered and chattered, far-off motorcycles stuttered, a coconut fell onto a roof.

AUHL WAITED THROUGH the morning as massive cloudbanks adorned with strange horizontal rainbow bands gathered in the west. There were no signs of life in Fanning's villa until mid-morning, when a woman arrived accompanied by a small child. She let herself in. Emerged later to shake out a broom. Later again to toss soapy water onto the garden. Lloyd Fanning finally appeared late morning sporting a bad case of bed hair, bum-crack pyjama pants and a vast white belly. He glared at the view, went inside and re-emerged later with damp hair, combed, and wearing shorts and a T-shirt. He sat at his veranda table with a laptop. When the woman brought him a tray of food he ignored her.

The hours passed. Mid-afternoon a man arrived with a machete, hacked at some dead palm fronds. Left again. The woman departed with her child. Auhl stirred to move but a taxi appeared in the street below, turning up Fanning's driveway. Fanning stepped out of the house wearing trousers and a short-sleeved Hawaiian shirt. As if the driver were deaf he shouted, 'You take me Apache Underground? Kuta?'

WHEN THEY WERE GONE Auhl hurried down to the main road and hailed a taxi to his hotel, where he showered and changed.

Early evening now, he took another taxi, this time to Kuta Beach.

It was a place of young Balinese men lounging—in doorways, on little Hondas—and Western families strolling, their daughters scuffing along in scraps of flimsy cotton; cars and mopeds crawling and tooting. Auhl found Apache Underground opposite the Discovery shopping mall and saw Fanning at a table with three other men; they were just leaving.

He went back outside and waited. Followed Fanning and his companions when they emerged, noting the way they crowded the footpath, peering drunkenly at restaurant menu boards. He drew nearer, unrecognised in a floppy hat, sunglasses and his new beard, as the men came to a decision. Heard one man say, 'This place suit you guys?' and another say, 'Good as any.'

The Sambal Beach Club restaurant was above a shop selling bootleg DVDs. Auhl waited for fifteen minutes, occasionally glancing up. Dim lights, discordant music, silhouetted people. He checked the time, seven-forty-five, and climbed the steps. Found himself in a large space overlooking the beach, with a scattering of dining tables, the bar a U-shaped island in the centre. Fanning and his friends were at a table on the other side of the bar.

Auhl hesitated. On his side of the bar there were tourists on stools; a single empty stool next to a woman wearing a thin cotton dress. That seat would give him a clear line of sight to Fanning. He found himself saying, 'May I?'

She flashed him a tired smile; he settled beside her and ordered a beer.

Cast the occasional glance Fanning's way.

Silhouetted against an extravagant sunset, the four men were tucking into nasi goreng and Tiger beer. Nothing distinctive about them. None of them young, all wearing the middle-aged holiday uniform of loose shirts and cargo pants. Auhl guessed they had known each other for a while: Fanning had been coming to Bali for years. Maybe the others had, too. Maybe they lived here.

He felt uneasy suddenly. What if other bar patrons were interested in Fanning and his fellow diners—Australian Federal Police, for example? He ran his gaze over the room. A handful of tourists, muted lighting, murmured voices. Too early for the dance music, or the wasted twenty-somethings from Melbourne, Auckland, Berlin, Los Angeles…Just then Fanning raised his head as if feeling the force of Auhl's scrutiny and Auhl immediately turned towards the woman beside him.

'Can I buy you a drink?'

She had been fiddling with her iPhone. Fiddling and muttering. 'You can tell me why my phone's frozen, that's what you can do.'

Australian. Slightly unfocused, not looking especially happy. Strong, bony hands and tanned arms, shoulders and thighs in a sleeveless dress. She leaned towards Auhl and peered at him. She was pretty, slightly sloshed, more friendly than wary. And, he thought, perfect cover. Fanning, glimpsed from the corner of Auhl's eye, had returned to his meal.

'Reboot it,' Auhl said.

'Pardon?'

'Switch it off and on again.'

'Huh.'

He watched as she did that, his shoulder touching hers now, and finally she was saying, 'Well, what do you know.'

She looked at him. 'I should be buying *you* a drink.'

'Sure.'

HER NAME WAS LOUISE. She was thirty-five and a little maudlin, but her mood lifted as they talked. In a land of holidaying nurses, schoolteachers and hairdressers, she was an anthropology postgrad taking a break from field work. Now she was coming to the end of her week at a Nusa Dua resort and was starved for company. 'You know who stays at those places? Teenage drunks too stupid to live and married couples who want to be waited on by native people while their kids go crazy.'

So she'd taken a taxi to Kuta Beach. More young drunks and middle-aged couples, thought Auhl. And me. Her knees bumped against his under the table. Once or twice their hands touched. It was nice.

THEN THEY WERE DINING at a table a few metres away from Fanning's. The day had been hot and humid; the evening was mild and humid, punctuated by a quick, fierce tropical downpour that drew a curtain over the sunset and freshened the air briefly, before the odours of cooked spices, garbage and piss drifted in on the tails of it. They talked and dined and Auhl, occasionally scratching the new beard, watched Fanning.

'It's not like I'm huge or anything,' Louise said at one point, 'but when I'm with them I *feel* huge, you know?'

Auhl nodded.

'Self-conscious,' she said. 'On account of Indonesian people are so…so…*petite*.'

'I understand.' He understood that she was lonely. So was he. He understood that she needed to vent a little. Well, so did he; that's why he was here.

'Like if I go out on one of the boats or help with the fish processing or just sit and have a meal with them—and they're *always* offering me food, I'm getting so fat—I feel like some great, lumbering water buffalo.'

'Take it from me,' Auhl said, 'you're not.'

Tall, yes, with those capable hands and broad feet. Hair bleached and flesh dusky from months of studying Sumatran fisher-folk on land and sea. But certainly no water buffalo. More slender than solid.

Then she was eyeing him, shrewd despite the wine she'd drunk.

'Alan, you're not going to start talking about your wife and kids, are you?'

He could talk at length about them but rarely felt the need. He smiled, shook his head. 'When do you return to the village?'

He wondered if the question was a misstep. It raised unspoken questions.

Louise gazed at him levelly and said, 'Tomorrow afternoon.'

He looked away. He'd not checked on Fanning for a while. Fanning was still there.

Returning to Louise, he said, 'Are you examining relationships, structures, men's work, women's work…?'

She winced, and it came out haltingly, how she'd come to Indonesia intending to study the fisher boys in the Straits of Malacca. Virtual slave labourers working far from shore on the rickety, unlicensed fishing platforms known as *jermals*. She'd had it all mapped out: a year and a half of field work and archival research, two or three years of writing, resulting in a stunning PhD and a powerful book…until she was chased off by fisheries inspectors and navy officials in the pay of *jermal* owners. But by then she was ready to quit anyway.

'Boys as young as twelve, working up to twenty-three hours a day,' she told Auhl. 'For months at a time. Paid a pittance if they're paid at all, crap food, back-breaking work. No toilets, no beds, no first aid, regular beatings, fierce storms. Some of them drown, no one cares. Broke my heart.'

The acts of talking, unburdening, had loosened some of her tightness. She grew rueful and comic, grinned at him, watched her fingers on his forearm. Auhl risked a glance. Fanning was still there.

Then Louise was resting her chin in her palms and eyeing Auhl. 'Enough about me. Tell me about *you*.'

Not quite so tipsy now. Warm, but he could see her thinking: solitary, middle-aged Australian male on holiday in Bali. Sleazebag? She would gather her things in a moment and call it a night. Auhl didn't want that. She was cover. And he liked her.

Putting on a non-sleazy face he said, 'I work for the Volcanic Ash Advisory Centre,' and gestured at the air—clear this evening but who knew what tomorrow would bring? The ash cloud from Mount Raung, on East Java, could close the airport at any time.

Louise relaxed. 'Working holiday.'

'Something like that.'

'I wish you could wave a magic wand. When I'm not sitting around the village feeling fat I'm coughing my lungs up.'

'You get the ash down there?'

She shook her head. 'Smoke from the jungle fires. Then I come to Bali and strike ash clouds.'

'Tell me about it,' said Auhl, wondering if his flight out would get cancelled. He couldn't afford to be stuck here.

He looked over the balcony railing at the darkening sand and sea of Kuta Bay, the eastern tip of Java a distant, smeary silhouette through the ash-filtered sunset. A Balinese family walked by but mostly the beach strollers were Westerners. An obese man lay flat on a low table on the sand, enduring the last massage of the evening: now and then one leg spasmed in protest. The odours of the day intensified: perfumed tropical plants, wok oil, beer, deodorant, cigarettes. Auhl felt Louise's warm hands around his.

'What does the job entail?'

Christ if Auhl knew. 'Monitoring.' That probably covered it.

Their meals arrived, a green curry for Auhl, salad for Louise. She picked at it and eyed Auhl's dish. 'Have some,' he urged.

She was torn. 'I have to be careful.'

'Can I say something?'

'Uh-oh. What?'

'I think you look lovely. I'd never get tired of looking at you.'

She blinked and took her hand away. 'Objectification is a key theme in my line of work. Whose gaze? Can we be neutral? Can we know the other? Can we, should we, avoid objectifying and representing the other in our own terms? Et cetera.' But then she grinned, as if she wouldn't dream of objectifying him as an old sleazebag. 'But thank you.'

Then she gave him a look. 'Crunch time. Tomorrow I have to return to the village and you have to go watch clouds, so can we pretend we're lovers on holiday?'

Auhl touched her taut forearm. 'Sure.'

But he needed to know Fanning's movements. His tension showed in his face.

Louise looked away. 'I mean, if you don't want to…'

Auhl was saved by Fanning himself saying to his friends, 'Sorry, guys, no clubbing, I need a sleep-in.'

'As they say in the classics'—Auhl's hand encircled Louise's wrist lightly—'your place or mine?'

SHE TOOK HIM TO the Sanur Paradise Lagoon, a resort east of Kuta. 'Certainly a step up from my crappy hotel,' Auhl said.

A collection of small villas set among swimming pools and coconut and bamboo groves, with further pools and restaurants overlooking the beach and out to Lembongan and Penida islands. Expensive, but Louise had been determined to treat herself, and Auhl found himself led in soft moonlight along a path and up steps and through a door to a vast suite: bedroom, sitting room, bathroom, a balcony brushed by palm tree fronds and overlooking yet another pool, glowing blue.

'I see what you mean by treating yourself.'

'It's an ongoing process,' Louise said, beginning with his top shirt button.

Then the shirt was off and she trailed her fingers over his chest, shoulders and back. 'What's this scar from?'

A nasty slash from the bottom of his rib cage to his navel. 'I was walking along, minding my own business, and came across this street gang robbing an old woman. After I'd saved her, they turned on me.'

'What happened?'

'They killed me, damn it.'

'What, and now you've been reincarnated as an environment protection bureaucrat?'

She looked up at him trustingly, still stroking his skin. Auhl wondered if he'd see her again. Unlikely. If he did, sooner or later he'd have to say he was a cop. He'd have to be truthful and tell her he'd been stabbed by a kid high on meth a few days after graduating from the academy. Or maybe she'd learn about him sooner than that. Maybe Indonesian or Australian Federal Police officers would track her down and grill her about the bearded man she'd spent a night with.

He said, 'It happened when I was a kid. I got cut by a nail when I was climbing a fence.'

She kissed it better.

'If I'd known I'd be performing cunnilingus,' he said later, not feeling entirely original, 'I'd have shaved more closely.'

But some things proved to be universal. Louise cuffed his ginger head and told him to get on with it.

He got on with it and woke at 5.00 a.m. to find a smooth thigh pressed against him. He stared at the ceiling and experienced a liberating sense of thankfulness. He hadn't felt wanted or attractive to someone for a long time. Finally, he stirred. Showered, dressed, scribbled his Melbourne landline number on a sheet of resort note-paper, along with a row of kisses, and let himself out.

In no particular hurry, he strolled along the beach, the air hazy, warm, the sand almost unpeopled in the last hour of moonlight, only ranks of empty deckchairs aimed at the sea. Yard servants were sweeping leaves, picking up palm fronds and tourist litter, clearing entrances. A decorative culture, he thought, passing a villa set back behind a low stone wall, amid palm trees and stone columns, vases, urns and figures from Hindu mythology. The stonework wore a patina of damp green moss, and a moist, oily heat was already seeping into the day.

He took a laneway that led away from the beach, passing small houses behind walls. At the end, he came to streetlights, a strip of motorcycle repairers and stone-carving businesses. Vehicles and noise now: cars, a truck, a family of four rolling by, balanced on the spine of a tiny sputtering Honda. A man on the other side of the road pissed against a wall, his back to Auhl, and then a taxi appeared.

Auhl gave the name of the yoga retreat in Fanning's village.

A REPEAT OF YESTERDAY, except that he was earlier.

But just as he was ducking into the cover of the villa wall, the air was torn open with sound and he jumped in fright. The mosque, broadcasting the call to prayer from four loudspeakers on a high pole in the front yard. Auhl had barely subsided back into the shade when Fanning emerged from the villa. An obese, determined figure in boxer shorts, carrying an axe. Certain he'd been spotted, Auhl ran back to the far corner of the wall and down into a ditch, his heart hammering.

Time went by. He risked a glance. Fanning was intent on the mosque. Auhl watched him enter the grounds and make straight for the loudspeaker pole. With a waggle of his large buttocks, Fanning swung the axe head high above his head, seemed to expand mightily, then brought down the blade in a savage, cleaving stroke.

Sudden silence. Satisfied, Fanning strode back across the lane, through his gate and into his house. Meanwhile the imam had appeared. He frowned up at the speakers. Spotted the severed cable, peered around helplessly.

POLICE, ELECTRICIANS, thought Auhl, cursing. And Fanning wide awake.

He gave it half an hour, concealed in the trees above the villa, occasionally sipping from a water bottle. Watching for the arrival of servants or visitors. Then, drawing on latex gloves, he moved at a crouch downhill, into Fanning's backyard, through the kitchen door.

Austerely white, mangosteens and rambutans in a wooden bowl, polished wooden floors, a small, glass-topped bamboo table. Finally an archway to a sitting room, also stark and modern. A massive home-theatre screen flickered, a game of soccer playing somewhere in the world, the sound off. A coffee table on a white rug, a chunky glass tumbler, an empty scotch bottle. The tropical fruit aside, Fanning might as well have been at home in Geelong.

A flicker in the corner of Auhl's eye. A gecko, halfway up the wall, utterly still now, as if playing a game of statues with him. At the far end of the hallway, open glass doors led to a deck, shadowy under ferns and blowsy hanging baskets, where bamboo wind chimes sounded softly, licked by a hill breeze. A neighbouring house, a rice paddy beyond it; a man wandered through in bare feet, carrying a sickle. Auhl sensed a busy, populated landscape, even though he'd barely seen or heard anyone yet.

He listened, and presently followed a rattly snore to a bedroom midway along the hallway. Fanning sprawled asleep in his boxer shorts, head down, his backside aimed at the ceiling.

Between the toes, Auhl decided. He removed the syringe from his pocket, filled the barrel with the succinylcholine, gave a tiny preparatory squirt and went straight in, plunger depressed, ten mils, no messing about.

Fanning jerked awake at the sudden pain and thrashed around onto his back. He stared wild-eyed at Auhl, then reared up at him with a roar. Auhl stepped back. He said, 'Intravenous would have been quicker, but I didn't want to fart around trying to find a vein.'

Fanning wavered. He grunted, spasmed, flopped onto his back.

'Even so, it's quick-acting,' Auhl said. He twinkled at Fanning. 'It's called sux. Appropriate, right? It mimics a heart attack.' He leaned into the heavy, panicked face. 'What's that? You want to know why? Your daughter, arsehole. Your wife.'

A last faint flicker in Fanning's eyes, a cessation of panic, an accommodation with fate.

AUHL CHECKED AGAIN for cleaners and gardeners then left the house by the back door. From the trees on the upper slope he could see into the grounds of the mosque. The imam had called the police. Three faces stared across at the villa. Soon they would make a decision and knock on Fanning's door. He slipped across the hillside and into a paddy field, and was skirting around it when he almost stepped on a woman.

She was young, blonde, with braided hair, tie-dyed skirt and top, bangles, beads, rings, piercings, tatts. An amalgam of 1960s hippie and contemporary hipster, and he had no idea where she'd sprung from. Seated in the lotus position, her face tilted in communion with the rising sun, she didn't stir when Auhl muttered, 'Sorry,' and hurried on. Potential witness, he thought, with a twist of panic.

He walked head-down along the narrow earthen banks between paddy ponds thick with new rice shoots, making for the coast road below. Then he left the paddy behind and found himself in a familiar urbanscape of small houses behind crumbling walls, lean dogs and popping Honda motorbikes. A breeze wrapped a blue supermarket bag around his ankles, but that was the street: look inside someone's yard and you'd not see a scrap of paper or plastic.

He reached the main road. Early commercial traffic snarled by, bikes, tiny vans and taxis, all tooting as if Auhl might want to buy a ride. He was relieved to see two girls and a boy striding ahead of him, maple leaf flags stitched to their packs, their legs long and tanned. He felt old and weary and trudged along behind them in the mounting exhaust gases until he reached a bus stop outside a motor repair business. Engine parts, five-litre oilcans, a faded Shell sign on the back wall.

The backpackers kept walking, but Auhl joined the people waiting for a bus. A couple of women in sarongs, others in knee-length office skirts, a handful of schoolgirls. Feeling absurdly large as he stood among them, Auhl thought of Louise; her warm lips kissing his scars.

One of the women spoke sharply, shaking her fist at an old man astride a tiny Honda scooter. He was holding aloft a pair of gold-fish in a clear Ziploc bag filled with water, urging the schoolgirls to buy. They were entranced. Another woman intervened, rebuking the girls this time, who withdrew, heads down, stifling giggles. Finally the old man gave up. Stowed the goldfish into a pannier and rode away, merging with the restless traffic. And to Auhl's relief the Canadian backpackers returned, the bus arrived and everyone trooped on. He was no longer a memorable lone Westerner in the vicinity of a vandalised mosque and a suspicious death.

AUHL RIDING A BUS, lulled into sleepiness, dreaming of Fanning's flabbiness, Louise making love with a kind of welcome relief, bells tinkling on the hippie girl's wrists. Realising as the bells dragged him awake that it was his phone ringing.

An Australian number—his, in fact. His landline in Melbourne, where the time was now mid-morning.

'Dad, where are you?'

He had told his daughter he'd be in Port Fairy for a few days, an old hit-and-run rumoured to be a murder. 'Still away,' he said.

'Okay. Look, I know it's too soon, but this friend of mine and her boyfriend were housesitting and the owners came back unexpectedly and can they doss down with us for a while?'

Auhl felt sad and relieved and half-mad. Around him the other passengers swayed and scratchy music leaked from the speaker above the driver's head. He breathed in and out, deep breaths. 'Of course, sweetheart.'

'They can move in tomorrow.'

'Not sure I'll get back by then,' Auhl said, thinking of the volcanic ash. The bus stopped. An old woman boarded with a rooster in a bamboo cage. The bus started again, trundling on.

AUHL LEFT THE BUS in Kuta Beach and took a taxi across to his hotel, where he checked out, paying cash, and walked to the main terminal. The airport was in turmoil: all Virgin and Jetstar flights cancelled. *Ash-cloud event*, said the website.

The cloud hovered between Denpasar and northern Australia. The skies to the north and west were clearer, but every Singapore and Kuala Lumpur flight was full. A waiting game now, Auhl thought.

The place teemed with stranded passengers, so he slumped on the floor next to a couple of kids in surf gear. His back, slouched against the wall, belied body and mind, which seemed to thrum. Although depleted of energy he was tight as a bowstring, an edginess running through him.

Not fear, he thought, or guilt, or dismay. He couldn't get his head around what it was.

Who he was.

Most of the killers he'd arrested in his long life had been men, and most had simply stuffed up in some way. He eyed the male passengers and airport staff now, young and old and in-between. Grumpy and harried and bored. Tired and alert and dozing and canoodling. Maimed, unblemished.

Seeing a tourist with his arm in a sling, Auhl thought of Claire Pascal's hacked-about forearm and he touched his stomach unconsciously, the thin worm of stitched flesh so recently kissed by a beautiful woman. Scarred by the job. He thought, what about the scars that can't be seen?

A little Chinese girl was watching him. She stood hedged between the knees of her parents, who were intent on their phones. It often happened that Auhl locked eyes with a child in a crowd of people; a solemn, wordless communication would pass between them, unwitnessed by the throng. Now he did what he always did. Pulled on one earlobe to release his tongue tip, pulled on the other to retract it. Would she duck her head? Send the trick back to him? He waited. She continued to stare.

Auhl looked away, not discomfited but wondering if the child had the savant eyes to see who he'd become and who he'd been. A man who'd plodded along, doing his best, righting a few wrongs— then suddenly righted two big ones. Stumbling in, initially; becoming decisive. Whether he was a better man, or one more resolute now, toned by recent sex and murder, Auhl didn't know.

But the energy was there in him and he stood. Waved to the child—who waved back with a transformative beam—and did business at one ticket counter after another, spending the last of his savings.

Soon he was on the way home. It took a day and a half, his route across the Pacific a series of oblique advances north, east and south. Coming home the back way—but coming home.

ACKNOWLEDGMENTS

My grateful thanks to Renata Alexander and Chris Atmore, who assisted me enormously by reading manuscript drafts and answering my dumb courtroom and family law questions— any subsequent mistakes are my own. And to all at Text Publishing, especially my editor, Mandy Brett, who for years now has made each of my novels a great deal better.

βK